"Dinah McCall knows how to bring emotions right off the page. Her characters are so alive."

—Curtiss Ann Matlock,
author of *If Wishes Were Horses*

# *Dreamcatcher*

"[Dinah McCall] has penned a gripping emotional story that satisfies on every level. It's a romance. It's a time travel. It's wonderful."

—Debbie Macomber,
author of *Denim and Diamonds*

"*Dreamcatcher* is a wonderfully provocative book, complimented by a fascinating story, characters you can't forget, and pacing that has you panting for breath. This book has it all."

—Carol Finch,
author of *Once Upon a Midnight Morn*

# LEGEND

## DINAH McCALL

HarperPaperbacks
*A Division of HarperCollinsPublishers*

**HarperPaperbacks**
*A Division of* HarperCollins*Publishers*
10 East 53rd Street, New York, NY 10022-5299

This is a work of fiction. The characters, incidents, and
dialogues are products of the author's imagination and are not to
be construed as real. Any resemblance to actual events or
persons, living or dead, is entirely coincidental.

ISBN 0-06-108701-7

HarperCollins®, 📖 ®, and HarperPaperbacks™
are trademarks of HarperCollins Publishers, Inc.

Cover illustration © 1998 by John Ennis

First printing: October 1998

Printed in the United States of America

Visit HarperPaperbacks on the World Wide Web at
http://www.harpercollins.com

❖ 10 9 8 7 6 5 4 3 2 1

It isn't so much the witnessing of a miracle that sets a person apart from the rest of the world. It's the fact that they believe one can occur.

I believe I have seen miracles. I know that I will see more.

This book is dedicated to those people who not only look for the miracles in life, but who celebrate and share them as joyfully as a rich man covets gold.

# NOTE TO MY READERS

I believe that faith really can move mountains and love really can change our world.

As is my story, *Legend,* the Apache legend in this book is a piece of fiction. There never was a healing place. There never was a place in the Superstition Mountains known as the mountain that embraces the sun.

The Apache are a strong and proud race of people. As an Oklahoman, born and bred, I honor the Native American culture in every way and appreciate their efforts to retain the uniqueness of their own people.

But I am first and foremost a storyteller. This is my story. I'm sharing it with you. Enjoy.

DINAH MCCALL
P.O. Box 127
Henryetta, OK 74437–0127

# THE HEALING PLACE

*Apache Legend*

Many, many lifetimes before the men in metal clothing came riding into the land of the People on the four-legged beasts, other men came out of the sky and stayed among the People. We could not hear their words, but we knew their thoughts. They dug deep into our land, taking the heart out of the mountain that embraces the setting sun.

There was one young warrior who'd seen them fall from the sky and had been brave enough to greet them. Among the People, he became known as He-Who-Saw-Them, and he became a friend to the Men-Who-Came-Out-of-the-Sky. Just as the Men-Who-Came-Out-of-the-Sky were ready to leave the land of the People, He-Who-Saw-Them fell ill, and no matter how much magic the medicine man made, He-Who-Saw-Them weakened. It became apparent to the People that He-Who-Saw-Them would soon die.

The Men-Who-Came-Out-of-the-Sky took great pity on He-Who-Saw-Them and built a chamber within the heart of the mountain that embraces the sun. Just as He-Who-Saw-Them was near death, the People were instructed to carry him into the chamber and then leave in haste and never look back. The People did as they were told and went back to their village.

When the sun was directly over Mother Earth, the air began to vibrate. A sound filled the air, not unlike that of the screams of a thousand eagles. The People were frightened and fled to their lodges and hid beneath their robes. The noise lessened as the sun began to move toward the horizon, and only when it could be heard no longer did the People venture out.

To their amazement, they were greeted by He-Who-Saw-Them, himself. Everyone crowded around to see him, to touch him. No one could believe that this was the same man they'd carried into the cave only hours earlier. Yet when they questioned He-Who-Saw-Them, all he would say was that the Men-Who-Came-Out-of-the-Sky had made great magic, and that he must now repay for saving his life. He said he'd been given the duty of watching over the great chamber, which he now called the Healing Place. He-Who-Saw-Them had also been given the secret to the magic and was to use it as he saw fit to help the People.

The People rejoiced that He-Who-Saw-Them had been returned to them. The Men-Who-Came-Out-of-the-Sky were never seen again. And as he'd predicted, He-Who-Saw-Them became the keeper of the Healing Place. As the years moved one into the other, the secret was passed from father to son, and so it has been for each generation after. To the People, the Healing Place is holy ground, and should it ever be desecrated, then it is the keeper's duty to destroy it forever.

So it is said.

So I believe.

# CHAPTER

# 1

Joseph Colorado was a man of many faces. He was the son of his father, Michael Colorado. He was a lover of horses and a caretaker of the land. He was a brother to Benny and a good neighbor to his friends. He could take an engine apart and put it back together without missing a lick. And he could pilot a helicopter as if it were a part of his body and not a machine. He was a man with deep roots to the past and a far-seeing eye to the future. He was an open and honest man, and he was a man with many secrets.

But today, he was a man with a mission. He glanced down at his watch, and then up at the sun's position in the sky before looking back over his shoulder to the woman on the stretcher behind him.

Unable to move, she met his gaze with a blinding intensity. For the last three years Wynema Littlefish had been battling full-blown AIDS, and had it not been for her father's intervention, she would have lost the war. But Duncan Littlefish was a man who lived his life in the old ways and he'd known a man—who'd known a man—who'd heard a story.

Duncan Littlefish's interference with the business of his daughter's dying had brought her to this place and to this man who was at the helicopter controls. Duncan had asked for her to be healed. And even now, unless Joseph hurried, it could still be too late.

As Joseph gauged the strain on Wynema's face, her dark eyes held a question he understood all too well.

Would they get there in time?

He gave her a nod of encouragement and then turned, giving the area over which they were flying his full attention.

Moments later he glanced to the west and saw it: the twin peaks of a long length of mountain range with the deep curved space in between. From the ground, the mountain peaks looked like two arms reaching up to the sky, and the valley between, breasts upon which a dying sun might pause. To the casual observer, they were a natural and beautiful frame for Arizona's majestic sunsets. To the Apache, they were the mountains that embrace the sun.

They'd made it, but with no time to spare. Like a warrior going into battle, he shoved the control stick forward, sending the helicopter hurtling toward the heat-laden earth like a dragonfly darting toward the shimmering surface of a pond.

The air was still thick with the dust of their landing as Joseph lifted Wynema Littlefish from the stretcher and began carrying her toward the face of the mountain. She moaned from the pain of being moved. Joseph murmured an anxious apology, but there was no time to waste. Her life depended on his haste.

Then suddenly he stopped, and the absence of motion was such a relief that Wynema roused. But when she looked up, her eyes widened in disbelief. There was nothing before them but a rock wall that seemed to go on forever. Her voice was weak, her anxiety evident as she gazed up at the sheer face of the mountain.

"Colorado . . . what is this?"

He laid her down on the ground and then took a deep breath. "Wynema . . . forgive me, but I must undress you before I take you any further."

There was a flutter of anxiety in her eyes, but the expression faded as she nodded and looked away.

He removed her clothing as if undressing a child, anxious not to cause her any more pain. Though he had prepared himself to witness the devastation of her disease, it was impossible to hide his dismay.

She was little more than skin and bones. Her teeth were so loose she could no longer chew, and she had sores on her body that would not heal. Her once thick, black hair was wispy and brittle. In a tender gesture meant to reassure, he brushed back her hair and was unable to hide his shock when several strands came away in his hand.

"I'm sorry," she whispered, closing her eyes in great shame.

Joseph stood. "There is no longer a need to be sorry." He made a fist and turned, thrusting his knuckles sharply against the rock. The band of pure silver on his finger had become a key, and the stone setting—a large chunk of green crystal—slipped into the odd-shaped niche like the last piece of a puzzle.

When a large portion of the rock began to slide away, he grunted with satisfaction. A dark, narrow chamber leading into the bowels of the mountain was slowly revealed.

When he turned to pick up her up, Wynema instinctively crossed her arms across her chest. Joseph ached for her shame, but there was no time for modesty.

"Forgive me."

Tears slid from the corners of her eyes and onto her cheeks, but she didn't speak.

Moments later, they were inside the mountain, but that was not enough. Until he had her inside the chamber, he could not relax, and time was not on their side. He shifted her to a more secure position and began to move with long, hurried strides.

The passageway was marked by translucent green crystals embedded deep into the walls and emitting a faint, pulsing light. Joseph's and Wynema's skin took on an unearthly appearance, and their eyes reflected the strange verdant glow. And even though he'd come this way many times before, he never got over a feeling of awe.

The air in the tunnel was cool, protected from the sun's heat by the mountain's density. And while the temperature was a drastic change from the one outside, sweat began to run from Joseph's temples and down the middle of his back. He was strong, very strong, but the exertion of haste and Wynema's weight was beginning to take its toll.

Five minutes later, he was close to exhaustion and she was bordering on unconsciousness from the constant jolts of pain. He heard her groaning, but was no time to stop and reassure her. Her father had entrusted him to a task he did not intend to fail.

Suddenly they emerged from the passageway into a large, spacious chamber. The faint glow from the nearby corridor cast strange, eerie shadows inside the domed vault, but Joseph didn't need to see to know where he was going. They'd made it. With a heartfelt sigh, he touched her arm, then her cheek as he laid her in the center of the floor.

"Wynema."

She didn't respond. He touched the base of her neck where her life's blood flowed. The throb was faint.

"Wynema . . . do you hear me?"

When she opened her eyes, he relaxed.

"Remember what I told you. When I leave, don't open your eyes and don't move or cry out, no matter what you hear or feel."

She blinked, indicating she understood. Joseph glanced at the luminous dial of his watch. It was time.

"Close your eyes . . . now!"

She did so. The only sign of her nervousness was the tremble in her lower lip.

"When it's over, follow the green lights back to me. I'll be waiting."

"Yes," she whispered. "Back to you."

He hurried to the doorway, once again using his ring as a key, and pressed the chunk of crystal into an indentation on the wall. A small opening suddenly appeared in the ceiling directly over where the woman lay. He looked back just as a single beam of sunlight broke through the darkness, beaming into one of the crystals on the floor near the top of Wynema's head. He began to run and never looked back.

When he emerged from inside the mountain, the sun was directly overhead. The intense heat felt good after the chill in the tunnels. Winded from his race against time, he leaned over, bracing his hands upon his thighs, and took slow deep breaths.

A few moments later he straightened. There was still a thing left undone. He knelt, gathering a handful of the Arizona earth, and then stood, holding it up to the sky. With the words of his ancestors spilling from his lips, he faced the four corners of the earth, at each point giving back a portion of the dust to the ever-present wind.

Sunlight burnished his smooth copper skin when he turned to face the mountain. He was as God had intended him to be. Strong and tall—a proud man—an Apache.

As he stood, the texture of the air began to shift, and then a faint but distinct humming sound could be heard. The air around him began to move, like water lapping at a shore. His blood began to heat and his heart began to pound. Again, the voices of his ancestors came through him. The cadence of his mother tongue matched the rhythm of the wail coming from inside the mountain that embraces the sun.

*Two months later—Oracle, Arizona*

Raine Beaumont was tired and hot. Bone-weary from driving and the lack of sleep she'd been suffering, she wasn't sure she could keep moving on. Her mind was blank, her soul as empty as the fuel gauge on her car. She'd been on the road for the better part of the last two days and this morning she'd started driving before daylight, stopping only for fuel. In little more than an hour it would be dark again, but her only thought had been to get back to Oracle.

She didn't know what would happen after that. It had been twelve years since she'd set foot in the small Arizona town where she'd been born and raised. All she knew was that she had a man to find and a favor to ask.

A man. It was a simple way of thinking about the only love of her life. Was Joseph Colorado a man now in every sense of the word, or would he be like so many of the men she'd known back in Chicago— definitely males, but not necessarily men?

She could only guess. The last time she'd seen him he'd been twenty to her seventeen. He would be thirty-two now, nearing thirty-three. Age didn't necessarily make a man out of the male of the species. But after the way she and Joseph had parted, she didn't much care what kind of a man he was. She'd come back to Oracle because she needed a favor. Nothing more.

Her gaze drifted slightly as she ventured a brief look at the nearby Catalina Mountains. As she did, the loneliness she carried within her shifted. After all those years on the flat plains of Chicago, nothing said home to her quite as clearly as this land.

An eighteen-wheeler drove up behind her and honked his horn four times in quick succession. Startled by the noise, she jumped and then realized she was weaving back and forth across the road. Thankful for nothing worse than being honked at, she swerved back to her lane. The truck quickly passed and the miles continued to unroll.

Just as exhaustion was about to claim her, she saw a green and white road marker off to her right. A little closer, and she was able to read it.

ORACLE—FIVE MILES

She set her chin in a obstinate thrust. Five miles. She had that much left in her.

But the closer she got, the farther it seemed from where her journey had begun. She was a long way from Chicago. If she let herself, she could very easily panic.

Another eighteen-wheeler blasted past her on the highway, this time rocking her car from the side draft of his rig. At least this time she'd been driving in her lane. She gritted her teeth and kept her sight on the highway before her. Nothing could deter her now.

For the better part of the last eight years, she'd been a journalist for the *Chicago Tribune* and had been good—damn good at her job. But she didn't work there anymore. Exactly four days ago she'd walked into the editor's office and quit. She'd given them no warning, no reason, and no notice. Today she was only minutes away from what was left of her past and counting.

ORACLE—NEXT EXIT

Her mind registered the fact as her heart began to race.

*Oh God, please let him still be there. Joseph of the laughing eyes and tender smile.*

She took a deep breath as she drove into town, then a few moments later exhaled on a shaky sigh. It had changed some, but not enough for her to get lost.

Suddenly the light on the fuel gauge came on, reminding her she'd been running on empty. As she pulled up to a small gas station and stopped at the pumps, she almost laughed.

That was her all right. Running on empty. Considering everything else going on in her life, an appropriate analogy.

She killed the engine. After so many miles of motor noise, the sound of silence was almost deafening. The urge to sleep was strong, but the need for food was stronger.

She got out.

As she refueled the car, she gave what was left of the small town a flat stare. Once she'd known these streets and alleys as well as she'd known her own name. But that was before the move. Before her daddy's job had transferred him to Chicago—before Joseph Colorado had broken her heart.

The attendant gawked when she entered to pay. She eyed him cautiously, wondering if he was someone she should remember.

" 'At'll be eighteen-fifty," he said shortly.

She slipped a twenty on the counter.

He handed her the change.

"Just passin' through?"

Raine stuffed the money in her pocket and ignored his question by firing one of her own at him instead.

"Do you know a family by the name of Colorado?"

His expression brightened. "Yeah, sure. They lived here a long time."

Her hopes plummeted. "Lived?"

"The old lady . . ." He paused and then shrugged. "I forget her name. Anyways, she took off to California years ago. Died out there, I'm told. The old man, Michael . . . he took sick and died a while back, too. His boys, Joseph and Benny, run the place now. Raise horses, you know."

Even though a thread of relief ran through her, hearing the sound of his name made her sad. Joseph. She sighed. So many wasted years.

"Is there a motel around here?"

"Yep. The Chalet. Only it's shut down for repairs. There's a whole passel of them bread-and-breakfast type places, though."

Raine wrinkled her nose. She'd counted on the anonymity of a motel. Right now the thought of facing people and having to converse on a normal level was more than she could accept.

Then the clerk added. "There's another place down at the other end of main street, but I don't think it's quite your style."

"Why not?" Raine asked.

His face turned red as he shrugged. "Well, ma'am, not many people spend the entire night there, if you know what I mean."

Her eyes widened. A no-tell motel? Then she thought about why she'd come. A no-tell motel would do just fine.

"Thanks for your help," she said shortly, and left.

A short while later, she emerged from her room at the Sleep-Inn and headed across the street to the café. All she needed was some food in her stomach and a good night's sleep. Then she would be fit enough to do what she'd come to do.


The scent of fresh-brewed coffee drifted down the hall and into Benny Colorado's bedroom. He sniffed and then smiled to himself as he rolled over on his back. The high-beamed ceilings and the thick adobe walls kept the house cool in summer and warm in winter. Comfort was a thing that he loved. He stretched lazily, contemplating the day ahead.

For Benny, it was a matter of first things first, and that would be coffee.

Coffee!

*Oh, man,* he thought. If the coffee was made, then that meant Joseph was up.

At that point, his smile faded. He'd overslept. With a groan, he kicked back the covers and crawled out of bed. Suddenly having an older brother when you'd been on your own was, for Benny, too much like having a father. He'd been raised without benefit of either and considered himself a man fully grown.

At the age of three his parents had separated. His mother had moved to California and taken him with her. Benny had grown up on the streets of L.A. Coming back to Oracle had been like stepping back in time. The pace was slower, the lifestyle less frantic, and the absence of excitement only added to the friction already present between the two brothers.

Two years ago Benny had returned unannounced, informing whomever cared to know that his mother was dead, and then proceeded to make himself at home as if he'd been here all of his life.

Less than a year later, his father, Michael, had died, leaving Joseph and Benny to deal with each other as they saw fit. At that point Benny had proclaimed loud and long that he would be heading back to L.A. Oracle was too small-town and laid back for this big-city boy. But that was over a year ago, and he was still in residence and still disagreeing with Joseph, the man he regarded as the yoke around his neck.

And then Joseph called to him from the kitchen. "Hey, Benny! You up?"

Benny reached for his boots and jeans. *Speak of the devil.* "Yeah! I'm up. Be there in a while."

A few moments later the back door slammed. Joseph was already starting his day, and Benny had yet to wash the sleep from his eyes.

It was almost noon. The horse tethered at the end of the rope looked as hot as Joseph felt. In deference to the heat, he'd unbuttoned his shirt. An errant gust of wind scattered the dust in the corral and set the shirt to flapping against the taut surface of his belly. His eyes narrowed against the blast of grit.

He settled his Stetson a little tighter on his head, ignoring the dust and welcoming the breeze as it dried the sweat on his body. And even as he continued to work the horse, he was aware of Benny's every movement.

They shared little except the blood that ran through their veins. His mother had seen to that, but that was old news. The pertinent facts were that he had a 22-year-old male on his hands who was a hell of a long way from becoming a man. The streets had made Benny tough, but they'd also made him weak. He had no concept of earning money, only spending it. But they *were* brothers. They shared parents.

Maybe one day they would learn how to share the same space, as well.

He glanced across the fence into the next corral. Benny was supposed to be cooling down one of Joseph's prize mares, but as usual, he was staring off into space.

"Hey, Benny, don't let her—"

Benny pointed and Joseph turned to see what his brother was looking at. Surprise caught him. There was a car parked in front of the house and he hadn't even heard it drive up.

He frowned, a bit startled he'd been caught unawares, and more than a little annoyed that someone was here. He had wanted to finish with this horse before noon, and this would be a delay.

Benny shoved back his hat and grinned. "Ooh, boy, would you look at those legs."

Joseph's eyes narrowed as a woman emerged from the car.

She was wearing tight black jeans and some sort of loose white shirt. Her dark, shoulder-length hair was loose and whipping with the wind. He tried to remember if he had an appointment with anyone and couldn't.

She saw them and started toward the corrals. The moment he saw her stride, his mind skipped gears and then slid back in time. He dropped the rope and started toward the fence without speaking.

Benny jumped forward as the horse Joseph had been working suddenly bolted toward the opposite end of the arena.

"Hey, Joseph, are you gonna let that horse—"

But Joseph wasn't listening. As he climbed over the corral, Benny's voice faded from his consciousness. Even after he started toward her he was unaware of the ground beneath his feet and the sun in his face.

Raine. Sweet Jesus, it was Raine.

Her hair was still the same rich shade of chocolate, but it was shorter now, just brushing the tops of her shoulders. Except for the push of her breasts against her shirt, she was whipcord thin, almost skinny. But she walked with that same lanky stride he remembered.

When she paused to brush the hair from her eyes, he couldn't do anything but stare. Only after he saw her stumble did reality return. It wasn't a dream. She was really here.

She was taller than he remembered. But his memories of her had stopped when she was seventeen. It stood to reason she could have grown more. As the distance closed between them, he tried to gauge her expression, but it was impossible.

Although she walked with purpose, there was no obvious emotion on her face.

No anger.

No joy.

No welcome.

No greeting.

No nothing.

He stopped in midstride as the skin suddenly crawled on the back of his neck. This didn't feel right.

When they were within a couple of yards of each other, he stopped, watching as another errant gust of wind lifted the hair from her neck. At that point, he was stunned by the longing that swept through him, but the instinct to keep his distance was strong. She'd burned him once. He didn't make the same mistakes twice. She'd been his world and she'd dumped him without so much as a kiss-my-ass or a thank-you. He'd spent years hating her, then a few more forgetting her. Or so he'd thought until now, standing almost toe-to-toe, and for the first time in many years sharing space.

Raine's heartbeat was hammering so loud against her eardrums that if he'd spoken right then, she wouldn't have been able to hear the sound of his voice. All she could think was, *Dear God, he's so beautiful.* And then she frowned. This instant attraction wasn't part of her plan.

His smooth, teak-colored skin was burned even darker by the years of Arizona summers. His face was leaner, his features hard and chiseled. His body had taken on the definition of a man's, with long, taut muscles, a flat belly, and eyes that seared clear through to her soul. She felt stripped beneath his gaze and knew a swift moment of fear. But then she remembered why she'd come.

"Joseph."

The sound of his name on her tongue sent a shockwave of longing through him that he didn't expect. Chalking it up to nothing more than auld lang syne, he almost smiled.

"Rainbow . . . long time no see."

She thought she'd prepared herself for the pain, but hearing her nickname brought back a world of memories. Ignoring her feelings, she nodded. *Just say it, Raine. Spit it out and get it over with.*

"You're looking well," she said.

This time he managed a smile. "From what I remember of our past, aren't we being a little too formal?"

A faint blush stained her cheeks. He was right. Being formal with a man who'd had her naked and begging on a regular basis was out of place. She shrugged.

"So . . . are you lost or what?" he asked.

The smile on her lips never reached her eyes. "Not any longer."

He frowned. The ambiguity of her words sounded threatening.

"So, if you're not lost, then what are you doing here?"

*He's given you the opening you were waiting for. Now say it!* Raine lifted her chin, staring him straight in the eyes.

"I came to ask you a favor."

It was the last thing he'd expected her to say, and because it took him aback, old anger surged, along with unanswered questions from their past that had plagued him for years. He glanced down at her left hand, searching for signs of a ring. To his surprise her fingers were bare.

"You dumped my ass twelve years ago. What in

hell could I possibly have now that you'd want?"

Shocked by his remark and the anger in his voice, she retaliated without thought for why she'd come.

"Dumped you? Like hell, Indian. The way I remember it, I'm the one who got dumped."

She wasn't making any sense. He frowned, sarcasm thick in his voice.

"I'm thinking the years have screwed with your memory."

*That and everything else.* "I don't think so. If I remember correctly, the last time I saw you, you swore you didn't want to lose me." Then to her disgust, tears blurred her vision and she choked on her last words. "You swore you'd love me forever."

"But that was before your last night in Oracle, remember?"

She frowned, thinking back through the years to a night long ago when her eyes had been rudely opened to the ways of the world.

"All I remember about that night was waiting and waiting for you to come."

He caught himself taking a step forward, wanting to reach out and grab her, to shake her into admitting the truth.

"And I remember going to your house and your father telling me you were out on a date."

She would have interrupted, but Joseph kept on talking, the words and the anger spilling out of him in waves.

"I didn't believe him until I saw you myself—

sitting in the car with some boy I'd never seen. He was feeding you french fries and you were laughing and touching him and—"

He stopped, then took a deep breath. An easy smile slid across his face.

"Well, hell, that was a long time ago. It's water under the bridge, right?"

She couldn't believe what he'd just said. It wasn't water under the bridge to her. It was twelve wasted years. Pain shafted through her. Twelve years she could never get back. She shook her head.

"He wasn't my date. That boy was my cousin, Robby. He came to help us move."

He couldn't hide his shock, but after all these years, Joseph finally understood. Her father had lied to him. Purposely. And he knew why. He glanced down at his fingers, flexing the muscles in his hands and feeling the warmth of the sun soaking into his skin—that ever-brown Indian skin.

"Hell."

This time Raine managed a smile, but it was brief and bitter. "My sentiments exactly."

Joseph reached for her, but she took a step back.

"No, don't bother. There's nothing between us but the past . . . and that's okay."

He didn't expect her words to hurt, but they did.

"Then why come? And what's the big favor you need to ask?"

Forcing herself to a calm she didn't feel, she met his gaze. "Eight months after we moved away, I gave birth to a stillborn baby. It was our baby, Joseph . . .

a little boy." She watched the blood drain from his face, but to his credit, his expression never wavered. She took a deep breath. "And now there's something we must do."

His voice was deep; rough and shaky from unshed emotion. "Ask."

"I want to bring our son back to Arizona and rebury him here on your ranch. He never got to feel the air on his face or the dust beneath his feet, but I would like to know that he sleeps on his father's land."

Tears shattered what was left of Joseph's view of the world as Raine's request ripped through him.

"Ah, God," he muttered, and pulled her into his arms.

The shock of being held came swiftly as Raine absorbed his touch, then his embrace. Once she would have rejected the overture, but not now. Not today. For a moment in time, they drew strength from the knowledge that once upon a time—in another part of their life—they had laughed and loved and made love with a joy they could never repeat.

When Raine could think past the flood of old memories, she stepped back, masking the tremble in her voice with a forthright attitude she didn't feel.

"Then it's okay?"

Joseph felt as if he'd been cut off at the knees. He saw her lips moving, even heard the sound of her voice, and still couldn't bring himself to speak.

Okay?

To bring their dead son back to this land?

Dear God, right now he felt as if nothing would ever be okay again. He blinked, his focus shifting from the ground beneath his feet to the look on her face. She seemed to be waiting, but for what? Then he remembered. She was waiting for an answer. It was all he could do to nod an acceptance.

She went limp with relief. One hurdle down. So many more to go.

"Good," she said shortly. "I'll be in touch."

Only after she started to turn away did Joseph rally.

"Wait! Where are you going?"

New pain shoved its way through old scars, adding to the burden of Raine Beaumont's grief. *I haven't the faintest idea.* But that isn't what she told him.

"Back to town. I set the groundwork for the exhumation before I left Chicago, but now I need to make some calls."

Unwilling to lose the tenuous connection they'd forged, he grabbed her arm.

"Use my phone."

She shook her head. "No, I'll use the one in my room."

"Room? What room?"

"I'm staying at a place in town."

But still he persisted. "Where?"

"The Sleep-Inn."

Joseph made no attempt to hide his disgust. "My God, Raine, that place is little more than a revolving door for prostitutes."

"It suits me," she said. "Besides, I need to be alone when—"

Anger shifted through his voice. "I would have thought you'd had enough of alone."

"Please don't, Joseph. I didn't come all this way to fight." And then she sighed. "Besides, I'm too tired to fight."

His rage died within moments of the sound of her voice. When he looked back at her, his eyes were dark and glistening with unshed tears.

"I'm sorry. It's just that your news was a difficult thing to hear."

Raine nodded. "This isn't easy for me, either."

Again, her words were almost an accusation. She obviously blamed him for not coming after her. Guilt pushed at him. All those years ago he should have confronted her and the boy he'd seen her with, but at the age of twenty he'd let his pride rule his head.

"I'm very, very sorry you went through that alone."

She bit her lip and then tilted her chin in a defensive manner.

Joseph kept staring at the changing expressions on her face, searching for the girl he'd known in the woman she'd become.

"Raine?"

"What?"

"Would you have told me? If he . . . if the baby . . . hadn't died, would you have told me?"

Her answer came without hesitation. "Yes."

His shoulders slumped. In a strange way, that helped.

"I'll call you when I know something," she said.

A horse nickered in a nearby corral. The wind shifted, blowing a fresh swath of grit into the air. A shadow passed upon the ground between them. Joseph looked up, squinting against the glare of the sun and judging the wingspan of the bird above them.

"Eagle?" she asked.

"No, buzzard."

*Carrion. A bird that feeds on carrion.* "It figures," she said shortly, and walked away.

Joseph stood in silence, watching until there was nothing left to mark her reappearance but a new wave of old pain. Unaware that his brother was walking up behind him, he jumped when Benny spoke.

"Who was that?" he asked.

Joseph looked back toward the road.

"The woman . . . who was she?" Benny repeated.

A shiver moved up Joseph's spine. "A ghost."

Then he turned and walked away.

A loud thump sounded on the wall above Raine's bed, followed by, "Oh baby, oh baby," and a high-pitched giggle.

She hated to admit it, but Joseph had been right about this motel. If that trucker in the next room didn't get what he paid for—and soon—she was going to scream.

She looked up, nervously eyeing a dusty matador and a big, bloody bull depicted on the black velvet painting above her head, hoping that Romeo and Juliet next door would finish what they'd started before the velvet matador met a less dignified end than the one the artist had intended.

A last thump sounded against the wall. The picture slid sideways upon the nail. She held her breath as a new wave of quiet descended. Thankful for the silence, she rolled over onto her belly and closed her eyes. There was a dull pain between her eyebrows and another around her heart. She kept reliving the moment of seeing Joseph's curiosity turn to grief. She wanted to hate him but the emotion wouldn't come.

Once the hate had been alive and well within her. For a time after the baby had died, it was all she'd been able to feel. Then she'd needed to blame someone. It had been easy to blame Joseph for his absence. It had taken more than a year for Raine to accept part of the responsibility for that fact. He'd been absent because he hadn't known. After that revelation had come and gone, she'd felt nothing at all. That was the year she was eighteen—going on seventy.

Somewhere between the ages of nineteen and twenty-two, her ambivalence toward life began to change. While at college, she started working at the *Tribune*. A year later, when her parents died in an accident, her job became the focus of her world. For the next seven years, Raine Beaumont lived for her work. Only rarely did she let herself remember the boy she'd once loved, or the baby who'd never drawn breath.

Suddenly, the picture above her bed began to thump once more, this time with a rapid and steady rhythm.

"Oh baby, oh baby, oh baby," Romeo moaned.

Raine rolled over on her back, glaring in disbelief at the velvet matador and the bloody bull now bouncing against the wall.

"Now, baby, now!" Juliet cried.

"I'll give you now," Raine muttered, and rolled off of the bed, grabbing one of her tennis shoes as she straightened.

Before she could talk herself out of the act, she threw the shoe just below the picture, grimacing in satisfaction as it bounced off the wall with a sharp thud. At that same moment, the velvet matador finally gave way. It fell off the wall and onto the mattress with a thump—still dusty, but none the worse for the fall.

Raine absorbed the sudden silence with an odd sort of glee, then stomped into the bathroom and turned on the shower, taking small pleasure in the loud wheeze and groan of the pipes as water came rushing through them.

"Let them listen to this for a while," she muttered, and stripped off her clothes, leaving them in a pile on the floor as she stepped beneath the spray.

*Raine Beaumont stood naked beneath the night sky. At sixteen, her slim, perfect body shimmered in the moonlight like a marble statue come to life.*

*At three years her senior, Joseph Colorado was a man fully grown, but at this moment he felt helpless. He took a deep, shaky breath, awed by her beauty as well as her willingness to let him be the first. He reached out to her, feeling her blood pulsing beneath his fingertips.*

*"Rainbow, are you sure?"*

*"I'm not afraid," she whispered.*

*"But I am," he answered, encircling her wrist with his fingers.*

*She moved closer, feeling the heat from his*

*body—that beautiful, naked brown body.*

*"Why, Joseph? What is there to fear? We love each other. Nothing else should matter."*

*He shook his head and pulled her close, shuddering with a sudden and overwhelming need for them to be body to body, flesh to flesh. Then he thrust his fingers through her hair, cupping the back of her head, then tracing the shape of her body with the tips of his fingers.*

*"I'm afraid I'll wake up and find out this was only a dream."*

*"Is this a dream?" she asked.*

*"Feel me." She thrust her breasts against his chest.*

*"Know me," she begged, and moved until the thrust of his manhood was pushing against her belly.*

*"Love me," she whispered, and knew a true moment of joy when he pushed her down onto the ground and slid between her legs.*

*He heard her gasp, then he felt the breath of her sigh as it passed by the side of his face.*

*"Did I hurt you?"*

*"Yes," she said softly, and clutched him a little bit tighter.*

*He gritted his teeth, knowing that it would be agony to quit, but he would rather die than hurt her.*

*"Do you want me to stop?"*

*"No."*

*Again, he was shaken by her bravery. He took a deep breath and raised up on his elbows, staring intently through the darkness to the girl beneath him.*

*"I love you, Raine Beaumont, more than you will ever know."*

*Raine shuddered as the clear, perfect pattern of his words broke the silence of the night. She wrapped her legs around his waist and tunneled her fingers through his hair.*

*"I already knew that, Colorado, or this wouldn't be happening."*

*A momentary silence was broken by Joseph's soft chuckle as he started to move within her. Sometime later, that same silence was shattered by a woman's soft cry, followed by a man's deep groan.*

Joseph sat straight up in bed, gasping for air and reaching for the light. Beaded in sweat, he breathed a sigh of relief as the room was bathed in a quick glow of white light. He shoved the heels of his palms against his eyelids, but the memory was still there. Disgusted with himself for wallowing in the past, he rolled out of bed, reaching for his jeans with one hand and his boots with another.

A few minutes later he was in the kitchen and heading for the door. As he passed through, he lifted a bridle from a nearby peg. When he stepped off the porch, the night breeze dried the last remnants of perspiration from his body. He lifted his head, inhaling deeply and testing the scents on the wind. Unlike the dream he'd just had, it was a reassuring act. Nothing seemed out of place.

Nearby a horse sensed his presence and nickered.

Joseph whistled once between his teeth and then headed toward the corrals. The horse tossed its head and started toward him at a trot.

Joseph climbed the rails, then jumped down, landing inside the corral just as the horse reached his side.

"Yes, Blanco, good boy," Joseph crooned, rubbing the horse's head as he slipped the bit between its teeth.

The horse pushed its head against Joseph's bare chest, begging to be scratched as Joseph worked the bridle over its ears. Within seconds, he was on the horse and riding as his ancestors had ridden. Bareback. Without caution or fear.

Rider and horse circled the corral twice, gaining momentum with each turn, unaware they were being watched. Moments later, Joseph kicked the horse sharply in the flanks and then tightened his legs around its belly. Just before the horse became airborne, Joseph leaned forward, flat against the horse's neck. They cleared the top rails with ease.

Benny watched with envy from the shadows of the porch. Joseph had a skill he would never acquire. The sheer beauty of that leap was still with him as he walked back in the house. Even after he returned to his bed and closed his eyes, he kept thinking of his brother. That jump. It was as if he and the horse had been one.

He cursed beneath his breath and rolled over. He

needed to get back to L.A. This life wasn't for him. Out here, Joseph lived too close to the old ways. Benny wanted fast cars, easy money, and pretty women, and he didn't much care how he got them. Besides, there were secrets in Joseph's life that he didn't understand. Like the days when Joseph would disappear, making no excuses as to where he was going or when he'd be back. All he would tell Benny is that it was business.

Benny snorted softly. Business. That was a likely story. The way he figured it, Joseph had something going on the side and was keeping all of the money to himself.

And in Benny's mind, that was another good reason for wanting to leave. Joseph didn't trust him. For that matter, none of their people trusted him. He punched his pillow into a comfortable wad and then closed his eyes. Joseph could ride all the way to hell as far as he was concerned. He was going back to sleep.

The night sky looked as if it had been showered with diamonds, but tonight it was hard for Joseph to see the beauty for the pain of the words going around and around in his head.

*Had a son . . . stillborn . . . bring him home. Bring him home. Bring him home.*

"Ah, God."

He pulled the horse to a stop, then slid off, dropping to his knees in the sand.

The horse nickered softly, nudging Joseph's

shoulder. The familiar scent of horseflesh, along with that warm, velvet brush of Blanco's nose, brought him back to a reality he didn't want to face.

He'd been a father.

He'd lost a child.

And there was a small part of him that wanted to add that he'd also lost the best woman he'd ever known. But he knew it was impossible to reclaim the past, and he let that thought go. Raine didn't belong to him anymore, and maybe she never had.

The ring on his finger glimmered in the moonlight. He watched the reflection catching fire in the crystal, then sighed. There were too many responsibilities in his life to dwell on maybes and what ifs. His only defense was that he'd been so damned young and so much in love. He was sorry—about as sorry as a man can get and still be breathing—but no amount of apologies could turn back time. And even if he had been of a mind to go after her all those years ago, he'd been tied to the healing place. Becoming guardian had changed everything, including his life.

He closed his eyes.

Remembering . . .


*"Joseph, wake up, my son."*

*Joseph rolled over in bed, staring up into his father's stern face in sudden confusion. Then he glanced toward the windows. It was still dark outside. Something dreadful must be wrong. His father never behaved in such a manner.*

"Dad?"

Michael Colorado tossed a pair of jeans and a shirt at the foot of Joseph's bed.

"Get dressed. We're going on a trip."

Joseph glanced at the clock as he rolled out of bed. It was a little after three in the morning.

"Where are we going? What do I need to pack?" he asked as he yanked on his clothes.

Michael gave his son a look that ended the questions.

Joseph's father was not a tall man, but at that moment, he looked like a giant. Joseph swallowed nervously and grabbed his boots on the way out the door. When they got to the truck, it was obvious to Joseph that his father had packed everything they might possibly need for an extended stay. That made Joseph even more nervous. He had a job. He had a girl who—

At that point, he corrected himself. Up until a month ago, he'd had a girl. It was still difficult for him to remember that Raine was gone from his life. It hurt even more to realize how little he'd meant to her.

The truck bounced in a pothole on the road and he gave his father a nervous glance.

"I told Danny Blaisdale you wouldn't be in until Monday. You won't lose your job."

Joseph nodded.

"Coffee in the thermos," his father said, pointing toward a small chest in the floor between Joseph's feet. "Egg sandwiches in the sack near your *elbow. I'm hungry, how about you?"*

*Joseph grinned as he thrust a hand through his hair, giving it the only combing it would have for hours.*

*"You know me," he said, reaching for the coffee to pour some for them both.*

*"Save me two," Michael said. "You can have the rest."*

*Joseph grinned. He didn't know what was going on, but this part was definitely all right. It wasn't until the sun started coming up that he realized they were driving north.*

*Mile after mile passed with little more than an occasional comment between them. Joseph could tell by the expression on his father's face that this was no hunting trip. But he knew his father well enough to know that when it was time, he would tell him the rest.*

*It wasn't until evening of that same day that Michael pulled off the road and into what amounted to little more than a natural cul-de-sac. An outcropping of rocks and brush marked the spot where Michael parked as he got out and locked down the truck. As he unloaded his pack, he glanced up at the sky.*

*"It will be dark in a couple of hours . . . maybe less," he said shortly. "Grab your backpack, boy. We need to make the campsite before sundown."*

*Joseph frowned. The campsite? They were in the Superstition Mountains, not a national park.*

*Although his patience was running thin and the*

*wonder of this adventure was wearing out, Joseph
knew better than to argue. He did as he was told.*

*"Are you ready, boy?"*

*Joseph nodded.*

*"Then follow me. There is much you must
learn."*


Blanco snorted softly, jerking Joseph back to the present.

"I hear you," he said, and pulled himself to his feet.

Dwelling on the past gained him nothing. What was done was done. He could never go back.

Exhaustion hit as he was mounting, and it was all he could do to remain upright. He looked up into the heavens, reorienting himself with the world by the stars. When he saw the Big Dipper, he grabbed Blanco's reins and nudged him forward.

"Let's go home, boy," Joseph said.

The big horse moved forward. Joseph never looked back.

Stuart Damon Rossi III came from money. He hadn't been born with just the proverbial silver spoon in his mouth. He'd had service for twelve. He was a Robert Redford lookalike with a penchant for fast cars and long-legged women. At the age of forty-two, he had the world in the palm of his hand . . . and he was dying.

The most aggravating part of the whole situation was the fact that his social status had no impact upon his disease. Even though Rossi was an uncommon man, none of his wealth or power could change what heredity and an excessive lifestyle had wrought. He was a hemophiliac with congestive heart failure. In Stuart's case, there were no options of transplants or miracles to save him.

Like the one he was making today, his trips to the Bel Air hospital were necessary. They'd been necessary all of his life. The periodic infusion of clotting factors into Stuart Rossi's blood had stood him in good stead all these years. It was the damnable news of his heart problems that had knocked him flat on his ass. But Stuart wasn't the kind of man to run from trouble. He had searched the world over for specialists who might consider taking on his case. Although he'd had nothing but negative responses, he wasn't ready to give up. Added to that, having to stop his search so he could go for treatments further frustrated him.

Late for his appointment, he bumped shoulders with a young woman on her way out the door and cursed beneath his breath. She whispered a quick apology he almost ignored. But there was something familiar about the tilt of her head and the swing in her walk that made him stop and look back.

Then he stared.

She wasn't the type of woman who moved within his social circles, yet he was certain he'd seen her before. His eyes narrowed thoughtfully. All that black hair . . . and that delicate jut of dark eyebrows above a proud nose. Where had he—?

Recognition dawned as he suddenly bolted after her, grabbing her arm before she could escape.

"Wynema? Wynema Littlefish . . . is that you?"

The woman paled, trying unsuccessfully to pull away from his grasp.

"I don't know you," she said, glancing nervously over her shoulder toward the parking lot.

"I know, I know," Stuart muttered. "So we haven't been properly introduced. But I'm certain I've seen you several times here in this hospital. I've heard them call out the name. I remembered it because was different."

The woman's panic increased. She gave him a beseeching look.

"I'm sorry, but you've made a mistake. Please, someone is waiting for me."

When she looked up, Stuart's pulse skipped a beat. "My God! It is you!"

He stared, unable to believe his eyes. He'd seen her off and on for months and each time he'd seen her, he'd been increasingly disgusted by her condition. Everyone had known what was wrong with her. And he remembered thinking that she should have had the decency to go off and die in private instead of rotting away in public view.

Just then a car pulled up to the curb, and a young man jumped out, rushing to Wynema's aid.

"Get your hands off my sister," he shouted, and shoved Stuart aside.

"I didn't mean any harm," Stuart said. "I was just wishing her well." There was a sneer on his face as he glanced at her smooth skin and silky black hair. "But it's quite obvious she doesn't need it."

"Wynema has no need of anything from you or anyone else here at this place. Indian medicine is stronger. Indian medicine cured her when the white man could not."

Wynema paled. "Donny! We do not speak of it!" she cried, and pushed him toward the car before getting in herself.

Stuart couldn't quit staring.

*Indian medicine?*

*Cured?*

Stuart started to shake. The man couldn't mean cured in the true sense of the word? No one was cured of AIDS. And then he looked at Wynema again. None of this was making any sense. By his reckoning, he would have bet every cent he had that this woman would be dead, and yet here she was, vibrant, healthy, and obviously very reluctant to talk about her sudden change of health.

"Wait!" Stuart cried. "Talk to me. Tell me what you know. Please! If there is some great healer among your people, won't you at least share your knowledge with me? I don't have long to live." Then, for added measure, Stuart threw in what he considered his ace in the hole. "I would pay any amount of money to be healed."

Stuart watched as the man stared at the diamond ring on his finger and the gold Rolex on his wrist.

He masked a grin. All men had their price. And then the moment was broken as Wynema cried.

"Donny! We must go now! You've already said too much."

Donny blinked and then straightened, as if suddenly remembering the indignation he was supposed to be feeling.

"All men die," he said shortly. "Besides, the healing place is not for white men."

"Donny! Enough!" Wynema screamed.

And then they drove away, leaving Stuart Rossi with a new avenue to search. He'd wanted answers and was pretty sure he knew how to get them. All he needed was a checkbook and five minutes alone with Donny Littlefish.

\*   \*   \*

"Hey, Donny, how 'bout another drink?"

Donny Littlefish grinned at his buddies and then emptied his beer.

"No thanks, boys. I'm outta here."

"Damn, Donny, you act like you was married. You ain't got no one to go home to."

Donny's smile widened. It was a constant source of amusement to his friends that he still lived at home with his father and his sister, Wynema. What was even harder for them to understand was that he did it because he liked it, not because he couldn't afford to do otherwise.

"Ooh, that's where you're wrong," Donny yelled as he headed out the door. "There's a big pan of chicken fajitas waiting for me. That's better than an old lady, any day."

Their laughter followed him out the door and across the parking lot as he headed for his car.

The Goal Line was a neighborhood bar. Nothing fancy. Nothing bad. A good-old-boy place to play pool or maybe watch some sports on the big-screen TV. Donny stopped there after work once or twice a week to unwind with his friends. But now he was ready to kick off his boots, listen to his dad's corny jokes, and eat some of Wynema's good food. He was still smiling as he pulled his keys out of his pocket to unlock his car.

"Donny Littlefish?"

Donny turned, his eyes widening as he spotted

the dark limousine. It wasn't unusual for someone to be out here at night, but not in a vehicle like this. Leery of things that seemed out of place, he took a quick step back. This was, after all, still L.A.

"Who wants to know?"

The back window slid down. Swiftly. Silently. Donny's eyes widened as a man's face appeared.

"I know you," Donny said.

"Not nearly as well as you should," Stuart said. "Get in. We have some business to discuss."

Donny's heart skipped a beat, and then his true nature took over.

"White man, there can be no business between us."

He turned his back on the limo and shoved his key in the lock of his car.

"Get him," Stuart ordered.

Within seconds, Donny's limp body was dumped unceremoniously inside the limousine, his keys lying on the pavement beside his car where he'd dropped them.


Stuart Rossi was livid, which elevated his blood pressure, which in turn put a strain on his heart. Right now, it felt as if it were trying to jump out of his chest. Four hours and counting he'd wasted on this excuse for a man. And they hadn't started with threats. Oh no. He'd been much more than fair. They'd started with the money. After all, it was what ran Stuart's world.

*  *  *

"Have you ever seen a million dollars?" Stuart asked.

Donny rubbed at the knot on the back of his head while staring down at the huge pile of loose bills in the floor before him. He looked up at Rossi, then at the matching muscle on either side of him. In that moment, he accepted the fact that he would not be home for fajitas, ever again.

"Have you ever seen a white man die?" he countered softly.

Stuart's mouth dropped open, and then he started to smile.

"Well now, boy. You're pretty feisty for someone on the wrong end of the stick."

Donny knew it was futile, but he took a swing at him anyway. Even if it never got there, he would know that he'd tried.

Shocked by the viciousness of the young man's attitude, Stuart froze. If it had not been for the persuasion he'd hired, he would have taken the blow straight in the face.

"You little son of a bitch," Stuart snarled. "I'm going to make you sorry—very, very sorry. Then I'm going to make you talk."

But that was four and a half hours ago, and now Donny Littlefish was holding onto life out of pure stubbornness. Worse yet, he hadn't told Stuart a thing more than what he'd blurted out at the hospital all those weeks ago.

Stuart leaned over the bed where Littlefish was lying. Blood bubbled from the young Indian's nose. It was the only indication Stuart had that the man was still breathing.

"Fine. You don't want to talk to me, maybe your sister will have more to say."

The words came through the black fog of Donny's pain, rousing him as nothing else had done.

"No," he muttered through split and swollen lips. "No."

Stuart grabbed him by the arm and yanked. Donny's head banged against the headboard.

"Then talk to me. Tell me what I need to know. Who healed your sister? Who took away her sores and her shame?"

Donny heard the words and then felt himself sigh. His last coherent thought was, *Sister, forgive me*. He pursed his lips, trying to speak, but his throat was too dry, his tongue too swollen inside his mouth.

Stuart pointed at a nearby pitcher of water. "Give him something to drink."

The bald-headed thug threw the contents in Donny's face.

Donny groaned and licked his lips, but there was just enough moisture to temper the fire in his throat.

"Don't hurt her," he croaked.

Stuart leaned close, so close he could smell Donny's sweat and the coppery scent of fresh blood.

"Then tell me what I want to know," he hissed.

✳   ✳   ✳

Donny heard a great roar, and in his mind's eye, saw a vast prairie behind him and before him a small rise. On the rise stood a horse about sixteen hands high. Its black spotted coat was like a star on the sea of brown grass. And he stood, watching in awe as the star began to pivot and then rear on hind legs, pawing the air in a slow, graceful dance. His heart swelled at the sight of such beauty. When the horse started toward him, Donny knew a great joy.

First at a walk.

Then a trot.

Then a full, all-out run.

Faster it moved.

Closer it came.

Donny shivered with anticipation. The dappled hindquarters of the majestic Appaloosa were familiar. He'd seen this horse once before. But he'd only been six and near death from pneumonia. Then the horse had appeared in a feverish dream and disappeared almost immediately.

Donny started to laugh. The horse had never come this close to him before. He heard himself whistle and then somehow he'd known of its name.

*"El muerte,"* he whispered.

The horse whinnied out loud, as if it had heard.

Donny laughed as it stopped before him, pushing a soft, velvet muzzle into the palm of his hand and nickering in the way horses do when they greet a good friend.

*"Finally, you have come."*

The horse ducked its head, as if showing Donny

the way to get on. Donny wrapped his hands in the long, flowing mane, preparing to mount.

But even then he hesitated, knowing that their journey would be long. In the distance, he could hear someone shouting his name. He wouldn't look back. Didn't want to look back.

But the horse did not move. Something was wrong. There was a magic word that came first, but he couldn't remember it.

He began to wail.

"Don't leave me behind . . . not again, not again."

The great horse reared in the air once again, coming down so hard that grass and sod tore beneath its hooves.

Donny looked down. There on the ground beneath the torn grass was the word he'd been trying to find. With a loud, joyful shout, he swung up on the horse's back.

"Colorado!" he yelled. "Joseph Colorado's the name."

Stuart cursed until he was physically blue in the face from lack of oxygen and then sat down on the foot of the bed where Donny Littlefish's body still lay. The son of a bitch had died before he'd told him everything he needed to know. Yes, he had a name. But there were fifty states and several million people to sort through.

"What do you want to do with the body, boss?"

Stuart didn't bother to look up.

"Take him back to his car."

"But boss! It's almost daylight. People might see."

Stuart looked up. He didn't see five hundred pounds of muscle accumulated between the two men. He saw no threat, felt no fear. All he saw was two men who had easily been bought.

"Then you'd better hurry, right?"

I t was almost sundown. Another day had passed, and Raine was no closer to peace of mind than she'd been when she arrived in Oracle. Still reeling from her meeting with Joseph, she hadn't been able to eat a bite all day and had retreated to the temporary safety of her room.

The call she'd made earlier to Chicago still echoed in her mind. "It's done," she'd told her lawyer. "Start the paperwork through now."

Paperwork. A generic term for such a monumental undertaking.

She lay on her back on the bed, staring at a water stain on the ceiling to the left of the door, trying to block out the image of that small marble cross back in a Chicago cemetery and the grave it marked. That cross . . . and her baby . . . would be following her to Oracle. Only she would be continuing on.

Tears came then, unbidden but impossible to stop, and she rolled out of bed, angry with their presence and herself for the weakness.

"I've got to get out of here," she muttered, and started grabbing at clothes.

Minutes later, she exited the motel on the run and slid behind the wheel of her car as if she were being chased. Although she had no particular destination in mind, when she got on the highway, she headed south out of town. A short while later she looked up to realize she was at the entrance to Spencer Canyon. Her heart dropped.

She had come back to where it had all begun. To the first place she and Joseph had made love. It seemed only fitting that it had also been the last place she'd seen him before she'd moved. She took the turn knowing that it would be dark in a short while, and well aware that it wasn't the safest place for a woman alone. She kept telling herself she just needed to see it one more time, if for no other reason to close a painful chapter of her life.

It had been twelve years since she'd set foot in this place, and yet when she parked the car and got out, the familiarity of it overwhelmed her. The trees were taller than she remembered, and some of the trails had been cleaned and marked for hikers and backpackers, but other than that, it seemed the same.

She lifted her face to the sky and then closed her eyes, inhaling the fresh, clean scent of the forest. Something rustled in the underbrush nearby and she turned just in time to see a rabbit dart into a thicket. There was a moment of empathy as she sensed the rabbit's fear.

She knew fear. For the last few weeks, it had been her constant companion.

Fear of facing Joseph.

Fear of change.

"Run, rabbit, run," she whispered, moving away from where she'd been standing and into the trees, following the sounds of running water toward the nearby creek.

The leafy canopy above her head threw thick, dense shadows upon the ground. Protected now by the trees through which she was walking, she felt her self-imposed isolation more keenly than ever before.

It was one thing to be solitary in a city like Chicago, because even when you were alone in your home, you were never really alone in the world. There were too many constant reminders of the multitudes of people within mere yards of where you lived. But here, in this place that marked the mouth of Spencer Canyon, Raine felt the true meaning of solitude. For as far as the eye could see and the ear could hear, she was truly alone.

It felt good.

Memory had brought her back to the place where she and Joseph had loved, but it was instinct that kept her moving deeper into the trees.

Toward sanctuary.

Toward peace.

And oh, God, she needed peace in her heart more than anything she'd ever needed before.

When she reached the banks of the creek, she dropped to her knees with a groan and rocked back on her heels.

"God help me," she whispered, and covered her face with her hands.

\*     \*     \*

Joseph was restless. His concentration was nil. Today he'd started to work the same horse twice before stopping himself in disgust. He'd been short-tempered with Benny and on the verge of anger all day. But with who? Raine for coming out of nowhere and rocking his world, or himself, for not being with her when she'd needed him most?

It was past suppertime, but he couldn't eat. His appetite was gone. Benny had left for town hours earlier, and for once, Joseph could find no solace in the beauty of a setting sun. Impatient with himself for dwelling on things he couldn't change, he grabbed his hat and car keys on the way out the door. He didn't know where he was going, but anything would beat this mental misery all to hell.

He was miles down the road before he realized he was almost at the entrance to Spencer Canyon. He tapped the brakes and took the turn without thinking, but when he pulled up at the parking area where the hiking trail began, knew he hadn't been the only one tonight who'd been led by memories. If he wasn't mistaken, the lone car to his right looked very much like the one Raine had been driving when she'd come to the ranch.

He killed the engine and then sat without moving, considering the wisdom of following his heart one last time.

"What the hell," he finally muttered, and got out of his truck. He'd come this far. It was too late to back out now.

As he moved though the trees toward the creek, a mental scenario of what he might say kept playing out in his head. But when he came out of the trees, he was completely unprepared for the sight he beheld.

It was Raine, down on her knees, her shoulders bent in sorrow. Even from here he could hear the soft, uneven sounds of sobs ripping up her throat.

He started toward her.

The sound of twigs snapping bought Raine upright and she stood and spun in one motion, her heart pounding with sudden fright as the tears still ran upon her face. When she recognized who it was, a rush of relief swept over her.

Joseph reached for her. "I'm sorry. I didn't mean to frighten you," he said quickly.

Raine stepped backward and Joseph stopped, his hand still outstretched. She didn't answer, and he couldn't find the words to express what her tears had done to his heart. Finally, it was Raine who found her voice.

"What are you doing here?" she asked.

Joseph shrugged and then stuffed his hands in his pockets to keep from touching her.

"The same thing you were, I guess. Looking for answers."

Raine almost laughed. "Then like me, you're looking in all the wrong places. There wasn't anything here but ghosts."

She started to push past him when he stopped
her with one word.

"Memories."

She paused.

He took a step toward her. "Memories aren't
ghosts."

She frowned. "Maybe not for you, but for me
they are."

Joseph sighed and then smiled, and it was that
small, heartfelt smile that wrapped around Raine's
bruised and battered heart.

"Bad memories maybe, but not good memories," he said. "Good memories are a blessing, and
we left nothing but good memories behind in this
place."

She shuddered on a breath and then dropped her
head. Before she could react, Joseph's arms were
around her and her head was on his chest. Her resis-
tance was almost instinctive after years of being hurt
and alone.

"Just let me hold you," he begged. "No strings,
no promises, no more than this touch."

She sighed. It was his strength that was her
undoing. She had none left of her own.

"Just this and nothing more," she muttered.

His arms tightened around her shoulders as he
laid his cheek against the crown of her head.

"Yes, Rainbow. Just this and nothing more."

Later they walked out of the forest, sharing an
uneasy silence as they unlocked the doors to their
cars.

Joseph paused at his pickup, watching as Raine slid behind the steering wheel of her car.

"Raine."

She looked up. Moonlight caught the glimmer of tears in her eyes, but he didn't remark upon them. He was too close to them himself.

"Will you be all right?" he asked.

He saw her take a deep breath, and then she lifted her chin.

"Yes. I'll be fine."

"We still need to talk," he said softly.

She closed her eye s and then looked up and nodded. "But not tonight."

He shook his head. "No, not tonight."

He watched as she drove away. When he could no longer see the taillights of her car, he got in his truck and drove away.

Benny Colorado was not in the mood for lost travelers. He was already late for his date with Shelley Bigger, and he knew she'd give him hell about it. But Joseph was nowhere in sight, and Benny couldn't pull his own vehicle past the Mercedes limousine that was coming to a stop in the driveway without at least seeing what he wanted. He tried to conceal his surprise when the driver opened the back door to let out a man attached to what looked to be an oxygen tank that he was dragging behind him.

"Can I help you, mister?"

"I'm looking for a Mr. Colorado."

Although Benny suspected the man meant Joseph, he couldn't resist.

"I'm Mr. Colorado."

"My name is Stuart Rossi from Bel Air, California, and I'd venture to say that this conversation is more about what I can do for you."

Benny laughed. He'd heard the same patter a million times back in L.A., although to be honest, this was the first time he'd ever seen a traveling salesman in a chauffeur-driven limo and sporting a portable oxygen tank instead of a briefcase.

"Look, mister," Benny said. "Whoever you are doesn't matter and whatever it is you're selling, we don't want any."

Stuart gasped and then choked. Not much, but enough that the driver bolted from the car and hastened to his employer's side.

"I'm fine," Stuart said, waving his driver back to the car. "My apologies," he told Benny. "Edward fusses too much to suit me. But your assumption of my presence here rather shocked me. On the contrary, Mr. Colorado, I don't want your money. I'm trying to give you some of mine."

Benny straightened. Even though it had to be a scam, the mention of free money was something he would never ignore.

"Who has to die?"

Stuart grinned. "As you can see, I'm not in the best of health."

Benny's gaze shifted to the tube in the guy's nose and the oxygen tank at his side, but he remained silent.

Stuart continued. "I was told that you guard the location to a very sacred place among your people. I was told that you could take me to this place and that I would be healed."

Benny gawked. He couldn't help it. This was off the scale of every come-on he had expected to hear. Finally he found the good sense to answer.

"I don't know what you're talking about, mister, but I'm late for a date and I need to—"

"Is your date worth a million dollars?"

Benny froze. "What?"

"I'm saying that I would pay a million dollars to be taken to your healing place, and that—"

The screen door behind Benny squeaked and then slammed. Stuart's attention moved from the man before him to the one just emerging from inside the house, missing Benny's sigh of disgust.

Joseph would have to show up just when it was getting good, Benny thought and turned, eyeing the cold, implacable expression on his brother's face.

Stuart couldn't quit staring. The man who'd just exited wore a mantle of authority that was impossible to ignore, and Stuart knew he'd been talking to the wrong man. His eyes narrowed, and he muttered, as much to himself as to them.

"Why wasn't I told there were two?"

Joseph didn't answer. He'd heard enough on his way out the door to know that somewhere a very serious confidence had been breached.

Although Benny could see that his brother was displeased about something, he was too excited about the stranger's offer of a million dollars to remain quiet.

"Joseph! This is Stuart Rossi from California. He says he'll give a million dollars to be taken to some health spa and that—"

Joseph silenced Benny with a look. When he turned to Rossi, there was no mistaking his displeasure.

"Mr. Rossi, I'm afraid you've come a long way for nothing. As much as I'd like to be able to direct you to your destination, there are no health spas in or around Oracle. Maybe you should try Phoenix."

Benny groaned beneath his breath, mentally picturing a cool million dollars going down the proverbial drain. Damn Joseph anyway. If he'd just kept his big mouth shut, they could have worked a quick scam. There were dozens of places around here that a smart man could make into an overnight health spa . . . especially for a fool such as Rossi appeared to be.

"I'm outta here," Benny muttered, and stalked down the steps and got into his car. He left a fantail of dust for the duo to breathe as he spun out of the drive.

When the air began to thicken, Stuart gasped and then began coughing anew.

"Sorry," Joseph said, and waved toward the driver who was standing beside the car. "I'd say the best thing for you is to get out of the dust and go back where you came from."

"Please! I wasn't looking for a health spa and

you know it. Take me to the place you took Wynema Littlefish. I'm dying. Why won't you help me? You helped her."

Joseph couldn't believe what he was hearing. He would have bet his life that Wynema would keep her vows of silence.

"I don't know anyone by that name," Joseph said.

Stuart began to panic. The implacable expression on this man's face was frightening in a way nothing had ever been before. Sensing his last chance slipping away, he grabbed Joseph by the wrist. It was a mistake.

"You don't understand. I'll pay! I'll pay anything!"

Joseph stared down at the hand gripping his arm and then slowly peeled Stuart's fingers away.

"Didn't anyone ever tell you that there are some things that money can't buy?"

Stuart started to shake. "I'm not trying to insult you. I just want my health back. If you won't help me, I won't live to see my next birthday."

Joseph shook his head. "I'm sorry, but someone has misled you. I'm not God. I cannot perform miracles."

Stuart suddenly yanked the tube from his nose and tossed it aside, letting his rage spill out into the air between them.

"You bastard . . . you dirty brown bastard! What are you trying to prove?" He began to pace, his face growing redder by the moment, his words coming out between grunts and gasps. "What is this—retribution for having your lands taken away all those centuries ago? Is that it? Is this your way of getting back at the white man?"

Joseph stood silent beneath Stuart's unexpected attack, watching the man's polished shell fall away to reveal his true personality.

"There is no such thing as a fountain of youth," Joseph said. "I would have thought that the odyssey into the Florida swamps a few centuries back already proved that."

"I don't want my youth!" Stuart shrieked. "Only my health. And you—you lying bastard—could help me. I know it! I saw Wynema Littlefish when she was dying of AIDS—and I saw her less than two months ago."

"Again, I know no such woman," Joseph said. "But maybe she was just in remission. I've heard of such things."

Spittle ran from the corner of Stuart's lip as he pointed an accusing finger in Joseph's face.

"Not according to her brother, Donny."

Joseph flinched. Damn! He couldn't believe that anyone from the Littlefish family would have betrayed him like this. But how else could this man have known even this much?

"Maybe this Donny lied to you," Joseph said. "Maybe he tricked you for your money."

A cold smile spread across Stuart's face. "I didn't give the man a dime. I didn't have to. He talked— and, I might add, voluntarily." *And the private investigator I hired to research the past three months of the Littlefish family did the rest.* But he kept those last thoughts to himself.

Joseph shrugged and then shook his head.

Frustration hit Stuart like a fist in the belly. Gasping for air, he doubled over, aware that he'd expounded too much energy in anger. His small reserve of strength was gone.

At this point, Edward came running back.

"Take him home," Joseph said shortly. "There is nothing for him here."

Halfway to the car Stuart turned. "Two million. I'll give you two million dollars to be healed."

Joseph turned his back on the pair and walked into the house.

The slamming of the door was as effective an end to their conversation as any handshake might have been. Moments later, Stuart collapsed in the back seat, grabbing for his oxygen tube and cursing every Indian who'd ever walked the face of the earth.

"They should have annihilated the lot of them," he whispered, and sank back against the opulence of the pure leather seats.

"Try to remain calm, sir," Edward said. "I'll find the nearest doctor and—"

"Hell no," Stuart muttered. "I don't want a doctor. I want you to take me back to Phoenix. I need to rest. Tomorrow we're going to approach the other Colorado. The one named Benny. Something tells me that he won't be as tight-assed about money as his big brother."

Inside the house, Joseph was scrambling through his desk, searching for the phone number to the Littlefish home outside of Los Angeles. Furious beyond words, it was all he could do to gather his thoughts as he counted the rings at the other end of the line. Just when he was about to hang up, a man answered.

"Hello."

Joseph took a deep breath, willing himself to a calm he didn't feel.

"Duncan Littlefish?"

"Yes?"

"This is Joseph Colorado."

Duncan's voice began to shake like a dying leaf in the wind. "It is a sign," he said softly. "The man who saved my daughter's life is again giving solace to our family in a time of great need. You will say a prayer for us?"

Joseph frowned. "I'm sorry, I don't know what you—"

"You have called at a time when our spirits are low."

Joseph stopped. Something was wrong. Surely Wynema hadn't relapsed. Not once in the span of centuries since the healing place began had anyone ever relapsed.

"Wynema . . . is she—"

"No," Duncan said. "It is Donny. He is dead, and my heart cries for justice we will never see."

"Justice?"

"Yes," Duncan said. "He was beaten to death about a month ago."

Joseph was in shock. "Sir . . . I am so sorry. I didn't know about this. Please give your family my condolences. I will say a prayer for you all."

"It will be appreciated," Duncan said, and then sighed. "But if not this, then why have you called?"

Joseph discarded the notion. The old man's voice was full of pain. This wasn't the time. In fact, the time for answers from this family was obviously over.

"It doesn't matter," Joseph said softly. "Again, I am sorry for your loss."

"Thank you," Duncan said, and then disconnected.

Joseph dropped the phone back in the cradle, then leaned his head against the wall. Donny Littlefish dead? Murdered? My God . . .

Joseph closed his eyes, but instead of the peace he sought, he kept seeing the smirk on Stuart Rossi's face—kept hearing Rossi's vow that Donny had talked voluntarily. But what if he hadn't? Joseph had seen Rossi's rage firsthand. What if—

He straightened, his thoughts in turmoil. He hadn't been able to believe that any of the Littlefish people would have talked about the healing, especially to an outsider. Maybe his first instincts had been right. Maybe they hadn't talked—at least not voluntarily. His mind blanked.

He stared down at the ring on his finger. The clear green crystal seemed cloudy . . . and no wonder. Two days ago Raine Beaumont had reappeared in his life like a restless ghost and then she'd shattered the orderliness of his life with the news that he'd fathered and lost a child without his ever knowing of either incident. Add Stuart Rossi's appearance today and that would be enough to cloud anything.

He shook off his doubts. Raine's presence in Oracle was temporary. And if he had anything to do with it, Stuart Rossi's would be as well. He looked up, staring around the emptiness of his home and suddenly wishing for the sound of someone else's voice. At this point, he would even settle for some of Benny's complaints. But it was Saturday night, and Benny wouldn't be home before morning.

Joseph paused just a moment and then reached for his hat. He'd been ignoring his conscience and putting off the inevitable, and he knew it. He had to see Raine. Even if it did neither one of them a bit of good, he wanted to look upon her face and let the sound of her voice settle in his bones.

Raine stepped out of the shower, reaching for a towel to wrap around her hair. She was tired. So tired. All she wanted to do was lie down on the small, lumpy bed and sleep. Sleep until this nightmare was over.

Disgusted with her maudlin feelings, she vigorously toweled her wet head, then tossed the towel on the floor and grabbed the last clean one to dry herself. A few moments later, she stood before the damp, cracked mirror, judging her image. Rivulets of condensation ran down the face of the glass, separating her reflection into bits and pieces. She frowned. In a way, it was a very apt description of the way she felt. Damaged, but still in one piece.

She leaned forward, staring at herself until her eyes burned. Finally, she pushed away, chiding herself for brooding. It did no good to dwell on how screwed up her life had become. It wouldn't change a thing.

Still naked, she threw herself facedown upon the sheets and closed her eyes. *I'll rest for a minute . . . then I'll eat.*

Two hours later she was awakened by a loud knock on her door. Momentarily confused by her surroundings, she rolled out of bed and staggered toward the door before it dawned on her that she had nothing on.

"Who is it?" she called, ready to turn away whoever it might be.

"Joseph."

She sighed. She know why he was here: he'd come to talk.

"Just a minute," she yelled, then grabbed at the first thing she could find—her Eskimo Joe nightshirt.

Although it was old and worn paper-thin, it reached well past her knees. It wasn't much, but it would afford the modesty she needed, especially with this man. She tunneled her fingers through her hair in lieu of combing and grabbed the doorknob before she could change her mind. But when she opened the door, she forgot the glib comment she'd been about to offer.

*Now I remember why I couldn't leave him alone.*

Joseph tried not to stare, but the truth was, his

cool had just up and died on the doorstep of the no-tell motel.

Raine waited for him to speak. When it became obvious that wasn't going to happen, she stepped aside and opened the door a bit wider.

"I suppose you should probably come in."

Joseph moved inside, trying to breathe around the sudden lump in his throat. All he could think was that it should be against the law for a blue-eyed woman to look so sexy in such pitiful gear.

"Sorry about the mess." Then she grinned slightly. "I fell asleep before I could hang up my stuff."

That explained the red mark on the side of her face and the matching one on the back of her hand. She'd obviously been using her hand for a pillow.

"I should have called," Joseph said.

Raine shrugged. "It's all right. I didn't mean to fall asleep. I'll probably be awake all night."

He shoved his hands in his pockets and let his gaze move from her face to the confines of the small, tacky room. There was a dusty painting leaning up against the dresser that matched a clean square of space on the wall above her bed. In lieu of a closet, her spare assortment of clothing was hanging from bent hangers on a rod beside the bathroom door. There was a burned-out light over what passed as a vanity and only one bulb burning in the night light by her bed. A tiny scrap of pink nylon was on the floor next to her shoes. He turned away, unwilling to look upon anything that reminded him of her body.

When he caught her watching him, he knew it was time to talk or start walking before he did something they both might regret.

"Well now, Miss Beaumont, if I were a betting man, I'd be willing to bet that this place is a little beneath your normal standards."

Raine dropped onto the corner of the bed and then waved him toward the one opposite her.

"Do shut up and have a seat. Since I'm missing any chairs, you'll have to settle for the other corner."

Joseph eyed the bed and then her and shook his head. "I'll stand."

She shrugged, trying not to stare. It was useless. And there was something about sitting when he was standing so close that made her antsy. She stood and then ambled toward the window, pretending great interest in what she could see beyond the part in the drapes. Finally she turned. Not because she was tired of the view, but because she could feel the heat of his gaze between her shoulder blades as clearly as if he'd touched her.

She crossed her arms across her breasts and lifted her chin.

"So, how have you been?"

Joseph snorted softly. "Are you referring to the last twelve years of my life . . . or the last thirty-six hours? Frankly, lady, the former was quite unremarkable. I wish I could say the same for the latter, but I can't."

There was so much pain on his face she felt ashamed. She couldn't bring herself to continue her charade. Her bravado was over. She wanted to walk across the room and into his arms—to be surrounded by that gentle strength just once more before—

She bit her lower lip to keep it from trembling and ran a shaky hand through her hair. This wasn't why she'd come.

"Look, this isn't easy for either one of us. Why don't you wait outside while I get dressed. Maybe I could talk you into buying me a hamburger, or whatever is good around here. I haven't eaten all day, and—"

Joseph interrupted. "No wonder you're so damned skinny. You should take better care of yourself and you know it."

She almost smiled. He'd been trying to fatten her up ever since the day they'd met.

"I like to think of myself as willowy . . . or maybe coltish."

He shoved his hat a little farther down his forehead and headed for the door.

"You have five minutes, after which time I will take you to eat steak in whatever condition I find you. Do I make myself clear?"

Startled by his anger, she started to argue and then caught a glimpse of his face as he passed by. There was a muscle jerking at the side of his jaw. She seemed to remember that wasn't a good sign.

"I'm agreeing, but only because I'm starving, not because I think you can tell me what to do."

He paused, glaring at her from beneath the shadows of that wide brim.

"I never could tell you what to do," he muttered, and let himself out, catching the door before it could slam.

Raine stood in the middle of the room, trying to catch her breath. She felt as if she'd just been sucked into the eye of a tornado and then spit out through the tail.

"Well now," she muttered.

"Four minutes and counting," Joseph yelled from the other side of the door.

Raine jumped as if she'd been shot and started grabbing at clothes.

The night air was cool. Raine shivered as she exited her room.

Joseph stepped out of the shadows where he'd been waiting for her. "Don't you have a jacket?"

She shook her head. "It's summer. I didn't think to bring one."

"You've been gone too long. Nights here are always cool."

"I'll be fine. Besides, I'm starving. That supersedes cold."

Again, he couldn't help but notice her pencil-thin figure and frowned as he opened the door for her to get in.

"There's probably a jacket or two behind the seat. Help yourself."

She slid into the seat, telling herself that her nervousness was nothing more than echoes of old feelings. But after she pulled a denim jacket out from behind the seat and slipped it on, she had to admit her heart was racing. Just for a moment she let herself pretend that it was Joseph who was holding her and not the fabric of some jacket. By the time he opened the door and slid behind the wheel, she was all business.

"Feels good," she said, rubbing at the jacket on her arms.

She looked so natural sitting beside him—and in his clothes—that it made him angrier. He gritted his teeth and jammed the key into the ignition. This was a damned stupid idea. He didn't need a trip down memory lane. He should have just asked her what he wanted to know and gotten the hell out of her face. Instead, here he was, about to spend what promised to be an interminably long evening with a woman from his past.

Then he looked at her again and his anger died. There was a fragility about her that made him want to protect her all over again. He put the truck in gear and pulled out of the parking lot, determined to make the best of a bad situation.

"Where are we going?"

"To get you a steak." When he stopped for a red light, he glanced over at her and added. "And maybe a baked potato or two covered with butter and sour cream."

Raine's chin jutted. "I don't need to gain weight."

The light turned green. "And I need a suntan," he retorted.

She hid a grin at the reference he'd just made to his perennially brown skin, but made no comment. They drove the rest of the way to the steak house in total silence. There was no common ground between them anymore, and whatever they might have made of their untimely reunion was muddied by the reason she'd come. To rebury a baby . . . their baby. Considering that, there was little left to be said.

An hour later, there was nothing remaining on their plates but steak bones and potato skins. Joseph was nursing a cup of coffee while Raine was polishing off the last few bites of a piece of chocolate cream pie.

"Good?" he asked.

Resisting the urge to lick the tines of her fork, she nodded.

"I can't remember the last time I ate like that."

He arched an eyebrow. "I'm not surprised."

Raine thought about arguing, but it was futile—and he was right. She had neglected her own well-being. She'd let her job take precedence over any personal life or hobbies she might have had. But that was then and this was now, and there was no more job. At this point, denying herself was stupid. She leaned back in her chair and for the first time since her return to Oracle, really let herself look at the man who'd once been the hub of her world.

"You're much bigger than I remember," she said thoughtfully, eyeing him as if he were a suspect in a police lineup.

Because she was staring so intently, he felt free to return the favor. "You grew, too. At least a couple more inches, didn't you?"

Her eyes narrowed thoughtfully as she let herself absorb what he'd become. The broad shoulders had always been there, as had the long legs, but the lankiness was gone. He was solid bulk, and there was a look about him that she couldn't quite place.

"You're very different, Joseph, but I can't quite put my finger on how or why."

He shrugged. "Twelve years is a long time. We all change."

"It's not that." She stared at his face, studying him as if he were a photograph. For a long time she was silent, and then she suddenly leaned forward. "It's your eyes! The difference is in your eyes."

Startled by her perception, he tried to change the subject. "They're still brown, and they've even been black and blue a few times since you left."

She frowned. "No, you're missing the point. It's not their color. There's something about them . . . like a knowing . . . or a—" Somewhere inside of her a knot started to form. It was almost as if another man—a stranger—was staring out at her through Joseph's eyes.

*Dear God.*

She bit her lower lip, trying to still its tremble.

"Your eyes . . . they look old."

A little stunned by what she'd just experienced, she glanced away. When she got the guts to look up, he was looking at her as if he'd never seen her before.

When Joseph realized he'd been caught, he began to stammer.

"Hell, Raine, twelve years is just twelve years. I can't have aged that much."

"That's not what I meant. I never noticed before.

Maybe because I was too young to recognize it, but you have an old soul, Joseph Colorado, and it shows in your eyes."

Then, embarrassed that she'd said too much, she excused herself and stood.

"I'll be right back," she said shortly, and headed for the ladies room.

Hair rose on the back of his neck as his memories turned inwardly, moving backward twelve long years to a ceremony between father and son, held within the valley of the mountain that embraces the sun. Back to the night that his father had taken the ring from his own finger and placed it in Joseph's hand.

*Joseph stared down at the ring he was holding—at the wide silver band and its stone, a chunk of clear green crystal. For as long as he could remember, that ring had been on his father's hand. What did this mean? Why was he giving it to him now? His heart skipped a beat as Michael began to talk.*

*"Many, many lifetimes before the men in metal clothing came riding into the land of the People on the four-legged beasts, other men came out of the sky . . ."*

*At this point, Joseph was hooked. An hour passed, maybe more. He lost track of everything except the words pouring from his father's lips.*

*And then Michael stopped.*

*"So it is said. So I believe."*

Joseph was stunned into silence and over-whelmed by the story his father had just told him. He was afraid to believe—didn't want to believe—but his father wasn't smiling . . . and there was the ring in his hand.

"Put it on, my son," Michael ordered. "To-morrow, when it is daylight, I will show you the truth of what you've been told."

Again Joseph stared at the ring. "But Dad, the ring is far too big. It will fall off."

Michael frowned. "It is not becoming of a guardian to doubt. You must be certain at all times and at all costs. Other lives will depend on you. Never forget! Now do as I say."

Suitably chastised, Joseph bowed his head and slipped the over-sized ring on the third finger of his right hand, expecting it to slide back off again. It did not. It was warm against his skin, and the longer he wore it the warmer it became. Quick beads of sweat broke out across his forehead. His heart began to pound. The heat was becoming intense. In dismay, he looked up at Michael, his eyes wide and filled with fright.

Instead of concern, there was an expression on his father's face that shocked Joseph. He was being judged. At that moment, he subconsciously accepted the role in which he'd been thrust.

Instead of yanking the ring from his finger, he closed his eyes, calming his breathing and making himself focus on the sounds around him rather than on the external pain.

*An owl called from a nearby tree.*

*He shivered. Owls were omens. Sometimes good—sometimes bad.*

*He took another deep breath. A coyote yipped from a faraway ridge while another answered closer by.*

*And then out of nowhere, images flooded the darkness in his mind, overwhelming in their intensity. Thousands upon thousands of years of his ancestors' knowledge slammed into his brain, imprinting him with a history he couldn't deny. Sounds tore through his ears—screams and shouts— war cries and laughter. Seasons passed before his eyes like dust before the wind. Words haunted him—old words long lost with the old ways. Ghostlike faces danced before him like bubbles in the air—there one moment and then gone.*

*His hands curled into fists, the muscles in his body grew tight, as if readying for a fight that never came. His heart was racing, his mind leaping from one thought to another so quickly that his memory couldn't follow.*

*And in the midst of the vision, he suddenly smelled sage, heard the wind rippling through the underbrush, and felt the ground vibrate as his father stood and walked away.*

*Startled that he had been left alone, Joseph opened his eyes and felt the burden of centuries weighing down upon his shoulders. He fell backward upon the earth, staring up in disbelief. The sky was peppered with heavenly lights, billions upon bil-*

lions of stars so far away that all they had left to show were their minuscule twinkles.

He dug the heels of his hands into his eyes, but he could no more wipe away the memory of what had transpired than he could quit breathing. With a groan, he rolled over and then stood. Besides everything else that had just happened, something was different. But what? He took a deep breath and then exhaled slowly, aware that the sounds around him had magnified. A faint scratching sounded to his left. He turned and looked just in time to see a small furry rodent scurrying out of sight. And as he did, the glow from the firelight seemed to catch and burn in midair. He looked down in disbelief.

The ring that had been two sizes too large was firm upon his finger, as if it had been made to fit. Emotion ripped through him, coming up his throat in a grunt. He stroked the green crystal stone. Although he could see fire, it felt cool to the touch.

He started to shake. There was a need within him for solitude that he didn't understand. Unaware that he was being watched, he walked away into the darkness.

Only after Joseph was gone did Michael Colorado return to the fire. He sat down with a thump. Tossing a small stick onto the blaze, he stretched out in his bedroll and pulled up the covers. When he had settled himself in for the night, he finally looked up at the stars.

"It is done," he said gruffly, and closed his eyes, knowing that whatever was happening to Joseph *now was nothing that hadn't happened a thousand times before to other men and other men's sons. It was their destiny.*

"I'm ready to go back to the motel."

Joseph jumped. He hadn't heard Raine return.

"Yeah, okay," he muttered, and tossed some bills onto the table to pay for their food. He'd take her back to the Sleep-Inn, but in his heart it wouldn't be far enough. Like it or not, Raine Beaumont had come back into his life too soon—and too late. She hadn't been gone long enough for him to forget her, and she'd hadn't come back in time for it to matter.

The drive back to the motel was far too short. Joseph had barely gotten up the nerve to speak when the lights of the motel appeared on his right. He pulled up in front of her door and killed the engine, then turned until he was facing her.

Raine glanced at him. As badly as she hated to remember the past, it was obvious he needed to talk about it. She turned, angling herself in the seat until they were facing each other.

"What?"

Joseph's chin lifted and his nostrils flared. Her challenge was unexpected.

"There are things I need to know."

"Then ask."

Again, her aggressiveness surprised him. The girl he remembered had been softer. Bitterness tinged almost everything she said.

"Why now?" he asked.

Raine's heart skipped a beat but her voice never faltered.

"Why what?"

Joseph frowned. Hedging an answer didn't fit the assessment he'd made of the woman she'd become.

"Why the sudden need to move the baby's body now?"

A flush of nervousness painted a quick flush on her cheeks, making her thankful for the darkness.

"Because I am moving from Chicago. As of last week, I no longer work for the *Tribune*. There's no telling where I'll be this time next year. In fact, my future plans are so up in the air it's uncertain if I'd ever return to Chicago again. I couldn't bear to think of that little grave lying unattended."

He managed a nod, although he was more than a little surprised by her answer. She didn't seem the type to be so unsettled.

"So where are you going?"

She hesitated, and in Joseph's opinion, the silence was a little too long for the truth.

"After all of this is settled, I'm starting a trip around the world."

Now he was really confused. "As a vacation, or does it have something to do with your work as a journalist?"

"Oh, I guess I'd say that it's a little of both."

Aware that she had said all she was going to about her personal life, he let it drop. After all, what she did was none of his business any more. He shifted subjects.

"The baby . . . did you name him? When was he born?"

A sad smile broke the somberness of her face as she looked into his eyes. Even in the half light, Joseph saw tears on her face.

Raine took a deep breath. "He was born on the first day of November, just before dawn. I named him Joseph Colorado Beaumont."

Joseph inhaled sharply. *Sweet mother of God.*

"Quite a coincidence, don't you think?" Raine asked.

Joseph looked away. The baby had been born and then died on the day Joseph was celebrating his twenty-first birthday. He took a slow shuddering breath, trying to come to terms with the fact that he'd been celebrating on the day that Raine's world had all but come to an end.

For a while, silence engulfed them. Neither could speak past the sheer emptiness of what lay between them. Finally it was Joseph who pulled himself together enough to ask.

"Did you hold him?"

Her voice finally broke. "They wouldn't let me."

Joseph groaned and when he would have pulled her into his arms, she bolted from the pickup and headed for her door on the run. Within seconds, Joseph was out of the truck and running after her. He caught her as she was jamming the key into the lock.

"Wait!"

She spun, her eyes wild with a panic he didn't understand. He lifted his hands and took a step back. "Sorry. I didn't mean to—oh hell. I just wanted to apologize for upsetting you, and to thank you."

Raine's heart was hammering within her chest like a trapped bird flailing itself against the bars of a cage. Clutching her purse to her breasts and the key in her hand, her first instincts were to put as much distance between them as possible. Unfortunately, the door behind her didn't give her much space.

She took a deep breath, making herself calm when she felt like screaming.

"I'll call you when I have a firm date for the arrival of the casket."

The image of a tiny, oblong box flashed through Joseph's mind and it was all he could do not to cry.

"All right. In the meantime, if there's anything you need, will you let me know?"

"Sure," Raine said.

"You're lying," he said softly and then started toward his truck. Just as he reached the door, he stopped and turned.

"Raine."

"What?"

"When you get up in the morning . . ."

"Yes?"

"Go eat some damned breakfast, will you?"

His concern surprised her.

"Okay."

"Swear?"

"I swear," she said softly.

A short distance away, a car wheeled into the parking lot, skidding to a halt in front of the office. Joseph recognized the car and the driver. It was Benny. And the woman beside him was already half-undressed. He looked back at Raine, not for the first time wishing she were in a safer location.

"Get inside and lock the door," he muttered.

Startled, Raine did as she was told. Only after she'd turned the lock and heard him driving away did she realize she hadn't told him good-bye. She sighed. It didn't really matter. The time for good-byes between them had long since passed. Now all she had to do was stay strong until the exhumation was over and she had reburied her son on the Colorado land. Then she was going to get in her car and drive until she reached an ocean—any ocean. After that she would—

She sighed. There would be time enough to decide about afters when she got there.


Stuart leaned back in the seat and closed his eyes. He shifted restlessly as he tried to let his mind go free, but it wasn't going to come easy. He kept seeing the implacable expression on that damned Indian's face—kept hearing him repeatedly deny knowing of any healing place. And the man could not be swayed to change his story in spite of everything Stuart had offered. He shook his head, knowing that for the second time in as many months, he'd seen a man who couldn't be bought. That they were both Native

Americans was not lost upon him, either. For two million dollars, one had died—the other had walked away.

The limousine hit a rough patch in the road, but Stuart barely felt it. It was one of the perks of being rich. The ride and the life nearly always ran smooth for men like Stuart. But there were the exceptions. Trouble was, Stuart didn't take well to being the exception. Somehow he'd find a way to persuade that Indian to heal him. Then Stuart's eyes narrowed angrily.

*By God, if he refuses me again, I'll make damn sure he never heals anyone again.*

His thoughts turned to the younger brother. Tomorrow he would concentrate on him. There had to be a way to get to Joseph Colorado, and he would find it.

Benny rolled over with a grunt and closed his eyes as Shelley Biggers disappeared into the bathroom. She had been pissed, but not enough to hold out on him. He rubbed his bare belly in satisfaction, savoring the afterglow of his climax without wondering or caring if he'd satisfied her.

His thoughts drifted back to that crazy man who'd been at the ranch. What was it he'd been looking for—oh yeah, a place to be healed.

Benny rolled over and then sat up on the side of the bed, listening to the sound of running water coming from the adjacent bathroom. He reached for his pants. He didn't smoke much anymore but there was something about a cigarette after sex that set his world right. He lit up and then lay back on the pillow, inhaling deeply and drawing great satisfaction from the kick of nicotine as it filtered through his body.

Benny grinned. He wanted to be healed? That crazy man should try a good whore. Good sex would heal a whole lot more than some wild story ever would. The bathroom door opened and Shelley stuck her head out the opening.

"Benny, baby, I'm going to shower real quick before you take me home, okay?"

"Yeah, whatever," he muttered, and took another draw on his smoke.

A million dollars. His pulse quickened just thinking about it. But then his mind skipped past the money to his brother's reaction.

*Why was Joseph so mad?*

And as soon as he asked himself that question, he sat up. That's what had been bugging him. If Joseph was as innocent as he claimed about the place the man was looking for, then why was he so defensive? Why didn't he just laugh it off?

He took a last drag on his cigarette and then stubbed it out in the ashtray and began looking for his pants. Something was going on, and he was determined to get answers. If there was the remotest possibility of getting his hands on that much money, there was no way in hell he was going to let the chance go.

"Hey, Shelley! Hurry it up in there!" he shouted and strode into the bathroom.

But Shelley's wet, buxom body and her tantalizing hands delayed the best of Benny's intentions. By the time she was through with him, they'd fallen asleep in the middle of the bed and didn't wake up until they both heard the screams.

Raine was dreaming. She was lost in the mountains in the middle of the night and had been shouting Joseph's name for hours. Deep in her heart she knew he wouldn't come—couldn't come. She didn't know whether to stay where she was and wait for morning or start walking toward the North Star and hope for the best. And while she was trying to make a decision, a fog began to descend.

She rolled over on her side, trying to escape the snaking tendrils of mist, but it was even thicker there. She moaned, kicking at the covers as she rolled onto her back. Fog everywhere with no light in sight. In the heartbeat between cognizance and a much deeper sleep, she caught the scent of a wood fire and opened her eyes.

The room was filled with smoke, and more was coming in with every passing second.

"Oh my God!"

She bolted from the bed, trying to remember which direction was out, and where she'd left her bag and shoes. She staggered into a wall and then gasped and fell backwards from the impact of the heat. It felt as if she'd just laid her face against a furnace. She rolled over onto her knees, feeling her way with outstretched hands.

Her bag! She'd just found her bag. Her eyes were burning—burning—her throat was on fire. She ventured a quick breath, then gasped and choked and dropped flat on the floor. It saved her life. With her face against the carpet, the slight draft of cooler air was more obvious. Again, she reached for her bag but this time it was nowhere to be found. There was no more time to waste. Panic hit hard as she began crawling on her belly, following the source of the air and praying that it would lead her to the front door.

Outside, she heard sirens and screams and then loud, frantic shouts.

"Help, help!" she screamed, choking harder as she swallowed more of the dark, acrid smoke.

Her elbow raked the corner of something sharp and she winced but kept on moving. Only afterward did she realize it was probably the picture of the velvet matador leaning against the wall. The disreputable work of art was about to go up in smoke. She didn't want to go with it.

Suddenly there was a wall before her. Tentatively she ran a hand up the surface, testing for heat, then tried to look through the smoke. It was useless. All she could see were swirls of what appeared to be a thick, black mist. She pulled herself up to her knees, desperately feeling along the wall for a windowsill or anything that would help orient her with where she was in the room. Something exploded behind her.

*God, please . . . not like this.*

At that moment, her hand touched the smooth, metallic surface of a doorknob. She tried to turn it. It wouldn't give.

*No . . . no.*

It took another couple of seconds for her to remember that she'd locked herself in for the night. With her last ounces of strength, she turned the lock and then pulled herself upward, feeling for the deadbolt she knew would be there. Within seconds, she was staggering out into the small parking lot, choking for breath. Someone grabbed her. A man screamed in her ear just to be heard above the sirens.

"Lady, are you all right?"

All she could do was nod.

"Over here!" he shouted. "Here's another one."

Someone put an oxygen mask over her face while someone else laid her on the ground and covered her with a blanket.

"Everything's going to be all right, lady. Just lie still and breathe deep."

Raine did as she was told, even though she knew he was wrong. It wasn't going to be all right. Nothing was ever going to be all right again.

Benny came to within seconds of the first scream. His first thought was that someone caught a cheating spouse in bed with someone else. And then he smelled the smoke and ran to the window. The other end of the Sleep-Inn was engulfed in flames, and they were rapidly spreading toward the room where he and Shelley had been sleeping.

"Shelley! Wake up! The place is on fire!"

They exited on the run, carrying their shoes in their hands. Benny took one look at the spreading fire and shoved Shelley in his car before sliding behind the wheel. He couldn't go far because the fire trucks had him blocked in, but he could move it enough to keep the heat from peeling the paint on his car.

Benny was so engrossed in saving his car that he didn't see the paramedic helping Raine across the parking lot to a makeshift ER, and if he had, probably wouldn't have offered a word of encouragement. She'd been just as much of a stranger to him as Stuart Rossi had been, and she hadn't made nearly as much of an impact.

A short while later the fire was out and everyone who was able was allowed to go home. Benny dropped Shelley off at her home with little more than a quick peck on the cheek and kept on driving. When he got to the ranch, he was still on an adrenaline high from having escaped certain death.

He glanced at his watch. It was four in the morning. He got out, stretching lazily and looking up at the sky. The color of night was already fading to a thin, dark gray. Soon it would be sunrise. In an unusual moment of reverence, Benny closed his eyes and said a quick prayer of thanksgiving that he had lived to see it, then he slipped the key in the lock and walked in. He was safe.

When Joseph heard the sound of Benny's car coming down the driveway, he rolled over and glanced at the clock. In another hour or so it would be daylight. When it came to work, Benny wouldn't be worth shooting tomorrow. He punched his pillow and then sighed. Heaven knows he hadn't slept much either. Might as well get up and make a pot of coffee.

But Benny wasn't ready to sleep. When he heard Joseph stirring, it was what he'd been waiting for. He burst into Joseph's room without knocking.

"Boy, oh boy! What a wild night in town."

Joseph pivoted, a little surprised by Benny's unusual offer to share a confidence, no matter how sordid it might be.

"Oh yeah?" he said, as he reached for his shirt. "So you and Shelley had a good time, did you?"

Benny frowned. "What? Oh . . . yeah . . . that. That was fine. But I was talking about the fire."

A chill moved up the middle of Joseph's spine. The last time he'd seen Benny had been at Raine's motel.

"What fire?" he asked.

"The motel! It caught on fire. Damned if there wasn't every fire truck in—"

Before Benny could finish, Joseph had him backed against the wall.

"Did everyone get out all right?"

Benny blinked, stunned by Joseph's vehemence. "Yeah, yeah. I'm fine and so was Shelley. As for the others . . . I couldn't say. The fire started at the opposite end of the motel from where we were at."

"Oh, God," Joseph muttered, and reached for his boots.

"Where the hell are you going?" Benny asked.

"To town. I've got to make sure Raine's okay."

Benny frowned. "You mean that woman . . . the one who was here earlier . . . she was staying at that motel?"

Joseph nodded as he yanked on one boot and then the other before grabbed his keys from the dresser.

"Damn, if I'd known she mattered to you, I could have looked for her."

*Mattered?* Joseph's heart sank. Until this moment, even he hadn't known how much.

"I'll be back," he said, and bolted out of the room.

Seconds later, Benny heard the sound of Joseph's truck engine coming to life, and then he was gone.

"Well, I'll be damned," Benny said, scratching his head in disbelief.

He lifted his arm to his nose, smelling his shirt sleeve and then wrinkling his nose. It smelled of smoke. In fact, everything he had on smelled of smoke. He stepped back out onto the porch and stripped where he stood. Leaving his hat and clothes in a pile on the porch, he went back inside to take a hot, steaming shower.

All eleven of the motel's displaced clients, including Raine, wound up on cots that had been set up at the free-throw line inside the high school gym. An elderly man moved between the makeshift beds, handing out extra blankets to those in need.

Raine sat huddled on the side of her cot and staring up at the bleachers from the playing floor. The last time she'd been inside this building, her situation had been reversed. She'd been in these very same bleachers, sitting beside Joseph and sharing a bag of popcorn, totally oblivious to the fact that there was a basketball game in progress. All she could remember was leaving before the game was over and getting home late.

Although she wasn't really cold, she pulled the blanket closer around her shoulders and then lay down. At the moment, the cot, rickety though it may be, was the only shelter she trusted. Behind her, she could hear the soft, muffled sobs of someone crying, and if she hadn't been so weary, she would have indulged in a bit of self-pity herself. Her throat was raw, her lungs and eyes burning from the smoke. As bad as it was, it could have been worse.

She turned over on her side, swaddling herself as she rolled and trying desperately to sleep. Her sigh evolved into a round of thick, choking coughs. Within moments, a doctor was at her side, checking her pulse and then helping her to an upright position that helped her breathe. He pulled a stethoscope from around his neck and began to examine her again.

"You've already done this," she said.

At first he didn't answer, and several times she saw him frown. Finally he stopped.

"Lady, you need to be in the hospital."

She shook her head. "No."

"Look, Miss . . ." He looked down at his notes. ". . . Beaumont, you inhaled a lot of smoke. It would be better for you if—"

"No."

He gave her a hard stare.

"Are you finished with me?" she asked.

"I suppose, but only for the time being."

Raine lay back down. Only after she heard him walking away was she able to relax. They didn't understand. She couldn't go to the hospital—didn't have time to go to a hospital. The authorities were supposed to call from Chicago tomorrow with an update on the exhumation. Then she groaned. The number she'd given them had gone up in smoke. When morning came, she'd have to remember to call them back and give them another location. The motel that had burned was the only one open in town. That meant she had to find one of the bed-and-breakfast establishments. Shuddering with exhaustion, she closed her eyes. She'd worry about that later. Right now she was trying hard not to cry. The last thing she could afford was losing control of her emotions.

A minute passed. Then another and another and the lull between noises was just enough to let Raine slide into a state of uneasy slumber. No sooner had she closed her eyes than she started dreaming. Of crawling on the floor through the smoke, then feeling the doorknob melting away in her hands.

After suffering through a third rerun of the same horror, she sat up and screamed just as he knelt at her side.

Joseph rocked back on his heels and then grabbed her. Before she knew what was happening, she was in his lap.

Only after he'd felt her alive and breathing in his arms had his panic begun to subside.

"Easy, sweetheart, it's just me."

Raine shivered as his words wrapped around her, soothing the horror from which she'd awakened. The solid comfort of his lap and the strength of his embrace were too much. His expression was full of sympathy, and she lost her composure. That suddenly. Tears welled, then spilled.

Joseph groaned and pulled her head beneath his chin, rocking her back and forth on the cot as if she were a child.

"It's all right," he kept saying. "It's all right. You're safe now. It's all right."

As dangerous as it was for her to let this be happening, she didn't have the strength to tell him no. She wrapped her arms around his neck and went limp.

"The smoke was everywhere. I couldn't see. I couldn't breathe."

"I know, baby," Joseph said, softly. "But you got out, didn't you? And you're safe now."

She choked on a sob. "Yes . . . now I'm safe."

Joseph's heart ached. He didn't know what he was feeling. Was it sympathy for what she'd endured, or was there something deeper involved? He tightened his grip and held her close, unwilling to decipher his true emotions.

"I'm taking you home with me," he said shortly. "And don't bother to argue, because you don't have any other options."

To his surprise, Raine agreed.

"Well, then," he muttered. "You'll feel better as soon as you can stretch out in a decent bed."

"And shower," Raine added, using the edge of her blanket to wipe at her tears. "All I can smell is the smoke. It's in my hair . . . on my clothes. I think it's even in the pores of my skin. I started out with my bag but I lost it. Except for this nightshirt, everything I had with me is gone."

"So we'll buy more," Joseph said, scooting her off his lap and standing abruptly. "Who's in charge around here? I need to tell them I'm taking you with me."

Raine shrugged. "I don't know."

"Never mind." He laid a hand on the top of her head. "Wait here. I'll be right back." And then he was gone.

Even though she could see him across the gym in deep conversation with the doctor, she imagined she could still feel the imprint of his hand upon her head. She knew it was silly and more than a little sacrilegious, but she felt as if she'd just been blessed. Her scalp was tingling, and her erratic pulse had smoothed into a slow, steady beat.

When he started toward her again, her gaze locked onto the rhythm of motion in his powerful body, and she caught herself breathing in and breathing out in perfect unison with his steps. She bit her lip and looked away. If she wasn't careful, everything she'd planned could come down around her ears.

And then he was there, lifting her off her feet and into his arms as if she weighed nothing at all. She stiffened.

"I can walk."

"So can I," he retorted, and started out the door.

She looked back over his shoulder to the hubbub that was still going on and knew a certain sense of inevitability. She'd left this gym with him once before. That night she'd gotten pregnant with their child.

A short while later, she woke up with her head in his lap to find that they had stopped.

"What?" she asked sleepily, raising up in the seat.

"We're home."

Her heart was aching as he carried her inside. If only it had been so. But for her, this place could never be home.

Raine awoke to the sound of a slamming door and opened her eyes, momentarily confused. Last night she'd crawled blindly into the bed Joseph had offered. But this morning was a different story. She lay without moving, staring at the pale blue walls and the rust-colored trim around the curtainless windows.

There was a painting of eagles in flight on the wall opposite the bed and she realized that its location was no accident. No matter where one slept in this bed, when you opened your eyes, the painting would be the first thing to see.

From where she was lying, she could see a small brass plate with an engraved inscription at the bottom of the frame. Curious, she crawled out of bed to go see.

*Isaiah 40:31*

It was biblical! Her eyes widened. This was a side of Joseph she hadn't known.

Having seen what she wanted to see, she crawled back into bed. Using the headboard for a backrest, she sat with her knees bent and hugging a pillow, intently studying the painting. The longer she stared, the more acute her senses became. And then in the middle of a blink, the painting seemed to come to life. Raine gasped, then leaned forward, reeling from the lift beneath the eagle's wings as it rode the currents of air between heaven and earth. And when a far-off cry of the other eagle's shriek echoed in her ears, she shuddered. What was happening to her? Only after a door slammed shut toward the front of the house did she realize she'd been holding her breath.

When a knock suddenly sounded at her door, she staggered to her feet on shaking legs and tugged at the long tail of her nightshirt.

"Come in."

Joseph peeked through the opening, and when he saw her up, came the rest of the way inside. At first glance, she seemed pale and shaky. He frowned as felt of her forehead, testing for fever.

"How are you feeling?"

Raine's answer was slow in coming, and she seemed dazed as she looked up at him.

"Do you hurt anywhere?" he asked.

She shook her head and then pointed toward the painting.

"That painting . . ."

Joseph turned in the direction of her point. "Ah, yes, the eagles. That painting has been in my family for many generations. My dad loved it. This was his room, you know."

Even though Joseph was only inches away, she almost forgot he was there.

"Do you like it?" he asked.

"Like what?" she mumbled.

He smiled. "The painting. Do you like it?"

"Like it? I don't think that's the correct terminology. My God, Joseph, it came alive."

He stilled.

"It what?" he whispered.

She shook her head, as if coming out of a trance.

"I know it sounds silly . . . but I was looking at the painting for so long that I forgot me." She stammered and then blushed. "Don't laugh. It's just the only way I know how to describe what I felt. One second I was looking at brushstrokes and the next thing I knew I felt the lift of air beneath my . . . I mean . . . the eagle's wings . . . and, oh, Joseph . . . I was flying. I heard the other eagle shriek." She clasped her hands against her chest, her eyes huge with disbelief. "It was the most unbelievable thing. I was almost at the point of knowing what they were thinking when a door slammed." She shrugged. "Then I lost the thought."

Joseph was stunned. The sound of breakers washing against a wide shore kept sounding in his ears, and his mouth was so dry it was impossible for him to speak. He kept staring at her face but hearing his grandfather's words on a day long ago.

*"Grandson, do you know what bird this is?"*

*At the age of six, Joseph was more than curious about the painting his grandfather was hanging on the wall of his daddy's room. He moved until he was right below the painting and then staring up. Before he could answer, his grandfather lifted him off his feet and set him a distance away in the middle of his parents' bed.*

*"Sometimes if you are too close to an object, you can not see everything there is to enjoy," his grandfather said. "Now, then. Look again and tell me what kind of bird that is."*

*"It is an eagle, isn't it, Grandpa?"*

*The old man nodded. "Yes. Eagles are the national bird of the United States of America, but more important, they are sacred to our people."*

*Joseph nodded solemnly. He didn't completely understand everything his grandpa was telling him, but he knew it was important.*

*"Did you paint this picture, Grandpa?" Joseph asked.*

*The old man shook his head while giving the painting a last thoughtful stare.*

*"Then who did?" Joseph asked as his grandfather lifted him from the bed and into his arms.*

*The old man paused at the door, checking the painting one last look.*

*"It's not who painted it that's important; it's the picture itself that matters."*

*Tired of this too-adult conversation, Joseph wiggled to be put down, but his grandfather held him fast.*

*"Wait, Joseph," he urged, pointing toward the painting. "Look. Tell me what you see."*

*Joseph glanced at the painting. "Birds, Grandpa. I see the birds."*

*"You're not looking hard enough," his grandfather said. "Look closer. There is more to be seen."*

And so they stood, two members of the same family with a mere sixty-some-odd years separating them in age, staring intently into a rather nondescript painting of two eagles on the wing, silhouetted against a near perfect sky.

Intrigued by the new game, the child's dark eyes danced with excitement as he searched the picture for some hidden image. He looked until his eyes began to burn and his head began to droop against his grandfather's shoulder.

Unwilling to admit he had failed, he continued to stare, waiting for Grandpa to end this strange game. He could feel his grandfather's breath against his cheek and smell the faint but familiar odor of barbecue that still lingered from their earlier meal.

Then, in that twilight moment of magic just before sleep comes and takes you away, Joseph heard the flutter of feathers against the wind and what sounded like the faraway cry of some bird. Suddenly frightened, he threw his arms around his grandfather's neck and hid his face.

"What, Grandson? What did you see?"

"It was the eagle, Grandpa. It was coming to get me."

"No, Joseph, it would never hurt you. It was only saying hello."

Joseph looked back at the flat surface of the painting. Both the sounds and the image he thought that he'd seen were gone.

"What happened?" Joseph asked. "Where did they go?"

"You had a vision, Grandson."

Joseph didn't understand and hid his face. Visions sounded bad. He didn't mean to be bad.

His grandfather patted his back.

"Joseph, there is something you must understand."

Joseph looked up. "What is it, Grandpa?"

"It's about the eagles."

Joseph glanced back at the painting as his grandfather continued to speak.

"The eagles . . . you know they were never really there."

"But Grandpa, I saw them. I heard them."

"No, Grandson, what you saw was like a dream. The People call them visions."

Joseph frowned. None of this was making much sense—besides that, he wanted to go play.

"I don't want a vision," he said shortly.

The old man smiled. "You were given no choice," he said. "Besides, you should feel blessed. Only the most special of boys are given such a thing to behold."

Joseph's interest was piqued again, but only slightly. Having visions was no good if you couldn't show them to your friends. "Why did I have it? Will it come again?"

"I do not know. What I do know is that when it's time, the Great Spirit will guide you in the way he wants you to go."

Joseph nodded. "Can I go play now?"

His grandfather smiled as he put him down. "Yes, boy. Go play now. There will be other days for us to talk about such things."

* * *

"Joseph?"

It was the frustrated tone of Raine's voice that yanked him back into the present.

"Sorry," he said. "I didn't mean to blank out on you, but something you said about the painting made me remember . . ."

Already convinced that she'd experienced nothing more dramatic than a daydream, she frowned.

"What about the painting?"

Joseph touched her arm, then her cheek, with the flat of his hand. Raine jerked as if she'd been slapped and took a giant step backward. But Joseph acted as if she hadn't moved at all. Instead, he followed her retreat until she was up against the wall and he was only inches away.

"Raine, exactly what did you see?"

She slipped out from beneath his arm and reached for a blanket, holding it up in front of her like a shield.

"It was nothing."

But Joseph wouldn't let it go. He had to know.

"Please . . . Rainbow."

"That's not playing fair," she muttered.

"This is not a game," he replied.

She glanced back at the painting, then closed her eyes, trying to remember the exact moment when dimension had shifted. When she looked again, Joseph was staring intently into her face.

"I heard something," she said.

"What?"

"I don't know."

"What did it sound like?" he persisted.

She shrugged. "Oh, Joseph, it was just a daydream. It happened so fast I'm not sure I remember."

"Please try. It's important."

She closed her eyes again. Moments passed and then she opened them suddenly.

"Feathers. It was the sound of wind blowing against feathers. Sort of like the sound a flag makes when it's popping in the wind."

Joseph's eyes narrowed.

"What else?" he asked.

"I heard an eagle cry." And then her voice rose an octave with remembered excitement. "But the best thing was I thought I understood what it meant." She grinned, more than a little embarrassed. "You know how silly dreams are. They never make sense when you awaken."

Joseph shook his head. "That was no dream."

She gave him an incredulous stare. "Well, yes, actually it was. I think I should know when—"

"That was no dream, Rainbow, it was a vision."

Her patience turned to anger as she thought of her life and all the sorrow it represented.

"I don't believe in visions, nor do I believe in miracles. Now if you don't mind, I would like to get dressed. I need to make some calls. I will put them on my calling card, of course."

Joseph turned on her, a little angry that she'd dismissed his beliefs so out of hand.

"While you are a guest beneath my roof, do not insult my hospitality by offering to pay for anything."

A little surprised by his anger, she stood without speaking as he walked away. Somehow, when he stopped at the doorway and turned, she wasn't surprised.

"You don't have to believe me," he said shortly. "One day you will see for yourself that you have been blessed."

Having said his piece, he disappeared. If he'd stayed long enough, he would have seen her shock turn to bitterness as she slammed the door behind him.

"Blessed? You call what's happening in my life a blessing?" she muttered, as she began to dress in the clean shirt and sweats he had loaned her.

Quick tears of self-pity blurred her vision, but she blinked them away. The time for crying was over.

She sat down on the edge of the bed and pulled on a pair of borrowed socks. Without meaning to, her gaze had drifted back to the painting, and to the eagles in full flight.

Blessed. She snorted beneath her breath. Right now, the only blessed thing in her life was the fact that she was still alive, which, considering the problems she was dealing with now, was almost a joke.

But she couldn't quit staring at the painting. Sunlight glinted off the metal plate on the frame below. Again, she wished for a Bible, and in that moment, stood up and walked to the bedside table as if someone had her by the hand. When she opened the small drawer and saw the edge of a black leather book, the hair rose on the back of her neck. How had she known to do that? And then she scoffed at herself. It was a logical place to look.

As she lifted it out, a verse she'd once memorized as a child took on new meaning.

*"Ask and ye shall receive . . ."*

Her fingers were shaking as she began to turn through the pages, searching for the book of Isaiah. Then to chapter forty. Then the thirty-first verse. After that, she began to read.

*"But they who wait for the Lord shall renew their strength, they shall mount up with wings like eagles, they shall run and not be weary, they shall walk and not faint."*

The words were chasing through her mind like whispers in the wind, leaving snippets of themselves behind as she gazed upon the painting once more. A quickening began down deep in her belly, warming and holding her fast within the thought until she forgot to breathe. She tore her gaze away from the painting and went to stand before the mirror. The woman looking back at her should have been familiar, but Raine had become a stranger to herself . . . and she knew why. She gazed back at the painting.

*Those who wait for the Lord . . .*

Then she closed her eyes. "If only it were—"

Somewhere in another part of the house, a phone began to ring. She began wiping her eyes, angry with herself for being so weak. Besides that, it reminded her she needed to contact her lawyer. She needed to notify him of her relocation.

She dug her fingers through her hair, massaging her scalp and trying to head off the onset of a headache she could well do without. It didn't work. She left her room with a frown on her face and the blanket wrapped around her like a cloak.

The scent of coffee was strong in the air. She followed the aroma into a bright, sunlit kitchen. A few minutes later she was sipping at the hot, steamy brew and gazing at the mountains in the distance when the back door opened. At first glance, Raine thought it was Joseph, but when she looked again, realized that this must be Benny.

They both stared, neither one certain of a proper greeting. Finally it was Raine who broke the silence.

"You must be Joseph's brother Benny. I'm Raine Beaumont. Looks like I'm going to be underfoot for a few days."

Benny's reaction was instinctive. He tipped his hat and turned on the charm.

"It will be a pleasure to see someone other than my brother every morning. Stay as long as you like, pretty lady."

Raine smiled in spite of herself and that was how Joseph found them. His brother had put a smile on Raine's face. So far, all he'd been able to do was make her cry. He didn't know who to be angry with, Benny for being charming, or himself for being so unyielding.

"Benny! Don't you have someplace to be?"

Benny shoved his hat to the back of his head and gave Joseph a long, considering look.

"Probably," he drawled. "But right now I'm introducing myself to our guest."

Embarrassed that she'd so soon become the bone of contention between the brothers, Raine would have walked away, but Joseph stopped her.

"My office is just down the hall, first door on your left. Breakfast is ready now. Eat first, then make your calls. I have called a friend from town. She's bringing out some clothes for you to borrow and will take you back to get your car."

*She? A friend?* The news shouldn't have mattered, but for some reason it did.

"Thank you for your consideration," she said.

He nodded and then fidgeted. There was something else he needed to broach, and he wasn't sure how to say it without insulting her. Then he sighed. What was wrong with him? This was Raine. She couldn't have changed *that* much in the twelve years she'd been gone.

"Raine, do you need any money? If you do, I would be glad to loan you some until you could—"

She smiled. "No, I'm fine. I'll call my bank and have them wire me some money, but thank you for asking."

"What about your driver's license?"

"Luckily, it was in the car."

"Well, then, I guess that would be that." Joseph was trying to concentrate, but her smile had wiped out his good sense. "Umm . . . I'm sure there are people who are worrying about you. Call anyone you need."

Raine looked startled. There was no mistaking the innuendo he'd just dropped. Joseph knew she wasn't married, but from what he'd just said, it sounded as if he'd convinced himself that she would have a significant other. She almost laughed. The last time she'd had a serious boyfriend had been over five years ago. Thirteen months into their relationship he had packed his bags, kissed her good-bye, and left to find himself. As far as Raine knew, he was still looking. She wished him all the best. She hadn't loved him. He'd just been someone to have around.

"Thank you, I will," she said.

Benny looked from one to the other. One minute they seemed to be at each other's throats, the next thing they were all friendly and smiling. It didn't make sense.

"Have you two known each other long?" Benny asked.

Joseph glanced at Raine. She seemed to be waiting for him to do the explaining.

"Yes," Joseph said.

Benny whistled beneath his breath. "So, the old girlfriend comes back to—"

At that point, Raine paled. Before Benny could finish, she'd done a neat pivot and exited the kitchen, unwilling to hear Joseph rehash their past.

Joseph felt sick. This kept going from bad to worse.

"Damn it, Benny, don't you know when to keep quiet?"

Benny shrugged. "I live here. I have a right to know what's going on beneath my own—"

"She came back to bury a child," Joseph said harshly. "Our child."

He turned and strode toward the door, slamming it behind him and rattling the glass in the nearby windows.

If someone had just handed him a snake, Benny couldn't have been more shocked. For once in his life, compassion for another human being took precedence over what he'd been thinking. Problem was, he didn't know who he felt sorrier for, his brother or the woman called Raine.

Stuart Rossi licked the flap on the envelope he was holding, sealing ten hundred-dollar bills inside. Then he picked up a pen and wrote Benny Colorado's name on the outside before handing it to Edward.

"Give this to Colorado when you meet. Tell him that's just a taste of the two million I'm willing to give."

Edward nodded. "Will do, sir."

"And Edward . . ."

"Sir?"

"I don't like to be kept waiting."

"Yes, sir. I know, sir."

"If he's interested, tell him I'll be at this number for a week. No longer. Just a week."

"Yes, sir."

"Well, then," Stuart said. "Hurry up. The sooner you get there, the sooner my healing will begin."


Benny pulled into the parking lot of the Mesquite and parked. It was early yet so the bar wouldn't be crowded for hours. He looked around before he got out, curious to see if the long limousine was anywhere in sight. It was not. He frowned and then shrugged. That was good. He would have time for a couple of beers. But not too many. Just enough to take the edge off the day.

A few minutes later he was at a table in the corner. His first drink was halfway gone and he was waving at the waitress for a refill. A pretty young thing in tight pants and an even tighter T-shirt served it up, smiling in delight at the five-dollar tip he dropped on her tray.

"That's just for openers," he said softly, and patted her on the back of her leg.

She took the five and winked as she walked away.

It was all Benny could do to stay seated. He had a sudden urge to shuffle some female drawers. But then he remembered the limo and the man with the money and took another deep swig of his drink instead. There would be time for sex later, after he had taken all the money that sick fool kept trying to give away.

Another half hour passed and just as Benny was about to order his third drink, several men entered. But it was the one who came in last that Benny had been waiting for. He stood, waving him over to his table.

Walking over, Edward reached inside his jacket and pulled out a fat envelope.

"Sit down! Sit down!" Benny said, waving the waitress over to their table, then leaning toward

Edward. "What's your poison, Eddie?"

Edward shook his head. "Oh no, sir. I couldn't. I'm driving, you know."

"Bullshit! So am I," Benny shrieked, and then slapped his leg and laughed out loud.

"You talked to Mr. Rossi earlier, am I right?" Edward asked as he slid the envelope toward Benny.

"We talked," Benny said.

"So, you know what he wants of you?"

Benny nodded. "For my brother to take him to some mystical Indian healing place."

Edward put the envelope in Benny's hands. "Mr. Rossi said to tell you that this was just a taste, if you'd agree to help."

"He said two million dollars on the phone," Benny reminded.

"Then that's what he means. Mr. Rossi never plays games with money."

Benny's fingers were itching to open the envelope. When hundred-dollar bills began falling onto the table, he groaned in disbelief. Suddenly aware that someone might see, he began grabbing them up and stuffing them into his pockets.

"You tell Mr. Rossi that I won't let him down," Benny said. Edward pushed back his chair and started to leave.

Benny looked up just as Edward turned and it occurred to him that he was losing contact with the man with the money.

"Hey! If I find out what Rossi wants to know, how do I contact him?"

Edward pointed to a sheet of paper that had fallen out of the envelope.

"He'll be at that number for a week, no longer."

Benny grabbed the paper, stuffing it into his pocket along with the money. That was one number he didn't intend to lose. He didn't know how, but he was going to find out what Rossi wanted to know. By God, he'd just gotten his ticket out of Oracle and back to L.A.

Half an hour later, Benny was still drinking and lost in a dream. He could see it all now—going back to his old neighborhood in style. Maybe he'd get a limo just like the one Rossi drove. Thinking of the money in his pocket made him smile. He downed the last of his drink and headed for the door. The thousand dollars in his pocket was just a spit in the bucket compared to what he would get out of Rossi before this he was through. And there was no time to waste. In his opinion, Stuart Rossi wasn't long for this world.

Raine glanced up from her magazine just in time to see a car coming down the driveway toward the house. She made a face. This would be the "friend" that Joseph had called who would be loaning her clothes. She stood abruptly, smoothing at the front of the shirt she was wearing. It was an old one of Joseph's, and even though it reached her knees, she felt exposed.

She watched from behind a curtain as the car

braked to a stop, then she caught a glimpse of delicate features as well as a cloud of blond hair. Oh great! Alice in Wonderland in the flesh.

When Joseph came out of nowhere and rushed to the car, Raine turned away, disgusted with herself for caring. What the man did was of no concern to her. It hadn't mattered for the last twelve years. There was no reason it should matter now. Especially now.

Footsteps sounded on the porch. She lifted her head and straightened her shoulders, bracing herself for the moment of truth. It wasn't long in coming. Joseph opened the front door and without even bothering to look in, shouted from the doorway.

"Raine, Evelyn is here!"

"Yes, I can see that."

Joseph turned, a bit startled and even more embarrassed that he'd yelled without looking to see where she was.

"Well, then," he said shortly, and stood aside.

The woman who came inside was about Raine's height, and from the appearance of her delicate bone structure, pretty close to her weight. But that was where similar ended. Evelyn was pregnant and looked due to deliver last week.

"Raine, this is Evelyn Hart. She's married to my buddy, Justin. Remember him?"

Raine's eyes widened. "Married? To Justin Hart?" She didn't know the slight grin on her face was one of relief. "Who could forget? I remember the night he got drunk on Teddy Pollock's home-made wine and ran into that utility pole outside the high school gym with his truck. Oracle went into a blackout and we had to forfeit the ball game that was in progress. Everyone went home in the dark."

Evelyn laughed. "That sounds like the Justin I know and love. Thank goodness his antics are far less hazardous than they used to be."

Then she clasped both of Raine's hands in her own. "I'm so sorry to hear about the fire, but equally glad that you're all right. When Joe called, I jumped at the opportunity to dig through my clothes. Even if I can't wear them just yet, it felt good to pretend."

Raine laughed. "I know just what you mean. I remember when I was—" But then she stopped without finishing her thought. The smile on her face froze and then faded. "Never mind. I appreciate the loan and I won't need them for long. I'll buy new clothes as soon as I get into town and pick up my car."

Evelyn motioned toward the door. "And like a goose, I forgot to bring them in. They're in the back seat. Joe, be a sweetheart and get them for me, will you?"

Joseph pivoted, glad to be out of the room and away from the stricken look in Raine's eyes. All the way to the car and back he kept thinking that he must have been out of his mind to have called Evelyn. There were a couple of other people he could have asked, but no—he had to call the one woman he knew who was ripe to bursting from the baby she carried. To Raine, it must be like rubbing salt in an open wound. Again, he would have to find a way to apologize for his thoughtlessness. He came back inside to find Evelyn had escaped to a bathroom.

Impulsively, he grabbed her fingers as he gave her the clothes.

"Raine, I'm so sorry."

But to his relief, she was already ahead of him. She took the clothes that he offered and then shook her head.

"It's okay," she said softly. "It was a long time ago."

His breath escaped on a long, heartfelt sigh. "Because the grief is so new to me, I keep forgetting that you've already let go."

*Oh Joseph, I don't know how to let go.* Raine took the clothes and moved away as Evelyn reentered the room.

"I won't be long," she told her.

"Take your time," Evelyn said. "Joseph can entertain me until your return."

He grinned and gently ruffled Evelyn's hair. "As long as you don't want to play cards. Last time I think you cheated."

Raine left in the middle of their friendly argument and was thankful to escape to her room. It was all too genuine and all too innocent for her liking. The sooner she was out of here, the better off she would be.

Raine squinted into the evening sun as she turned off the main highway and headed for the Colorado Ranch. It felt good to be on familiar ground. Her car.

Her clothes. Although paint was peeling on her car from exposure to the fire's heat, and her clothes were still stiff and new, it was a small price to pay for still being alive. Evelyn Hart had been a dear and for a moment, Raine thought that in a different situation, they might have been friends. But her one trip by the house to return the borrowed clothes had been her first and her last.

She bit her lower lip and returned her attention to the road. There were more important things at stake. She'd left a message earlier in the day with her lawyer. He'd promised to call back to give her a date and time.

If she could wish this to be over, she would have done it immediately. Her mother had always said it was a sin to wish your life away, but Raine had suffered with this far too long. Just thinking of that tiny casket in the belly of a cargo plane with crates of machine parts made her sick. Then she reminded herself that the baby's earthly remains were going to be where they belonged. On his father's land.

A great ache bloomed within her, spilling misery into every living cell of her body. When Joseph had said that she'd already let go, she'd almost cried. She didn't know how to let go. All these years and it still hurt as if it was yesterday.

She shifted her thoughts, making herself focus on anything but what lay ahead, and as she did, she glanced out the windshield. Overhead a large bird was circling the sky, weaving and dipping through the air currents like a kite on a string.

She watched it for a moment, marveling at its freedom. There were no strings tying it to earth, and yet it belonged to this land. Once she could have made the same claim, but no longer. She looked back at the road stretching out in front of her, accepting the fact that she didn't belong anywhere now. Truth be told, she hadn't belonged anywhere for a very long time. In a way, that was making everything easier.

A short while later, she reached the ranch. Her steps were hurried as she entered the house.

There were two messages on the answering machine. One from Evelyn. The other from her lawyer.

She smiled during the first, but the smile quickly ended as she listened to the other. There was a problem. It wasn't a big deal, he'd said, but there was going to be a delay in exhumation.

She groaned. At this point, any delay was a problem. Not only was she going to have to wait before she began her journey, but she was going to have to do her waiting under Joseph Colorado's roof. She dropped into the nearest chair and closed her eyes in defeat.

Joseph could not have described his emotions when Raine announced the delay at supper last night, but today, the truth was weighted in his belly like a hunk of uncooked dough.

Like her, it hadn't really mattered to him what had caused the delay. That it was happening at all gave him pause for concern. Every time he looked at her, it made him remember things he'd be better off forgetting. Like the way her breath caught when he entered her body, and the way her eyelids got all heavy and sleepy-looking when they began to make love.

They'd made love in broad daylight. They'd made love in the pitch black of night. They'd made love underneath the pale glow of a full moon and skinny-dipped in a creek full of bone-chilling water. Even now, if he closed his eyes and thought about it real hard, he could remember the soft, uneven gasps that she made when a climax was upon her.

He shuddered. What he needed to remember was the way they'd parted and why she'd come back. That was enough to take the want straight out of a man.

At least it should have been.

But it wasn't.

And if that wasn't enough to contend with, Benny had been acting strange. Every time Joseph turned around, Benny was underfoot and asking if he needed some help. Joseph didn't know what was going on. In a way, it was almost scary. This Benny was a stranger. Joseph didn't take well to strangers.

He reached for a bridle and started down the aisle of the stables toward the last stall on the right where a bay gelding belonging to Harlan Winslow of Yuma, Arizona, temporarily resided. The horse heard Joseph's footsteps, poked out his head, pricked up his ears, and watched him coming.

Joseph grinned. Dancer was like a little kid. He would do anything—for anybody—for a price. Harlan Winslow's fourteen-year-old daughter, Corkie, had spoiled Dancer rotten. Short of having a saddle on his back, the horse was most happy to go through any paces Joseph might put him through—as long as someone had a pocket full of treats.

Joseph eyed the big gelding with a knowing eye. His conformation was good, and, except for this one tiny character flaw, he had a great disposition.

He grinned to himself, remembering the day he'd gotten Harlan's call.

"Hey, Colorado, can you take the rotten out of my horse?"

Joseph had laughed, then listened to the rest of the story before accepting the job.

Even though he was optimistic, Dancer had been here a week and Joseph had yet to get a bridle on him without a struggle. But Joseph knew something Dancer didn't. The only treat Dancer was going to get around here was a good head-scratching.

"Hey, big boy," Joseph called softly. "How about you and me . . . outside . . . no holds barred."

Then he laughed to himself at the absurdity of his challenge and opened the stall door. Almost immediately, he had to push Dancer's head away as the horse began nuzzling at Joseph's hands and pockets.

"No apples in there," he said, slipping the bridle over Dancer's head and trying to slide the bit between his teeth.

The big horse blew out through its nose, and the

game was on. It sniffed at every pocket Joseph had, at his hands, even his hat. Joseph kept grinning and working and talking, reminding the horse that he, and not a four-legged baby with a terrific sweet tooth, was in charge. No apples—no carrots—no sugar.

Finally, in a quick sleight-of-hand, Joseph slipped the bit between the horse's teeth. Dancer took a short two-step backward, as if in disbelief. Before the horse could pull any other shenanigans, Joseph gathered up the reins and led the horse out of its stall.

The north end of the aisle opened into the corrals. Now that Joseph had Dancer in tow, he let his mind wander into other areas as they headed out of the shady walls of the stables into the bright light of day.


Benny was almost through with his chores and glad of it. These were the tasks he hated worst. Shoveling shit—as he put it—was not high on his list of important things to do. It didn't matter to him that Joseph also cleaned stalls on a regular basis. In Benny's eyes, the ranch belonged to Joseph—the profits belonged to Joseph—therefore the dirty work should be his as well. He refused to admit that he was profiting as much, if not more, than Joseph. He got room, board, and money to spend without putting forth nearly as much effort.

At any rate, this stall was the last one and then he would be through. If he was lucky, he could get cleaned up and out of the house before Joseph even knew he was gone.

He gave the clean straw a quick kick and then tossed the pitchfork out into the passageway without looking.

It came out of nowhere, the tines glinting in the sunlight and spooking the horse as if it had been a striking snake. Instinctively Joseph dropped the reins and struck out, trying to deflect the pitchfork from piercing the horse. Dancer whinnied wildly and reared. At the sound, Benny spun, his eyes wide with disbelief.

"Oh no," he muttered, and bolted out of the empty stall. Expecting to see the pitchfork embedded in horseflesh, he sighed with relief as Dancer raced past him into the corral beyond. And then he saw Joseph, writhing upon the floor.

"Oh man," he groaned, and hurried to his brother's side. "Joseph, I am so sorry. I had no idea you were anywhere around. Don't move! Let me—"

Joseph grabbed Benny by the arm. "Don't talk, just pull . . . and be damned quick about it."

Benny was shaking as he wrapped his fingers around the shaft, but he did as he'd been told, yanking swiftly and pulling out the tines that had penetrated the upper portion of Joseph's leg.

At the moment of his release, Joseph rolled to a sitting position and dropped his head between his knees. The last thing he needed to do was pass out.

"Wait here," Benny said. "I'll get Raine."

Joseph shook his head. "No. Take care of the animals first."

"But your leg. You need a doctor."

Joseph looked up, his voice was deep with anger and pain.

"Just once, Benny . . . just once could you do what you're told?"

At that moment, Benny could have gladly added to his brother's pain. He spun and headed out into the corrals, caught the trailing reins of the skittish Dancer, and quickly returned him to his stall. Then he stalked to the pickup truck without telling Raine what had happened and drove back to the barn, skidding to a halt in the breezeway and sending a fine cloud of dust into the air.

"Now will you get in the damned truck?" Benny yelled.

Joseph was on his feet. He limped toward the cab and slid into the passenger side, slamming the door behind him.

The drive into town was silent. Benny drove too fast, too guilt-ridden to speak, and Joseph was so angry that he didn't trust himself to talk. If they'd been a second or two later in coming out of the stable, the pitchfork would have killed the horse. The fact that it had come closer to killing him instead had yet to sink in.

A short while later, Benny paced the waiting-room floor while the doctor worked on Joseph's leg. Within an hour of the incident, they were on their way home. Joseph had been pumped full of antibiotics to prevent infections, plus a tetanus shot for good measure. The puncture wounds were ugly, but required only light bandages. Benny was all too aware of the dark seeping stains on Joseph's right leg.

When they pulled up back at the ranch, Benny's face was pale, his voice shaking.

"Joseph, wait," Benny said.

Joseph hesitated, his hand on the door handle. "What?"

"Man, I am *so* sorry."

Joseph leaned back in the seat and momentarily closed his eyes. His leg was throbbing and so was his head.

"I know that," he replied.

"I never meant for—"

Joseph turned, fixing Benny with a dark, icy stare. "Just think next time, okay?"

Benny nodded as Joseph opened the door.

"Wait," Benny said. "Let me help you."

Joseph shook his head. "You only poked holes in my leg, not cut it off. I *can* walk."

"But the doctor said you shouldn't be—"

Joseph waved and kept walking toward the stables. Although there would be no workout for Dancer today, he needed to make sure that all the other horses were in their stalls.

Meanwhile, Benny stalked into the house, carrying the small sack of medicine that the doctor had sent home with them.

Raine came out of the kitchen, a little taken aback that it was Benny and not Joseph.

"Hello," she said. "I hope you two don't mind, but I decided to make supper tonight. Sort of paying for my own keep, so to speak."

Benny stuffed the sack of medicine in her hands as he stalked past.

"That's real nice of you," he said shortly. "But I won't be here to eat. If Joseph asks, which I doubt, tell him that I won't be home until sometime tomorrow. I'm going to Phoenix."

She stared after his retreating figure. "Why didn't you tell him yourself?" she called. "I thought you both drove up together."

Benny stopped in the hallway. "Long story," he growled, then pointed at the sack in her hand. "Just make sure he takes the damned medicine. I don't want to be responsible for his death, however delayed it might be."

Raine paled and spun toward the doorway. Death? What on earth had happened between these two?

That night, Raine put the finishing touches on their supper while Joseph finished shaving. In a way, he was relieved Benny was gone. Although the incident was an accident, in Joseph's mind, it was just another mistake to add to the many Benny had made over the years. Every time he convinced himself that Benny might actually be maturing, he would pull something like this. His brother was a walking disaster, and for Joseph, it was like constantly waiting for the other shoe to drop.

He gave his hair a final combing and hung his towel back on the rack before limping into the kitchen.

"Supper is ready," Raine said, eyeing his dragging leg without comment.

"Smells good," Joseph said.

When she turned away, Joseph frowned. Why was it so difficult to find common ground with the two people he should have felt most at ease? Intent on trying to explain his distant behavior, he reached for her, his fingers cupping her shoulder.

At the moment of his touch, Raine pivoted. There was an inscrutable expression on her face that Joseph misread.

"Easy," he drawled. "Your virtue is safe with me. I was just—"

"My virtue is pushing thirty. Safety is no longer an issue," she snapped. She set a meat loaf in the middle of the table and then wiped her hands on her apron. "Supper is ready."

Joseph sat down, unaware of whether he'd just been insulted or given the green light to proceed into a different level of a relationship. Either way, he thought he was pissed. But everything smelled so good. Maybe he should eat first and fight later.

It proved to be a good decision, because by the time they were through, the atmosphere around the table had eased. Joseph explained a little about what had happened between him and Benny without placing any blame. But he didn't have to. Raine was no fool. She was well aware of how careless Benny's actions had been. And the longer she listened to Joseph's story, the more angry she became on his behalf. Joseph could have been killed.

But before she could comment, the doorbell was ringing and he was gone.

She pushed herself up from the table and began to gather the dirty dishes into the sink. It was just as well. Within a few days she'd be gone. After that, what they did to each other couldn't matter, at least not to her.

A minute passed, and she was putting leftovers into the refrigerator when a faint cry broke the silence in which she was working. She paused, listening—and soon heard it again.

That sounded like a baby. What on earth would a baby be doing in this house, and at this time of night? Curious, she dried her hands and went to see for herself.

The sound came again before she had reached the living room. The weak, mewling cry of a very young baby was impossible to miss. Moments later, voices blended with the infant's cries until nothing was distinguishable except a sense of rising panic.

The baby looked like a doll. A tiny wax doll. Only after it began to squirm and then offered up a thin, high-pitched wail, had Joseph let himself believe that the baby was real. But there was no mistaking the torment on Ken and Lisa Blue's faces. Before they had started to explain, Joseph knew why they were here. Taking an adult to the healing place was one thing. But a child? There were rules to follow that a child would not understand, never mind a helpless infant. But his worries were not evident as he let the parents present their case, all the while trying not to react to the panic he kept hearing in Ken Blue's voice.

"We live in Oklahoma," Ken Blue said. "We've been driving for the better part of two days now, but John Standing Bear said you would help us."

John Standing Bear. Joseph remembered him well.

An expert marksman, John Standing Bear had done the unthinkable and shot himself in the leg. It wasn't a bad wound as gunshot wounds go, but John Standing Bear was a diabetic and the wound wouldn't heal. Days away from amputation, John Standing Bear appeared at Joseph's ranch. Two days later, he left the Colorado ranch for his home back in Kiowa, Oklahoma, a whole and healthy man. Not only was his leg healed, but his diabetes had miraculously disappeared.

Joseph sighed. John Standing Bear had done as he'd been told. He had not talked about his cure to anyone, yet when the time had come for him to pass it on, he had done so without compunction.

When Lisa Blue began to cry, Joseph knew that he would try. They were asking something of him that he'd never done before.

Yes, he *could* take the baby to the mountain that

embraces the sun, but for the healing to take place, he would have to stay in that chamber with the baby in his arms. According to what he'd been taught, it would be safe. He had to trust it would be so.

The baby's cries began to lessen. Joseph saw the parents glance anxiously at their child. The baby wasn't necessarily happy, just too weak to register protest. And it was that same soft sound dragging from weakened lungs that the parents feared and that firmed Joseph's resolve.

He held out his hands for the baby, silently asking for permission.

Raine walked into the room just as Lisa Blue laid her baby in Joseph's arms. In the moment it took to recycle a breath, her concern for the crying child was replaced by a wash of great pain. It was something about the tenderness in Joseph's touch as he sheltered the child with his body that overwhelmed her. Blinking quick tears, she took a deep breath.

"Is there anything I can do?"

The parents turned, startled by the woman's appearance. They'd been warned many times over about the need for secrecy and looked nervous, as if they'd been caught in the act of something foul.

Joseph heard her concern, but it was the torture in her eyes that hurt most.

"Sure," Joseph said softly, and motioned her over with a toss of his chin. "Say hello to Adam Blue, why don't you? He's a pretty sick little boy, but he sure likes to be held." Joseph glanced at Lisa Blue, silently asking her permission to hand over her child to a stranger.

"Mr. Colorado is right," the woman said. "I've spoiled him, but that's part of the fun of having a baby." She gestured toward Raine. "If you'd like to hold him, I don't mind."

Raine's smile froze. She didn't know whether to run screaming from the room or fall down on her knees at Joseph's feet in thanksgiving. But she knew why he'd done it. Within a few days, they would be putting a child in the ground. Here was a chance to hold a living, breathing baby before they laid their own to rest.

"Raine?"

"I would love to," she said softly. "But I think I'd better sit down."

She dropped into a nearby chair and then held her breath as Joseph laid the baby in her arms. The moment she felt the tiny bit of warmth squirming beneath the blankets, what was left of her heart finally broke. This was what she'd been born to be. A mother. But she'd been cheated. It hadn't lasted long enough to enjoy.

The baby squirmed and then opened his eyes, giving Raine a clear view of very large, very dark, round eyes. She stroked the side of his cheek with the tip of her finger.

"Hello there, little man. I hear you're not well? I'm so sorry," she said softly. "I know just how you feel."

Joseph frowned. It was an odd thing for Raine to

say, but it was obvious that she was smitten. It was all he could do to refocus, but from the condition of the child that he'd held, there was no time to waste.

"Raine, I need to talk to the parents in private. Do you mind if we leave you on your own for a couple of minutes? We'll just be in the other room."

Raine never looked up. "No," she said softly. "I don't mind. I don't mind a bit."

## 8

Joseph's expression was serious. "Do you understand what I'm telling you?"

Both Ken and Lisa Blue nodded. They knew the risks of the unknown, but they were also aware of their baby's fate. Unless a miracle occurred, Adam Blue would not live to see his first birthday.

Joseph felt their panic, but there was something else the Blue family needed to know. Something that might cause them to change their minds, yet it had to be said.

"Mr. and Mrs. Blue, there's something I need to tell you, and there are no exceptions. After we get to the airport, the baby and I go alone."

Lisa started crying, but her gaze never faltered. "I have to trust you, Mr. Colorado. You're Adam's last chance. But there's something you need to know, too."

Joseph tensed. "And that would be?"

"Besides his birth defects, Adam's breathing stops periodically."

Never had the responsibility of being the

guardian weighed heavier on Joseph than it did right now. He gave her arm a reassuring squeeze.

"Just show me what to do."

She nodded.

"Where are you staying?" he asked.

"We have a travel trailer parked outside of Oracle. We can meet you in the morning," Ken Blue said.

"No, you tell me where you're parked," Joseph said. "I'll pick you up around seven. You can go with me as far as Tucson, which is where I keep my helicopter. After that, Adam and I go alone."

"Gladly, and for as long as it takes," Lisa Blue said. Then she glanced toward the living room. "I'd better rescue your friend before Adam gets fussy. It's past his bedtime, you know."

Joseph nodded, although he suspected that Raine wouldn't have cared how much the baby fussed.

A short while later, the Blue family was gone. Benny had long since taken himself off to Oracle in a cloud of dust, and Raine and Joseph were alone.

Raine's arms felt empty. She wouldn't have admitted it to anyone, not even herself, but being in Joseph's house with a baby in her arms had seemed right. That in itself was enough to give her cause for concern. She had to find something else on which to focus besides the memory of that soft little body and the baby-sweet smell still clinging to her clothes. She got up from her chair and headed for the kitchen.

"I'm going to finish the dishes."

"No," Joseph said. "You cooked. I'll clean up. Why don't you go soak in the tub for a while. If memory serves, you were real partial to bubble baths."

She paused, her eyebrows slightly arched. It was the only sign she gave of her surprise.

"You don't forget much, do you?"

He gave her a long, considering stare and then shrugged.

"No, I guess I don't."

Raine watched him leave, and there was a moment, just before he disappeared, when the urge to call him back was overwhelming. Instead of giving in, she bit her lip and headed for her bath. She didn't need any more grief—not from Joseph—not from anyone. All she wanted to do was just get the next few days over with. As soon as it was possible, she was going to get in her car and drive until she ran out of land, then get on a plane and fly until she found some again. It wasn't much of a plan, but it was the best one she had.

Just after sunrise, Joseph tossed a small bag into the back of his truck and then got into the cab, wincing at the pull of sore muscles in his leg from yesterday's injury. Just before he started the engine, he glanced up at the house, picturing Raine still asleep in her bed and Benny sleeping it off in his own. Sometimes the secrets and the loneliness got to him, and then he thought of people like Wynema Littlefish—and the baby, Adam Blue—and smiled. They were what balanced out the loneliness. He leaned forward and turned the key. Within minutes he was gone.

Inside the house, Raine shifted in her sleep. The sound of an engine running pushed at the perimeter of her mind, but she was too comfortable to focus. Instead, she drifted back into a deeper slumber.

It was after 10:00 A.M. before she made it to the kitchen. Benny was only steps behind her. They each saw Joseph's note at the same time, and while it was addressed to both of them, Raine stood back.

Benny frowned as he yanked it from the refrigerator and began to read.

Raine waited, her curiosity growing. She watched Benny's face growing darker by the minute. By the time he was finished, he was cursing. He wadded the note into a ball and flung it across the room.

"Hell's fire, he's gone and done it again! I'd bet any amount of money he's up in that chopper. Every time I ask him what he does when he leaves like this, he makes up some poor-ass excuse. He doesn't know it, but I've had just about all I can take of these damned secrets."

Raine was more than a little surprised to learn that Joseph could pilot a helicopter and that Benny seemed to think something illicit was connected with it.

"What secrets?" Raine asked.

But Benny was too furious to answer. Instead, he grabbed his hat and headed for his truck. He had no intentions of training any damned horse, no matter what Joseph said.

Raine picked up the note, smoothing it out on the countertop before tilting it toward the window to read. She skipped the parts that had been directed toward Benny, since he had ignored them, too. It was only after she got farther down the note that she began to frown.

Raine—I'm going to Tucson to get the heli-copter. The baby you saw last night needs to see a specialist. I told the family I'd help get them there. Be back tonight or early tomor-row. —J.

"So what's the big deal about that?" Raine mut-tered, but there was no one around to answer her question.

For a moment, she stood within the silence of the house, listening to the hum of the refrigerator and the distant whinny of a horse in the corrals. Food no longer seemed important.

She stepped outside, absorbing the sweet warmth of the day and the thick green of the lawn beyond the steps. She sat down at the edge of the porch, letting her bare legs dangle in the sunshine while an intermittent breeze played havoc with her hair. Her jeans shorts were new and stiff. The tag inside the neck of her blue T-shirt was itchy. And the longer she sat there, the more pronounced her dis-comfort became. Suddenly she bolted up from where she'd been sitting and headed inside.

Joseph was sharing his house. She was going to

take it one step farther and borrow some of his clothes as well. Once the stiffness was laundered out of the fabrics, she was certain she'd feel much better.

When lunchtime came, Benny's absence was noted and ignored. Truth be told, Raine could have cared less. Somewhere within the space of this day, she had found a peace her life had been missing. And while she couldn't take the feeling with her when she left, she made up her mind to enjoy it for as long as she could.

The sun was within an hour of its zenith when the helicopter topped the west ridge of the mountains that embrace the sun. Only after Joseph could see the mountain face did he start to relax. This trip had been like no other he'd ever taken. Instead of strapping the baby in the back, he'd buckled the infant carrier into the seat beside him.

The flight had been harrowing. More than once he'd imagined that the baby's breathing had stopped, but each time he had thrust a shaking hand against the baby's neck, his fears had been unjustified. He kept looking at Adam Blue's pale, unnatural color and picturing a tiny heart pumping madly to compensate for a hole that wasn't supposed to be there.

More than once, the baby's dark gaze had lingered on Joseph's face, and he'd wondered if the child was afraid. It was strange, these looks that passed between two men—one at the beginning of his life, the other nearing a peak. It was Joseph who was forced to look away.

The knowledge that his own son had never had the chance that he was giving Adam Blue was almost too painful to contemplate, and yet he accepted that there were things on this earth beyond man's control. His heart ached, both for Raine and for the loss that they shared. Somehow, when their baby had died, he feared a part of Raine had died, too. She laughed and talked and ate and slept, but it was almost as if she was just going through the motions of life.

The baby wiggled in the car seat and then whimpered in complaint. Joseph gave him a quick, urgent glance.

"Just a little while longer," he said softly, and gently cupped the top of the baby's small head, feeling the cotton-soft hair and the delicate structure of Adam Blue's bones. At the touch of Joseph's hand, the baby's eyes began to droop.

A short while later they touched down, and then once again, it became a race against time. Joseph glanced up into the sky. The sun was almost directly overhead. Quickly, he lifted the baby out of the seat, cradling him as carefully as he knew how and cupping his tiny cheek.

"Well, little man. Are you ready for this?"

The baby looked at Joseph, then squawked like an angry little bird that had been disturbed in its nest. Joseph laughed.

"My sentiments exactly."

Moments later, they were out of the chopper and

moving toward the face of the mountain. Joseph reached the wall; again he made a fist and thrust the ring into the niche, then grunted with satisfaction as the opening was revealed.

Without wasted motion, he laid the baby down on a blanket and took off its clothes. Tiny arms and legs windmilled in sudden delight at the unfettered feeling. Joseph laughed. Then, this time, he shed his clothes as well. He grabbed a handful of dirt as he gathered the child into his arms. The words of his people flowed from his lips as he turned to the four corners of the earth, letting the dirt flow with the breeze. Never had the prayers been stronger within him. Within seconds they were inside the tunnel and moving quickly through the passage.

Sheltered by a sudden darkness, the baby's eyes opened wide. As he focused on the verdant glow emanating from the walls, he grew silent. Joseph glanced at him nervously. The quiet made him uneasy.

"We're almost there, buddy," he promised, and hastened his steps.

He shifted the child's body slightly, holding it firmer against his chest as he hurried along the passageway. Today, the eerie green lights that marked the way into the belly of the mountain did not pull at Joseph's emotions. There was no time to indulge himself with fantasies about the centuries that had come and gone or of the men who had walked this way before him. Adam Blue had become more to Joseph than just another person to be healed. He'd become the symbol of his own son—the baby who had never drawn breath on this earth. He hadn't been able to save the one, but he could save the other.

And then he glanced down and his heart skipped a beat. The baby's eyes were closed, and he was lying so still against Joseph's chest that he could feel bones through the thin, fragile skin. Oh God, oh no, was he—

Suddenly the baby puckered his mouth and made sucking noises. Joseph went weak with relief. He'd only fallen asleep. But the fear had been enough to hasten his stride. He broke into an all-out run.

A few minutes later he reached the chamber. Uneasy about what lay ahead, Joseph closed his eyes, making himself picture his father's face, hearing his father's words, remembering his father's strength. Then a calm came over him. He knew what must be done.

Without hesitation, he shoved the ring into the second lock and was flat on his back in the center of the chamber before the first ray of sunlight pierced the gloom. The wound in his leg was pulling from the strain of moving so fast. He winced as a muscle began to spasm, then glanced down at the baby one last time. Satisfied that the sleeping child was secure in his arms, he whispered aloud.

"Stay asleep, little fellow. When you wake up, it will be in a whole new world."

He turned his hand so that his ring was facing up to the sky, then closed his eyes.

A spear of green light pierced the darkness like

fire from an avenging angel's sword. The hum it made was not unlike the sound a tuning fork makes when struck. Joseph exhaled deeply and let go of his soul.

It was beginning.

The afternoon came and went. Sunset was only an hour or so away and Raine was outside again, this time on the back porch, alone—but not lonely. Although her clothes had long since been washed and dried, she still wore one of Joseph's shirt over a pair of her shorts. It was long-sleeved and denim, and the tail hit the middle of her thighs. Her legs had taken on a light golden tan and her bare feet were covered in dust. To keep her hair off her neck, she had pulled it up into a knot on her head.

At first glance, the shirt appeared to be all she was wearing. Her acquaintances back in Chicago would not have recognized this woman as the associate they had known for years. The cool, collected journalist who had breezed in and out of the offices in her unisex clothes had virtually disappeared. They would have had no point of reference with this earthy, carefree woman.

Raine lay back and lifted her face to the waning sun. Today she had made a monumental discovery. Resting was good for the soul. She wondered why it had taken her so long to figure this out. Then she closed her eyes, telling herself that she'd just take a short nap. Her last conscious thought was of Joseph and the family who'd come to him in need.

*   *   *

The sun was balancing upon the horizon like a balle-
rina *en pointe* when Raine heard the sounds of a
vehicle coming down the driveway. Whichever
brother it was, she was in no mood to move. The
lethargy of the lazy afternoon was still with her. She
felt light in her heart but heavy in her bones. Like a
sleeping cat in the noonday sun, she was reluctant to
move an inch more than was demanded.

When the vehicle drove past the house and
turned toward the barns, she knew that it was
Joseph. Benny would not be checking on the horses.
There was a part of her that hoped Benny didn't
bother to come back tonight. If he did, she feared the
brothers would argue. Benny seemed reluctant to
accept any responsibility. Something wasn't right
between them. She just didn't know what.

So she lay there until the sun fell off its perch and
sank into oblivion, leaving behind a great splash of
color as a parting gesture.

"So beautiful," she whispered, watching until
the sky had turned to gray and the moon was just
visible overhead.

With great reluctance, she dragged herself up
from the lounger and turned around to go inside.

"Oh!" she gasped, and then a bit embarrassed,
unconsciously pulled at the tail of Joseph's shirt. "I
thought you were still with the horses."

He walked out of the house, stopping only
inches away from where she was standing. Raine

frowned. Although it was getting dark, it was still light enough to see his face.

He looked stunned. And then she remembered where he'd been and her heart sank. The baby. Something must have happened to it. Dear God, it had been so blessedly sweet.

"Oh, Joseph, the baby . . . did he—"

Joseph shook his head. "No, he's fine," he said slowly. "He got care in time."

"Thank God," Raine said, and felt a great sense of relief knowing she meant it.

For the first time in as long as she could remember, she had not begrudged someone else a healthy child.

But Joseph couldn't quit staring. Today, he had died and been reborn in a way he could never have explained. He'd been shattered like glass and pierced with the heat of a cleansing green fire. In his arms, a baby had been given new life, and the parents a miracle.

There was no way to say what he had experienced other than that he felt as if his soul had danced with angels. He had little to no memory of anything, not even hearing a sound, although he knew from past experience that a terrible roar did occur.

But for the soul within the chamber of the mountain that embraces the sun, it would seem there was nothing to experience but an unearthly peace. He took a deep breath, wanting to cry, wanting to shout, knowing that he would do neither, although for the rest of his life, he would always believe he'd seen the face of God.

Raine knew she was staring, but she couldn't look away. It was almost dark now, but he seemed to be standing in light.

"Are you all right?" she asked.

He nodded.

"Do you want something to eat? I didn't cook today, but I suppose it wouldn't take long to—"

He shook his head and then cleared his throat. "No, please, I'm not hungry, but there is something I have to say. Something I need to tell you before another day goes by."

She shrugged. After all the hospitality he'd offered, listening seemed harmless.

"I'm listening."

"I want to make love to you."

She took a quick step back, suddenly angry, suddenly afraid.

"I don't know why," she said harshly, "but I wasn't prepared for that."

Joseph didn't move. After what he'd been through today, deceit, both to himself and to her, was no longer possible.

"I won't lie to you," he said. "Not any longer. I shouldn't feel this way. Maybe it's just a case of trying to turn back time, but there is a want inside of me that I haven't felt in years. I remember what it was like with us. I can't quit thinking about you lying in my arms. I remember you, Rainbow." His voice shook as it deepened with emotion. "My God, but I remember you."

Raine felt as if she'd just been slapped into reality. "And you think I don't?" She spun and stumbled off the porch. "Damn you, Joseph, don't you understand? I don't want to remember what it was like. I can't afford to care—not anymore."

Even though this was no more than he'd expected, the disappointment still hurt.

"I understand. But after today, I needed truth between us." He sighed. "And now I suppose it is there."

Without another word, he turned and walked away, leaving her alone in the darkness, nursing a heartache that couldn't be fixed.


It was just after 3:00 A.M. when Benny unlocked the front door and stepped inside. The drunk he'd been on was almost gone, leaving him with a pounding head and a guilty conscience. He started to take off his boots to sneak into his room when he paused, cursing himself and his lack of backbone. This was his house. He was a grown man. He shouldn't have to tiptoe around like a naughty teenager.

He turned the lock on the door, tossed his keys on the hall table, and stalked down the hall. In spite of his mental pep talk, every click of his boot heels on the red Spanish tile made him nervous. He kept seeing Joseph burst out of a room, pointing a finger and telling him he was worthless. But it didn't happen. He got all the way to his room before he began to relax, willing his racing heart to a calm.

He sat down on the bed to pull off his boots, but

the room started to roll. His stomach pitched and he bolted for the bathroom with only seconds to spare as his body rejected what was left inside.

A short while later, he staggered out of the bathroom with a wet washcloth clasped to his face. When he got to the bed, he fell facedown across it, his boots dangling off one side, his head from the other. He slapped the wet washcloth on the back of his neck and closed his eyes. The next thing he knew it was morning.

Joseph was just getting out of the shower when Benny staggered into the bathroom.

"Sorry," Benny muttered, as he opened the door to the medicine cabinet and began rummaging through bottles. "Got a headache."

The urge to blame was overwhelming, but Joseph held his tongue. Instead, he stepped forward, water dripping from his bare body, and reached for the top shelf.

"Here's something that might help," he said, and handed Benny the bottle.

Benny had the grace to flush. He looked away, shaking several pills into his hand and then downing them without any water.

"How's the new colt?" Joseph asked.

Benny spun, his anger at the ready. "I have no idea and you know it," he snapped, glaring at his big brother and wishing that they could trade places for just one day. Then Joseph would know what it was like to live in the shadow of a man like himself.

He stared, hating Joseph for everything, including his size and stature. At that moment, he wished the pitchfork had caught Joseph in the chest and not the leg. That accident would have ended Benny's indenture to a life he was forced to live.

When Joseph did nothing but reach for a towel, Benny's anger diffused. How could you argue with someone who wouldn't talk back?

Sick at heart and frustrated beyond words, Joseph wrapped the towel around his waist and then got another one to dry off his hair. He thought nothing of the fact that Benny was still standing in the doorway. His brother never did know when to shut up, so he was probably waiting for another opportunity to argue. But when the silence lengthened, out of curiosity, he glanced over his shoulder. Benny was staring at him as if he'd just seen a ghost.

"If you're going to be sick, throw up in your own bathroom," Joseph snapped.

Benny shook his head and pointed.

"What?" Joseph asked.

Benny took a deep breath, trying to form words around the roar in his ears.

"Your leg."

Confused by the question, Joseph looked down, and the moment he did, groaned inwardly. Oh, hell.

"The wounds . . . they're gone," Benny mumbled.

Joseph pretended a lack of interest as he pushed past Benny and into his bedroom, reaching for his jeans hanging on a hook inside the closet door.

"You're imagining things." Then he dropped his towel and pulled on his jeans.

Benny bolted forward, grabbing Joseph's hand and stopping him in midstep.

"Don't lie to me!" he muttered, his voice shaking as hard as his hands. "I'm the one who pulled that pitchfork out! You were hurt . . . hurt bad."

Joseph pushed him away and quickly yanked up his jeans. "And don't I know it," Joseph snapped, then reached for a shirt. "But you weren't inside the doctor's office with me. Yes, it bled, but they were only punctures. Nothing was cut. There was no torn flesh. Punctures seal over almost instantly."

Benny frowned. Yes, that much was true, but there should still be marks—red, angry marks. He started to argue, but Joseph had already put on his boots and was on his way out the door.

"Damn it," Benny shouted, and bolted after him. "You're lying to me and we both know it."

And then he thought of Stuart Rossi and his crazy claims of a healing place. He thought of the couple who'd come with a sick baby in tow—then of all the other strangers who came out of nowhere. Always, always, asking for Joseph. He stopped, staggered by what he was thinking, then grabbed Joseph by the arm, needing to look him in the face when the words were said.

"It's true, isn't it?" he whispered.

Joseph rolled his eyes and sighed. "What's true, Benny? That you don't pull your own weight around here? Yes, that's true. That you drink more than you work and I'm sick of picking up your bad debts and living down your bad name? Hell yes, that's true, too."

Benny's face turned a dark, angry red. He doubled up his fists and swung.

Joseph grabbed Benny's wrist before a connection was made. And the look on his face was enough to scare Benny into silence. Joseph yanked Benny forward until his breath was hot against his little brother's face.

"Don't raise your hand to me again. Not in this house. Never in this house."

Then he dropped Benny's wrist as if it had become something foul and walked out of the door without looking back.

Benny stood in shamed silence, aware that he'd done an unforgivable thing. He'd raised his hand against his own blood. Even Benny, who refused to acknowledge his heritage, knew he'd crossed over a line. It took several minutes for him to realize that Joseph had never answered his question. And it was at that moment, Benny knew. There was something out there that had healed a terrible wound to Joseph's leg overnight.

That's when his nerves began to jump. All he could hear was Stuart Rossi's promise echoing in his ears.

*Two million dollars.* The man was willing to pay two million dollars for something that his brother was giving away.

# 9

The motel bed was too firm, and the pillows were too soft for Stuart's liking. For a man accustomed to the best of everything, it was the spark that set him off.

"Son of a holy bitch," Stuart growled, and flung both of them across the room. "Edward! Get in here, goddamn it!"

"Sir?"

"Call room service," Stuart snapped, then pointed to the pillows on the floor. "Get me some other pillows. Those things are too soft."

"Yes, sir," Edward said, and then bolted.

Stuart flopped back onto the bed, pissed off at the world and as desperate as he'd ever been in his life. Six days had passed since he'd sent Edward to meet with Benny Colorado, and he had yet to get a response.

He wondered if he'd been had. What if Colorado had just taken the money with no intention of helping? For the first time since he'd been diagnosed, he was beginning to fear he *would* have to face his mortality after all.

"No," he muttered, and flung his arm over his eyes.

It was bad enough that he'd been born a hemophiliac. That alone had curtailed much of the wild life he might have enjoyed, and for a rich, single man from L.A., that was a death knell in itself. Where Stuart came from, people like him didn't rot away like pieces of uneaten fruit. They outlived their heirs—or at the very least, died drunk in their cars or overdosed on some fancy designer drug.

Stuart's disease wasn't glamorous, but it *was* debilitating and deadly. He closed his eyes, hoping for peace. Instead, he kept seeing Wynema Littlefish's face, and it was like looking at her in rewind. From oozing sores and emaciated body to the picture of health. Back and forth. Back and forth. In a fresh burst of rage, he bolted up from the bed, ripped the oxygen tube from his nose and stalked to the wet bar to pour himself a drink.

Edward came in just as Stuart tossed the first one down.

"Sir! Mr. Rossi! You're not supposed to—"

Stuart pivoted.

"Not supposed to what? Drink? Why not? I can't party. I can't swim. I can't sail my own goddamned boat. It's been six months since I even had enough strength to fuck a woman. At least allow me a measly drink."

Edward blanched. "I only meant to—"

"Are they sending my pillows?"

Edward sighed.

"Yes, sir. They're on their way."

"When they arrive, bring them to me. I want to take a nap."

Edward nodded and left.

Stuart lifted the glass, then paused with it halfway to his lips to stare at his reflection in the mirror over the bar. The man looking back at him made him sick. He was pale and thin and his hair, once his pride and joy, hung limp and lifeless over his forehead. As he continued to stare, a snarl appeared on his face.

"It's four o'clock in the afternoon on a beautiful sunny day and I want to take a nap . . . a fucking, goddamned nap."

Suddenly he spun and flung his drink against the opposite wall. It shattered in a spray of bourbon and crystal.

A car stopped at the intersection, pausing for traffic, then turning right in the opposite direction from the phone booth in which Benny was standing. He kept staring at the phone number on the piece of paper he was holding and telling himself there was nothing wrong with trying to get ahead. It wasn't as if someone had to die before he could get this money. On the contrary, if Benny was right, someone was going to live.

By the time he'd talked to himself for another five minutes, he was completely convinced that Joseph was the evil one for holding back such a wonderful opportunity from the world. In Benny's mind, if the healing place was real, it should be available to everyone, not just a bunch of blanket-ass Indians who don't want to live in the twenty-first century.

Having justified everything weighing on his fair-weather conscience, he set his beer down on a shelf and dropped some coins into the slots, dialing the number Rossi's chauffeur had given him. It rang once, then twice, then three times. On the fourth ring, his hopes began to drop. What if the man was already gone? He'd said he'd be there at least a week. Benny shifted his weight from one leg to the other and transferred the phone to the other ear.

"Come on, come on," he muttered. "Someone answer the damned phone." Just as he was about to hang up, he heard a man's breathless voice, as if he'd been running.

"Hello."

"Hey, Eddie, is that you?" Then he laughed.

"Mr. Colorado?"

Benny grinned. It made him feel good to be called mister.

"Yeah, it's me," he said. "What took you so long to answer the phone? Got yourself a woman there with you?"

"No," Edward said. "There's no woman here."

Now that the chitchat had been accomplished, Benny went straight to the point.

"How's your boss?"

"Would you care to speak to Mr. Rossi?"

Benny took a quick swig of his beer. For some

reason, the man with the money made him nervous.

"Yeah, I suppose," he said. "But if he's busy or something, I can tell you what—"

"Just a moment. I'll put him on," Edward said.

The line went dead in Benny's ear and just for a moment, he thought the man had hung up. And then seconds later, another click sounded. Even though it was long distance, Benny heard himself sniveling and fawning to a man he'd only seen once.

He tried a little foreplay before laying his cards out on the table, but Rossi was obviously in no mood for chitchat.

"Mr. Colorado, do you have what I want?" Rossi asked.

Another surge of guilt hit belly-high, but Benny kept thinking of the lies, always the lies. He gritted his teeth and then grinned.

"I'm thinking I do," he said shortly. "Let me share a little story with you, sir. After you hear what I have to say, then you be the judge."

The tension between Joseph and Raine was as tight as a newly strung fence. But there wasn't a moment of what he'd told her that he would willingly take back. After what he'd experienced with Adam Blue in his arms, his leg wasn't the only thing that had been healed.

That's why his brother's questions had pushed him to panic. He couldn't tell his secrets—wouldn't tell—but the very fact that he didn't answer his brother's questions was, in a way, an answer in itself. He could only imagine what Benny was thinking.

And then there was Raine. Once she'd been his world. But her presence here was so cold, so formal. She was little more than a faded shadow of the real rainbow he'd known and loved.

And if he'd be honest with himself, her refusal was not unexpected, but it was the anger that came with it that was startling. Twelve years was a long time to hang onto revenge. Sometimes he could convince himself that it wasn't revenge that kept her anger on boil. But if not that, then what else could it be? Yes, he had gotten her pregnant, but he would never have abandoned her. She was the one who had left.

Then his conscience kicked.

*And you're the one who let her go.*

He spun, startled by the voice, only to realize it was inside his head.

A door slammed in the back of the house. It had to be Raine.

Raine's shoulders drooped and her steps were lagging. When she walked into the living room and saw Joseph standing there, she almost broke down. She needed to be held. She wanted to cry to the heavens for taking away her joy. But after what he'd said the other night, whatever comfort she'd felt in his presence was gone. So instead of couching her words, she blurted out her news for the bad taste that it was.

"My lawyer called while you were down at the barns."

Joseph's belly knotted.

"They're shipping the body tomorrow. It will be in Tucson around seven o'clock tomorrow night. I have the particulars right here."

She held out her hand, offering the small scrap of paper as if it were filth.

When he took it from her, the need to hold her was strong. He kept telling himself to say something wise that would take away all of this hurt. But it was as if he'd been struck dumb by the pain on her face. Instead, he took the piece of paper and watched as she walked away.

The day ended with an overcast sky, which suited the mood within the house quite accurately.

Then Benny called.

Joseph talked to him long enough to get mad and then hung up before he got to the point of shouting. Benny had never been what one could call amenable, but his rebellion had never been this apparent. Joseph didn't know what to do next. There was a sick feeling in the pit of his stomach. He couldn't prove it, but he suspected Benny was involved in something bad.

He turned away from the phone to stare out the window. It was getting dark. Although he'd already fed and watered the stock, he decided to make one last trip out to the barns.

Dancer, the bay gelding, was coming along nicely.

Once Joseph had gotten the message across that treats were not a constant part of the horse's life, it had taken to affection like a tied-up pup. Nothing more than the sound of footsteps would bring Dancer to the door, waiting to see what came next.

When Joseph stepped out on the front porch, the tightness within him began to subside. He took a deep breath and looked up at the sky, then lowered his gaze to the ragged horizon beyond. There were storms in the mountains, but they wouldn't come this far. Sometimes he longed for the feel of rain upon his face, but this land of his forefathers was not one given to constant downpours and lingering humidity. Then he gazed upon his land and felt great satisfaction. The soil was rich and when irrigated, turned a thin, brown soil into a blanket of green. For all its shortcomings, for all its blessings, this Arizona land was his home.

Just as he would have stepped off the porch, he sensed he was no longer alone. He turned. Raine was standing on the other side of the screen door, looking out.

"I'm going to the barn," he said. "Want to come?"

She hesitated.

"If you've got an apple handy, there's a big guy out there who will love you forever—or at least as long as the apple lasts."

Raine laughed, and because it was an unexpected invitation she nodded.

"Give me a second," she said, and bolted toward the kitchen.

Moments later she caught up with him at the edge of the yard, an apple clutched tightly in her hand.

They walked in easy silence together for a short distance, and then Raine looked up and sighed. She should have known. Without missing a step, Joseph had been watching her every move.

"You okay?" he asked.

She nodded. "I will be, when this is over."

He knew what she meant. It was as if a great swinging sword were hanging over their heads and gaining in momentum with every pass.

When he stopped suddenly, Raine stopped as well, her heart accelerating slightly.

"No big deal," he said lightly, and slid his arm across her shoulder as they resumed their stride. "Just between friends, okay?"

*Just between friends.*

A few days ago, she would have said that was impossible. But now, in light of everything else, she could afford the small concession.

She almost smiled. "Yes, just between friends."

And then they reached the barns. No sooner had they entered the long aisle between stalls when a horse poked its head out over the half door and whinnied.

Joseph grinned. "There's the big guy I was talking about. His name is Dancer, and he's an unabashed beggar. Wait a minute," he said, and then got out his knife and cut the apple into several small pieces. "Here you go," he said. "And watch your fingers. He's not only a beggar, he's a pig."

Raine's delight in the unexpected meeting grew as she offered the first bite of apple to the begging horse. The velvet softness of the horse's nose tickled the palm of her hand, and in spite of Joseph's warnings to the contrary, Dancer ate the pieces of apple with dainty precision.

Only after it was gone did she move closer. Dancer nickered softly as if to say, "Is that all?" and then laid his great head across Raine's shoulder. Startled, she stepped back. Joseph laughed. Dancer was begging for his head-scratching after all.

"You big old baby," Joseph said, but his touch was gentle as he rubbed his hand along the bay's powerful neck.

Raine watched Joseph's transformation. Out here he was a different man, more like the boy she remembered. The stern expression he usually wore was replaced by carefree joy. Just before he took his leave of the horse, he hugged its neck. Raine closed her eyes and then looked away. It reminded her of things better left in the past.

When Joseph turned around, Raine's expression was bland, and the smile on her face didn't go past her eyes.

They started toward the house.

"Give me your hand," Joseph said. Before she could argue, he added. "It's dark. I don't want you to stumble and fall."

"What about you?" she countered.

When he answered, there was a gentleness in his voice that caught her unaware.

"Well, now, Rainbow, I don't fall down anymore."

She frowned. It was an odd, almost conceited thing to say.

"Those words could be hard to live up to."

"It doesn't mean what you think," he said. "It just means that my life is on track. I know where I'm going."

A big ache hit her chest-high and it took several breaths before she trusted herself to speak.

"That must be a very satisfying thing to know. Not many people can say that," she said, and started forward alone.

"Hey, lady."

She paused. He took her hand and then gave it a gentle tug. "But just in case I'm wrong, maybe I'd better hold on."

Raine gave in, not because he was too persuasive, but because she so very badly wanted Joseph Colorado's touch.

When they reached the house, he opened the front door, reached inside to turn on the lights, and then stepped aside for her to enter.

"You go on ahead," he said. "There's something I still need to do."

Raine glanced beyond Joseph's shoulder. "But it's dark."

He nodded. "I know, but I'll be all right. Besides, there's a full moon, or didn't you notice?"

Raine shook her head. "No, actually I didn't. I've gotten so used to my world being dark, I guess I forgot to look."

Then she walked past him and into the house, pausing once in the hallway. She turned. As she'd suspected, he was still in the doorway, watching.

"Joseph."

"What?"

"Thank you."

"For what, Rainbow?"

She shrugged. "Oh, everything, I guess. You know ... the horse ... the apple ... the company ... and for holding my hand."

A bitter smile slipped across his face. "You're welcome," he said softly. "I'm just sorry it's all been a little too late."

Then he closed the door. She could hear his footsteps as he walked off the porch. The silence afterward was disconcerting, and she had a sudden impulse to go after him and call him back into the light. But she didn't. Instead, she went into the bedroom, closing—and for the first time since her arrival—locking the door behind her. Not because she didn't trust Joseph, but because she was beginning to distrust herself.

A short while later she was down on her knees by the side of her bed. Her hair was still damp on the ends from her shower, her face scrubbed of all makeup. The T-shirt in which she was sleeping fell way past her thighs. She looked like a child about to say her bedtime prayers. But she wasn't a child. She was a woman in mourning. Her child's eternal rest had been disturbed and it weighed upon her like an anchor around her heart. She couldn't quit thinking about a very small casket on a very large plane. The cargo area would be filled with the remnants of other people's belongings and other people's lives. For Raine, the casket represented the only remnant of her life that counted, and until she saw it, until she touched it again—

Her head dipped. She stretched her arms out across the side of the bed in supplication and closed her eyes.

"God, help me. I can't do this alone anymore."

Later she crawled into bed and slept. It was a deep and dreamless sleep—an answer to a prayer.


Raine jerked and then sat straight up in bed. She cocked her head, listening and trying to discern what it was that she'd heard that had awakened her from such a deep sleep. There was nothing but silence. She glanced at the clock. It was just after 4:00 A.M. She got up and looked out the window. The hood of a car gleamed beneath the light of a full moon.

Benny! He was home. Maybe that's what she'd heard.

She reached for her shorts, pulling them on underneath her nightshirt, then tiptoed out into the hall to make sure all was well.

A kitchen light was on. She paused in the hallway, contemplating the wisdom of taking a look or going back to bed and minding her own business. Before she had time to decide, Benny walked into the hallway. The forced cheerfulness of his demeanor wasn't lost on her. He was more than a little bit drunk. She thought of the innocent people who'd been on the road and at the mercy of his indulgences.

"Hey, what are you doing up so early?" he asked.

"I heard something. Couldn't go back to sleep until I made sure everything was okay."

"Sorry, honey," he joked. "I guess I slammed the front door a little too hard when I came in. It won't happen again."

Raine continued to watch him without comment, but she couldn't help wondering how many times Joseph had heard that before.

"So, how about joining me in a cup of coffee?" Benny asked.

Raine shook her head. "No, thanks. Now that I know it was you I heard, I think I'll go back to bed."

"Want some company?" Benny asked and then winked.

Raine's expression stilled. It didn't take Benny long to know that his joke had fallen very flat.

"Hey, I was just kidding."

Before she was forced to answer, the kitchen door suddenly opened.

It was Joseph. His steps were dragging, his shoulders slumped. He was dust from head to toe and he was carrying his shirt in his hands.

"What the hell?" Benny asked.

Joseph stared, obviously stunned by the fact that everyone in the house was up.

"It's after four. What's going on? Is everything all right?"

Benny took instant offense. "I should be asking you that," he snapped. "What the hell were *you* doing—waiting up for me just so you could play daddy again?"

Joseph flinched as if he'd been struck. His shoulders straightened and he looked past Benny to the woman beyond.

In that moment, Raine sensed he was close to coming undone.

Joseph blinked and then looked away, his nostrils flaring in anger as he focused on Benny's face.

"In a way I guess I was playing daddy, but not for the likes of you. It will be the only thing in this lifetime that I can do for my son, but I was digging his grave."

Benny paled and looked away, then turned off the coffeepot and headed for his room. After the time he'd just spent in pursuit of his own glory, he felt very ugly and very small.

Raine shuddered uncontrollably, then pushed past Benny, needing to get to Joseph, needing to take away that awful look in his eyes.

When they were close enough to touch, she stopped. He was shaking. Whether from anger or exhaustion, she knew the feeling. She reached toward him.

"Give me your hand," she said softly.

Joseph shook his head. Right now one touch of sympathy too much would be his undoing. But Raine wouldn't stop.

"Then do it for me," she said. "I might stumble and fall."

"Ah, God," he muttered, then walked into her arms.

Joseph couldn't quit shaking. If it hadn't been for Raine's arms he wouldn't have gotten further than the door. She smelled so sweet and felt so damned good.

"I'll get you dirty."

Stunned by what she'd just done, she kept her nose pressed to his chest and hoped that this moment would pass.

"Probably," she admitted.

His hug tightened, not much, but enough to squeeze out a small groan.

"Am I hurting you?" he whispered.

A single tear rolled down her cheek. Hurting her? Oh, God, in more ways than he would ever know. Then she lied.

"I'm fine. It's late. You're exhausted. Come on, I'll walk you to the bathroom. After that, you're on your own."

Joseph felt her withdrawal and tried a smile, but it just wouldn't come.

"Thanks for the lift, Rainbow, but I think I can make it from here. Lock up for me, will you?"

With that, he walked out of the kitchen, leaving her with an aching heart and the dusty imprint of his body upon her shirt.

Five hours later, Raine emerged once more from her bedroom. Her hair was freshly washed. Her makeup in place. Her jeans were clean, her only good shirt freshly ironed. There were butterflies in her belly and an ache in her heart. When she went into the kitchen, there was a note propped against the sugar bowl next to a pot of coffee.

> Benny and I are in the back pasture. I'll be home
> by noon. We'll leave for Tucson around four.

She dropped the note onto the counter, poured herself a cup of coffee and went outside to look at the day. Weatherwise, it seemed ordinary, but it was deceiving. This was no ordinary day. She took a sip and then sighed. This day had been a long time in coming. Her journey from Chicago to Oracle had been more than just a trip of miles. It had been a journey into the past—and it was almost over.

She glanced out across the land that Joseph called home and wondered where he'd dug the grave. And then she blinked back a quick spill of tears. That much was Joseph's call. It was his land. He would know better than anyone where the best place would be.

Funeral.

Just the word made her sick.

Her stomach fluttered anxiously, remembering the first time she'd gone through this alone. Her parents had been present, but their mourning had not been the same as hers.

In a way, they'd mourned the loss of her innocence more than they'd mourned the loss of her child. She'd suffered their judgmental stares during her entire pregnancy. The accusations were always there in their eyes. She'd played with fire. She should suffer the consequences.

More than once, they'd pressured her to put the baby up for adoption, but Raine wouldn't be swayed. Joseph might not want her any more, but she wanted their child—her child. That's what she'd tried to get across to her family. But they hadn't understood. When the baby was born dead, she'd sensed their relief. And she'd never forgiven them for it.

But today there was a peace within her that she hadn't expected. Today the baby would be laid to rest where he belonged. Where he'd always belonged.

At the thought, her chin set and she tossed her coffee into the bushes and headed into the house to get her purse. This wasn't a day for celebrations, but she wanted to wear something special, and jeans and T-shirts didn't quite fit.

A short while later she drove down the main street of Oracle, searching for a dress shop or a boutique. To her dismay, there didn't seem to be anything in sight. But when she turned the corner heading east, she spied what she'd been looking for.

## Jo-Nell's

The sign was feminine and tastefully done, a good indication that the contents would be the same. The dress in the window was simple. The accessories on display were stylish and colorful. She wheeled into a parking place and then grabbed her purse. It was almost ten. With a little less than two hours before lunch, she should be able to find something here.

A small bell over the door signaled her arrival. A

woman came out from the back, smiling a welcome. To Raine's surprise, it was Evelyn Hart.

"Well, hello," Evelyn said. "You're looking great."

Raine smiled. "At least this time I'm not wearing blankets and sheets."

Evelyn laughed and rubbed her more than ample tummy. "And at this point, that's about all that will fit me."

"I can't believe you're still working," Raine said. "Aren't you just about due?"

Evelyn shrugged. "Past, actually. But like I told Justin, I don't feel any worse here than I do sitting at home. Now, what can I do for you?"

Raine glanced around the shop. "I need a dress."

Evelyn laughed again. "Well, you came to the right place." She headed toward the racks along the wall. "For anything special, or just a dress?"

Raine's smile didn't quite meet her eyes. "Sort of in between."

"Size?"

"Seven."

Evelyn gave her a pretend glare. "Just thought you should know that at this moment I hate you." Then she giggled. "But it will pass."

Raine's smile widened. The woman's charm was infectious.

"Now," Evelyn said. "Down to work."

A half an hour and four dresses later, Raine stepped out of the dressing room and stood before the full-length mirror.

"Oooh," Evelyn said. "That's so pretty on you."

The sheer blue fabric was soft upon her skin, and when Raine got her first look, she knew this was it. Completely lined except for the billowing long sleeves, the scoop neck and full, knee-length skirt would be proper for any occasion. Even a very small funeral.

"Got shoes to match?" Evelyn asked, eyeing Raine's bare feet.

Raine groaned. She hadn't thought of that.

"Don't suppose there's a shoe store in town?" she asked.

Evelyn shook her head. "I wear eights. At least I used to when I could still see my toes. Want to borrow some of mine again?"

Raine teared and then turned away. This just wasn't fair. Here was the makings of the first woman friend she'd had in years and she couldn't stay around long enough to enjoy her.

"Yes. I would like to borrow." Then she turned. "But I have to have them today. Is that a problem?"

Evelyn laughed. "Nope. I own the place. I can do what I want."

Raine glanced back at the name outside on the sign. "Then who's Jo-Nell?"

She shrugged. "Beats me. It was the name on the store when I bought it. I just never bothered to change."

Raine laughed.

Even after she was on her way home with her new dress on the seat beside her and her borrowed shoes in a sack on the floor, she was still smiling to herself about Evelyn Hart's quirky humor. If things were different, they would have become fast friends.

It was late evening, and they were in the westbound lane of Interstate 10, when the Tucson skyline began to loom upon the horizon. Raine's pulse skipped a beat as she glanced down at her watch. It was just after five. Two hours until the plane was due in. Although Joseph was only inches away from where she was sitting, it was almost as she were riding alone.

For the most part, the trip had been silent. Once in a while he would inquire about her comfort—once interrupting their trip for a pit stop. The silence should have been an uneasy one. Instead, there was a sense of comfort between them. Raine leaned back in the seat and momentarily closed her eyes.

Instantly aware of Raine's mood, Joseph gave her a quick glance. To him, she looked like a very sad angel. Having seen her only in shorts or jeans since her arrival, the new dress had surprised him. But there'd been a warning in her eyes that he hadn't quite understood. Instead of telling her she was beautiful, he'd just kissed her.

It hadn't been threatening. Just a kiss between old friends sharing a very sad day.

Now he sensed her restlessness. The urge to touch her was strong. He turned off the radio, instead.

"Tired?"

She looked at him. "Not really. Just . . . you know."

He nodded and tightened his grip on the steering wheel. Yes, he knew all too well.

Raine straightened. "You're the one who should be tired. You didn't sleep all night and you were gone before I got up."

"I slept some." Then he surprised himself by adding. "I didn't really want to close my eyes. Kept seeing things I wasn't ready to face."

"I know."

He sighed. She probably did know. And in a way, that's what made all this bearable. Their pain was shared.

She fidgeted with her dress as she had dozens of times since they'd left the ranch. Joseph knew she was nervous, maybe even afraid. If only she would tell him what was in her heart, then maybe he could help.

He glanced down at her fingers and the knot she was worrying in the fabric of her skirt.

"That's an awful big mess you're making on that very pretty dress."

She frowned as she turned loose of the fabric. "What a mess," she muttered. "I wasn't paying attention."

Joseph grabbed her fingers, giving them an

apologetic tug. "I still say it's a very pretty dress. It's almost the same color as your eyes."

She leaned back and looked away, but there was a small smile on her face.

"Thank you, Joseph. I think I needed to hear that."

"Truth is the truth, no matter what circumstances you hear it under. This isn't the best day of our lives, but it doesn't mean we shouldn't look our best, does it?"

She turned her head, meeting the impact of his gaze. "You understood."

He ached. Dear God, if only things were different. "I always understood you," he said softly.

She thought for a moment and then nodded. He was right. He had always understood her, maybe better than she'd understood herself. She began to relax.

A few miles further, with the Tucson skyline growing larger and larger, Raine suddenly panicked.

"Oh, no."

"What?" Joseph asked.

"The plane. It doesn't arrive until after seven P.M. You must be exhausted. We can't make the long drive back tonight. Where will we put the casket? We can't leave it in the back of the truck."

"Already taken care of," Joseph said.

"But—"

"Just let me worry about things for a while," he said, and clasped her hand again.

The need to touch her was constant within him. In a way, he was afraid to let go. She said she would be leaving. He wasn't ready to face that. Then he shifted the thought to a fact closer to the truth. He would never be ready to lose her again.

Raine stared out the window without seeing the passing scenery. Trusting Joseph, or, for that matter, any man, was a new thing for her. She leaned back in the seat with a frown on her face, unaware that she still had hold of his hand.

The summer evening was drawing to a close. Before long it would be dark. Already the landing lights were visible on the runway beyond where Raine and Joseph stood. It was almost seven, and they'd been told that the cargo plane was on time. All they had to do was wait inside the hangar.

Raine's stomach was in knots, and she kept fighting a need to cry. Joseph had blanked out his emotions, instead using his energies to get ready for their own departure later. His Bell Jet Ranger was waiting a short distance away. The casket would be unloaded and then reloaded directly onto the waiting chopper. Once they took off, they would be back home on the ranch outside of Oracle in less than an hour. Before they went to bed that night, the baby's casket would have been laid to rest.

It was all Raine could do to look at Joseph. He stood a distance away with his hands in his pockets. Even though she could feel his pain, she drew comfort from his presence. Ever since she'd walked onto the ranch and told him why she'd come, he'd done nothing but back her up one hundred percent. When she'd begun her journey from Chicago, she'd hoped that he would help, but she hadn't been prepared for his complete capitulation.

There was a part of her that drew comfort from the man Joseph Colorado had become. It was a personal affirmation for her that the boy she'd fallen in love with had turned out to be a very good man. Laying the baby to rest on his father's land was right.

But she'd had no idea how difficult it would be emotionally. It was almost as if this burial were happening for the first time rather than being a replay of the original ceremony twelve years earlier. Part of the reason was seeing it through Joseph's eyes. For him, this was the first time—and he was as devastated as a man could get.

She glanced down at the flowers in her arms and then lifted them to her nose, inhaling the sweet fragrance. They'd been handed to her less than an hour ago by a young man in coveralls. It was obvious by the state of his clothes that he was a mechanic and not a delivery boy for a florist. But she'd seen Joseph slip some money in his hand and then watched as they exchanged a solemn handshake. After that, she'd looked away. Thanks to Joseph, she would have flowers to lay on the grave.

Suddenly she looked up. Joseph was watching her. She shivered, knowing that she'd felt his gaze as clearly as if he'd touched her skin. She should go to him—thank him for the flowers and maybe hold his hand as he'd held hers. Just as she took a step forward, he turned away. Her heart sank, but she told herself it was just as well.

*Don't get close. Don't care. Remember, when this is over, you'll be gone.*

Joseph kept watching the skies, every now and then turning to check on Raine. To his relief, she was holding her own. The girl that he'd loved so long ago had grown into a strong, articulate woman. It gave him a sense of pride to know that even though their baby had not lived, she'd been the mother of his child.

He shifted his weight from one leg to the other and felt as if he'd been in these clothes for a year. His jeans were shiny with starch and the knife-sharp creases in the fabric made his legs look even longer. His white shirt was open at the throat, the cuffs unbuttoned and turned a couple of times, exposing a length of brown forearm. His silver-belly Stetson rode low on his head, pulled down over his forehead and shading his dark eyes from the setting sun. His expression was fixed.

But inside, he kept fighting an impending sense of doom. It was silly and he knew it, but he'd played mind games with himself all day. He hadn't admitted it yet, but there was a part of him that kept saying if the plane doesn't come, then the baby won't be dead. If the plane doesn't land, reality wouldn't have to be faced. And each time the danger of the lie  became too real, all he'd have to do was look at Raine. She'd borne twelve years of grief alone. Truth was there in her eyes and in the set of her shoulders that she kept squared with the world. For her, this was already real. He could do no less than follow her lead.

Then someone shouted at him from inside the hangar. He turned. The same man who'd brought Raine her flowers was pointing to the sky.

Joseph spun. The plane must be on approach. His gaze slid to Raine. Her face was pale as marble and even from here, he could see her shaking.

*God give me strength.*

He went to get her. As he slid an arm across her shoulders, he couldn't help thinking that the constant intimacy they'd been forced to share was becoming too familiar—too easy. His belly knotted. He wouldn't think about never seeing her again. First came the business of burying their child.

"Come on, Rainbow. We're in this together, remember?"

She walked to the edge of the doorway within the shelter of his care. Even though her heart was racing, she had her emotions under control. But when the casket came out of the plane, her control went south.

Two airport employees lifted a small blue casket out of the cargo hold. At the sight, her knees went weak. If she hadn't been leaning on Joseph, she would have dropped where she stood.

Twelve years had come and gone since she'd seen it, but it still had the power to elicit the same wave of great pain. And then to her shock, they set it down with an unceremonious thump. Her pain shifted to anger.

"No," she groaned, more to herself than to Joseph.

But she needn't have worried. He was already running. She hesitated, but only for a moment. Seconds later she was right behind him.

"Don't put it there!" he yelled sharply. Both men spun, a little startled by his approach. But after understanding his orders, they picked it back up and started toward him.

"In the chopper," he said, pointing toward the gleaming black machine sitting off to one side. "Slide it in the back behind the pilot's seat. I'll fasten it down myself."

"Yes, sir," they both answered, and quickly did as they'd been told.

Moments later, Joseph was alone and standing at the doorway, staring down at what amounted to little more than a small blue box. Yes, there were fancy trappings: chrome handles and locks and a blue the color of Arizona sky. But it was still a very small box. And it held his only son.

Tears came swiftly, burning the back of his throat and blurring his vision.

"Oh, God," he whispered, and reached out, letting his hand rest upon the surface.

It felt cool to the touch, and he knew that was from the drop in nighttime temperature. His first thought was instinctive as he pulled a quilt from behind the pilot's seat and draped it across the top.

Raine walked up just as he stepped back. She

saw the quilt and leaned inside the doorway.

"What's wrong? Is something damaged?"

He shook his head and then laid his hand on the quilt, feeling the solid surface of the lid beneath.

"No," he said softly. "It's just cold."

Raine went instantly numb. Her flowers slid from her fingers onto the tarmac below. She couldn't think. She couldn't feel. All she could see was that patchwork quilt.

*Cold. It's just cold.* She drew a deep shuddering breath, but composure wouldn't come.

Joseph's hand was upon her back, then cupping her shoulder. When he turned her toward him, she leaned against his chest and let the tears go. They spilled without warning, silently tracking the salty flavor of her grief down her face.

Later, she stood to one side, watching as Joseph strapped their small cargo down. After that, everything seemed to move in slow motion.

Joseph buckling her in the seat and then handing her back her flowers.

The stern expression on his face as he slid into the pilot's seat and put his earphones in place.

The calm and orderly manner in which he went through a takeoff checklist.

And then the feeling of suddenly having grown wings as they went straight up and then forward into the night.

The only lights she could see were on the instrument panel in front of them and on the landing struts down below. She suspected there were more, but there was too much darkness beyond the windows to encourage further exploration.

She glanced at Joseph. His face was a study in concentration. She bit her lip and looked away. Whatever she needed to say could wait until they were on firm ground.

Joseph looked out the window to his left. He never ceased to marvel at the beauty of flight. Even though the sky was dark, there was a sensation of weightlessness that he knew was deceiving. One wrong move—one innocent mistake—and they would be hurtling to earth within seconds.

Down below he recognized landmarks by the patterns of manmade lights. He'd already charted a flight path, but now he went over it again in his mind, wanting to make sure that nothing went wrong.

He'd seen Raine's tears, but it had been beyond him to speak. He'd been so staggered by the sight of that casket that words had left him. He couldn't quit thinking that he'd devoted his entire adult life to the service of others, but that when it had counted most for the woman he had loved, not only had he not been there for her, he'd missed looking upon his own son's face.

Benny hurried through the chores, feeding and watering the horses and making sure everything was locked up tight. There was a rare urgency to his movements as he shut the door on the last stall and hung the pitchfork on its hook. The only funeral he'd ever attended had been his mother's, and that day he'd been higher than a kite.

He had vague memories of neighbors coming and going at their house and of their disapproving stares. They hadn't understood. The only way he'd been able to get through the fear of being alone was to block it out with the mind-bending blur of drugs. He still remembered what he'd felt like when he'd awakened the next morning, coming down from the high. His head was throbbing, his tongue felt fuzzy and dry. When he moved, the bed on which he was lying began to roll like the pitch of a ship on high seas. He'd barely made it to the bathroom before he'd become horribly sick. But that wasn't the worst. It was afterwards, when he'd walked through the house, absorbing the pervasive silence that he'd known he wouldn't stay.

His mother—the short, laughing woman who wore her dresses too short and her pants too tight— the woman who liked to party, but whose fry bread was more delicious than a fine French croissant— was gone.

It wasn't long afterward that he sold the small house and gave his mother's clothes away. When he was through, he packed his own belongings into the family car and headed out of L.A. He had no plan in mind, but two days later, when he crossed the Arizona border heading east, he realized that he'd been heading home all along.

Now he'd been here the better part of two years

and had yet to feel like he belonged. When he was honest with himself, Benny figured that there would never be a place where he really belonged. He'd been born into one world and raised in another. The ever-spreading tentacles of family roots were not a part of him. Sometimes the knowledge made him sad, but he accepted it as his truth.

Nervous now about Joseph's arrival, he glanced up at the darkening sky, gauging the time it would take them to fly home as opposed to what he still needed to do. If he hurried, he should have just about enough time to shower and change. He turned toward the house and started running.

When they came home this time, he would be fully sober. But it wasn't because he'd matured enough to realize the error of his ways. It was because he feared his big brother's wrath. From the way Joseph had been behaving since Raine Beaumont's arrival, this wasn't the time to mess up.

The phone was ringing when he opened the back door. He ran to answer, expecting to hear Joseph's voice at the other end of the line.

"Hello," he said breathlessly. "I was just out in—"

"Benny, this is Stuart Rossi."

Benny's knees went weak, and even though he knew he was alone, he spun nervously toward the back door.

"Yeah, what's up?"

Rossi frowned. This casual, almost backhanded attitude surprised him. When last they'd spoken, Benny Colorado had been gung-ho about helping him. Now Stuart sensed a definite reticence.

"Is something wrong?" Rossi asked. "If I've called at a bad time, I will be glad to call back at a—"

"No!" Benny said, and then took a deep breath. "No, it's not that. It's just that we've got a pretty heavy family situation going right now."

Stuart's nostrils flared angrily.

"Yes, well, I might say the same thing about myself," he snapped. "Time is not on my side."

Benny swallowed nervously. "Look, Mr. Rossi. I said I would call when I knew something. Obviously, until my brother makes a move to go on one of his trips, I will have nothing new to tell you. If you'd rather get someone else to help you, it's fine with me."

Stuart flinched. This was bad. The little bastard was trying to back out on him.

"Look, asshole, you took my money. You made promises. You owe me!" Then his voice lowered warningly. "Don't fuck with me, Colorado. You'll live to regret it."

Before Benny could say anything further, the line went dead in his ear. He laid the receiver back in the cradle and then walked out of the room. All the way to the shower he kept trying to come up with a way to get out of the mess that he'd gotten himself in. But the longer he dwelled on it, the more convoluted the problem became.

He had options.

Just tell Joseph what he'd done.

Give Rossi the money back.

Forget any of this ever happened.

But he kept remembering the underlying threat in Stuart Rossi's voice. Something told him that no matter what he did, Stuart Rossi wasn't going to go away.

Joseph's pulse was beginning to accelerate. About five more minutes and then they would be home. He looked out into the sky, beyond the halo of lights on the chopper, beyond the pale glow of full moon to the star-shot sky. There was a line from the children's book, *Peter Pan,* that kept running through his head. It had to do with finding the way to Never-Never Land. It was something about looking for the second star to the right and going straight on until morning.

If there had been such a place, he would have charted a course. There was something to be said for escaping the complications of being an adult.

He glanced over at Raine. Her eyes were closed and her flowers were lying in her lap. He looked behind him. Everything was still in place, fastened as securely as it had been when he'd taken off. Although he turned his attention back to the business of flying, he kept wanting to cry.

There was a huge hole in his chest where his heart used to be. For the first time since he'd begun the duties as guardian, he truly understood the pain of the people who'd come knocking on his door.

A muscle jerked in his jaw as he looked down at the instrument panel. A few seconds later, he began a gradual descent, still wrestling with his conscience.

He'd loved. But he hadn't trusted. Because of that, he and Raine were over before they'd had a chance to begin. In a way, the baby was symbolic of their relationship. It was the bud of a love that had never opened.

And he would give just about anything to be able to take it all back, to be able to start over and live the last twelve years of his life differently. Instead, he was faced with the knowledge that in spite of all the people he'd helped save, as well as all those who had yet to come, he'd failed those he loved most.

With a grim expression on his face, he shoved the stick forward. A heartbeat later, the chopper was diving toward the circle of lights in the pasture below like a moth to a distant flame.


Benny sat scrunched behind the wheel of his car. The motor was running, the radio playing softly in the background. He kept staring through the windshield to the circle of lights beyond. He'd known they were there. More than once he'd seen Joseph replacing one of the powerful bulbs. But it was the first time since he'd come back to Oracle that he'd seen the landing pad put to use.

He shifted restlessly and then closed his eyes. As badly as he would have liked to be sitting at a bar somewhere in town, it would have to wait. Benny wasn't good at waiting, but tonight he waited just the same. Tonight, he would fulfill his first real duties as a man of the family. As the baby's only uncle, he was going to carry one side of a very small casket to its final resting place on the hill above Eagle Creek.

Just as he was about to doze off, he heard them coming. He jumped out of his car and then stood to one side, listening as the familiar *whup, whup* sound of powerful rotors grew louder and louder. Suddenly it was overhead. Blinded by the landing lights and the gusts of flying debris, Benny ducked instinctively.

Joseph had made good on his promise. The baby was home.

"Raine."

She straightened slowly, as one does when coming out of deep sleep. Grabbing for her flowers with one hand and smoothing her hair and dress with the other, she blinked several times in succession. And then she saw Benny coming toward her from beyond a ring of bright lights and remembered. She stifled a moan.

They were here.

It was almost over.

She looked at Joseph, unaware that her fear was magnified many times over through her eyes.

"We're here already?"

He nodded. "Wait. The rotors are winding down. Let me come around and get you."

He was gone before she had time to agree. Moments later the door on her right was yanked open. A series of images flashed through her mind.

The whipping rotors sounding like the wings of angry angels.

The expression on Joseph's face as he leaned in to unbuckle her from the seat.

The way Benny was holding on to his hat as he helped her out of the cabin.

The smell of sweet grass and dry dust as she moved out of harms way.

And then standing beyond the rim of lights, watching as Joseph and his brother lifted the tiny casket from the belly of the chopper and started toward her.

Everything seemed to shift to slow motion. She saw the length of Joseph's stride shorten to accommodate his brother's walk. And there was the complete lack of expression on either man's face as they moved into the darkness.

As they drew even with where she was standing, Joseph thrust something at her. She caught it without really looking. Only after they'd passed her by did she think to look down. It was the quilt. She lifted it to her face and then covered her eyes. It was all too much too bear.

Joseph signaled to Benny to stop. He looked back. Raine still hadn't moved.

"Raine . . . you need to come with us, sweetheart."

She moved without thinking, clutching the quilt

to her chest as tightly as she held the flowers, letting instinct take her where she still had to go.

When she caught up, Joseph asked. "Are you all right?"

She paused, looking at his face silhouetted in the full moon's glow.

"Yes."

"I didn't think to ask, but do you need a few minutes to freshen up? Benny can take you to the house if—"

Her answer came swiftly. "No." Then she looked down at the casket. It looked silver in the moonlight, reminiscent of the little silver keepsake boxes women kept on their dressers. That was fitting, she thought. This one held what was left of her dreams. "I'm fine."

"Are you afraid of the dark?" Joseph asked. "There's a flashlight in the chopper."

She reached out, for the first time, giving herself permission to feel the cool, smooth surface of the lid.

"I'm not afraid."

He nodded. So be it.

They began to move, a man to each side, a rainbow behind.

Having once laid hands on the casket, Raine couldn't let go. It was her last chance to touch what was left of the child she'd never held. They walked together, each locked into their own thoughts, their own pain. When they suddenly stopped, Raine almost tripped. She looked up, startled by the abrupt cessation of motion.

Off to her right was a small, dark hole.

She took a deep, shaky breath, eyeing the size of the opening as compared to the casket the men were carrying. Joseph had done a good job. This would just about fit.

Benny was nervous. He didn't believe in ghosts. And even if he had, he didn't have it in him to be afraid of a dead baby's spirit. Still, the yellow spill of light from a nearby lantern couldn't take away the sinister aspect of burying in the dark.

"Shouldn't we have waited until morning . . . or at the least called a preacher?" he asked.

"No," Joseph said and then looked at Raine, though they'd discussed that very thing earlier.

Anyone Joseph might have asked would have been a stranger to her, and in this situation, strangers did not belong. As for waiting until morning, she had finally said no to that, too. She knew it would sound crazy if she had to explain, but in her mind, she'd brought the baby home. And it was dark and it was late and it was past time—about twelve years past the time—to put this baby to bed.

Because this was her call to make, Joseph had gone along with whatever she chose. But right now Raine wasn't listening to Benny's muttering. She was standing at the edge of the grave and staring down into the hole.

"Besides," he added, "there's nothing a preacher would say that we can't say for ourselves. This is Colorado land. The words that need to be said tonight will come from me."

Still holding the casket, he looked back at Raine.

"Raine."

She didn't respond.

"Raine . . . sweetheart."

Raine shuddered and then tore her gaze away from the grave.

"It's awfully dark," she said softly and clutched the quilt a little tighter.

"This baby is not in darkness . . . was never in darkness."

She sighed. Mentally, she knew that. Emotionally, well, that was a different story.

"Spread out the quilt," Joseph said.

Raine did as he asked and then stepped aside, watching as he and Benny laid the casket in the center, right on top of a starburst design. Then they picked up the quilt by the edges and carried it to the open grave. Holding the quilt taut between them, they began to lower the casket into the ground. Buffered by the layers of fabric and batting, it touched bottom without a sound.

The brothers looked at each other, then Joseph nodded. First Benny let go, then Joseph. They stood at the edge of the grave, watching as the quilt edges dropped; overlapping each other and forever swaddling the small blue box. Cocooned in the piecework of a grandmother he had never known, Joseph Colorado Beaumont was once again, laid to rest.

When the first shovelful of dirt splattered softly against the small mound below, Raine flinched. The sound was obscene. She gritted her teeth and took a deep breath. In spite of her fierce determination to remain strong, she began to shake. The sounds became less pronounced as the hole was slowly filled, but it became easier to watch Joseph than to watch what he was doing.

His hat was hanging from a nearby limb. His watch was in his pocket. The pile of dirt that he'd dug out of the ground was just to his left. When Benny offered to help fill in the grave, Joseph shook his head.

"No. This I do alone."

Benny nodded and stepped back beside Raine. An odd silence engulfed them. For a time there was nothing to be heard except the *splat* of dirt upon dirt, the sound of one's own breathing, and the swoosh and scoop of Joseph's shovel as he returned the soil into the hole.

Once he paused to wipe the sweat from his brow with the back of his shirtsleeve. Benny, who was unusually quiet, moved forward, touching him lightly on the shoulder.

"Please, Joseph, let me help," he offered.

Joseph looked down. Half the job was yet to be done. He looked at Raine. In the dark, she reminded him more of the girl he'd known. There was less definition of age, and the defensive manner he'd come to see as part of her persona was missing. Still clutching the flowers he'd given her earlier, she just seemed to be waiting.

He touched Benny's shoulder. "You will never know what your offer means to me . . . and to Raine as well. But you must understand. This is the only thing I will ever be able to do for my son. I have to do it alone."

Embarrassed and more than a little touched by their unexpected moment of brotherhood, Benny turned away. As Joseph resumed his task, Benny reacted without thinking and slipped his arm across Raine's shoulders, pulling her close, sharing in the only way he knew how his regret for what had happened to their lives.

After a short while, a soft breeze came up, wafting the scent of newly turned earth and fresh-cut flowers into the air. Raine looked up to see a scraggly bit of cloud moving between earth and moon. From the corner of her eye, she saw a quick flash of light. Her focus shifted.

*A falling star!*

It was gone as suddenly as it had appeared, leaving Raine with the distinct impression that she'd just gotten a sign from heaven. Bitterly, she shook off the thought and looked back at the hole slowly filling with dirt. It was a little late for heavenly signs. She'd already gotten the message.


One scoop at a time. It was the only way Joseph could concentrate on what he was doing. Less than two weeks ago he'd been going through life with the belief that he was, for the most part, doing things right. And then Raine came, and from that day on his world would never be the same. She'd shattered his image of himself and his trust in all things right and just.

Why, he wondered, had their lives gone so wrong? What was it about one person's life that would set them on a path of sorrow while another would go through life unscathed? The more he searched the Words, the more convinced he became that there weren't always answers—only faith.

Faith that each sunrise is the promise of a new beginning. Faith that when man can not stand alone, God is within him, keeping him strong.

That was what he believed. That was what carried him through. But what hurt him, probably more than anything else, was Raine's bitterness. Not only had she shut herself off from God, but it seemed as if she'd shut the rest of the world away, too. Why else would she quit her job, the one thing that had given her purpose, and start off on some fruitless search for personal fulfillment? Didn't she know that fulfillment comes from within, not from gaining worldly knowledge or goods?

He didn't know what to think or do to change her attitude, and right now he wouldn't let himself care. It was all he could do to scoop the next shovelful of dirt. There would be time later to deal with the fact that he was burying his own son.

A short while later he bent to thrust the shovel

back into the dirt and realized there was none to be had. He looked up in surprise. Raine's face was all he could see.

"Joseph."

He blinked, confused by the sound of voices when before they'd just been in his mind.

"It's time to stop now. You're done," she said.

He swayed slightly and then looked down at the ground. Even in the dark, the small mound of fresh earth was like a sore upon the land. It would take time for it to heal. It would be weeks before the earth would settle and even longer before nature would blanket it with a fresh growth of grass. Without thinking, he dropped to his knees and began smoothing the surface with the palms of his hands, tossing out anything that felt as if it didn't belong.

When Benny saw his brother go down, he took a deep breath. It didn't help the sudden blur of his vision or the knot that kept growing in the back of his throat. He'd never seen his brother this way. It made him seem all too human, which for Benny was a weakness he couldn't afford. But the baby that they'd buried had been family. His family. Part of his blood. Muttering something beneath his breath about turning off the landing lights, he stalked away into the night, unable to watch any longer.

Joseph patted and smoothed until there was nothing left to be done. He rocked back on his heels, wanting to prolong the moment, hating to break the only bond he would have with this long-dead child. A sound came up from his lungs and out through his lips; more like a groan than a sigh.

It was over.

The burying was done.

He dragged himself to his feet and then looked around for Raine.

She came out of the darkness, moving toward him, then past him, kneeling in the place where Joseph had just been. The earth was still warm from the contact of his body, and she took comfort in that ephemeral touch.

"There," she said softly, and laid her flowers on the apex of the mound. "Now you can rest."

Joseph was behind her, and then beside her, pulling her up and into his arms. Too weary to argue, she turned her face against his chest and pretended this was where she belonged.

His shirt was still damp with sweat, his hands smelled of the earth. She took strength from his nearness and courage from his unwavering stand in the face of such sorrow. In that moment, Raine faced a truth she'd been trying to ignore. She cared for this man, more than she should, more than she could.

And then Joseph began to speak. A whisper at first, like a communion between himself and God, and then his voice became clearer and his words became stronger. Wrapped within the confines of his embrace and with her ear against his chest, after a time, Raine didn't know where Joseph ended and she began.

"My son, God holds you when I cannot. My

heart is broken, but my spirit is at rest. I will see you in the sunrise and in the sparkle of an early morning dew. You will color all my rainbows and fly higher than the moon. This earthly journey has been a long time coming, but you can rest easy now. Your mother brought you home."

Raine choked on a sob. She'd already shed twelve years of bitter tears. She didn't want to cry anymore. But she made the mistake of looking up. Joseph was staring off into the darkness, his face a study in sorrow. He made no excuses for the tears on his cheeks or the tremble of his lip.

"Thank you for this," she said.

Joseph shuddered and looked down, focusing on her eyes, then on her mouth. In that moment, before this heartbeat and the next, she thought he was going to kiss her.

And because she so very badly wanted it to happen, she set her jaw and pushed out of his arms before turning away. Down below she could hear the trickle of water as it ran along the stream bed. The blowing breeze rustled the leaves in the nearby tree, making a soft shushing sound, like a mother would make when putting a baby to sleep. The motion of air passed by her, pulling at her clothes like long, teasing fingers, cooling the spot at the back of her neck where her hair was the heaviest.

It should have been refreshing. Instead, she wrapped her arms around herself to stop the shaking and tried to focus on something else.

"Why did you choose this place?" she asked.

Joseph bent down to pick up his shovel as well as the one Benny had dropped nearby. He gave her a long, considering look.

"Because it is a good place for him to be."

She couldn't believe what he'd said. A good place? There was no good place to bury a child.

"I don't see how," she said, her voice thick with angry tears. "Six feet down is six feet down, no matter where you put it."

Joseph stared at her for a long, silent minute, watching the shadows that the lamplight made on her face. Then he shook his head and turned away, staring off into the night and seeing the land through memory.

"You've changed, Rainbow. There's a hard side of you that I don't understand."

His words slammed into her, hurting clear to the bone, as truth often does. But she couldn't bring herself to argue, not here—not over the grave of their child.

Joseph's words drifted over her like silk settling on water, clinging, then sinking slowly until they'd been totally absorbed.

"You see what you want to see. You see a grave. I see a creek and a tree that gives shade." He turned, and even in the dark, she was pierced by the dark glitter in his eyes. "I chose this place because little boys need water to play in and big trees to climb."

She tried to speak but words wouldn't come. The image he'd just drawn was too powerful—and too beautiful. She looked down into the darkness.

Although she couldn't see it, she could hear the water trickling along the bed of the creek. She looked back at the tree, partially lit by the lantern hanging from the lowest branch. In her mind's eye, night became day and she could see the tree and the large patch of shade splashed across the ground beneath it. Somewhere within the thick cover of leaves she heard a child's quick burst of laughter and then saw a branch give way from an invisible weight.

She tried to swallow, choking on the lump in her throat, and then found herself sobbing instead. Before she knew it, Joseph was holding her.

"It's okay, baby. Cry now. Cry tomorrow. Cry as long as it takes until the pain goes away."

"But it won't," she sobbed. "I've been crying for twelve years and it still hurts. Oh, God, it hurts so bad."

Joseph groaned and then buried his lips in the crown of her hair. She smelled so sweet, felt so soft, and she still didn't understand.

"I know it hurts, baby. I know. But you've held on to the pain because that's all you had. Cry now and then let it all go. You're not alone anymore. You've got me, Rainbow, now and for as long as you want."

Her fear of being alone was greater than her fear of being hurt all over again. And for this reason only, she clung to him, pretending to herself that one night couldn't hurt, that stealing this last bit of joy for herself wasn't going to change the outcome of anyone's life.

Joseph closed his eyes, saying a quick prayer of thanksgiving. There was a part of him that wanted to be greedy, to demand that she come back to him now and forever. But if this was all she would give, then he would take it. He gave her a hug and then tilted her chin so that he could see clearly into her face.

"Are you ready to go home?"

Home. The word was a physical pain. But she was unable to deny herself this last luxury. She looked back at the flowers lying alone in the dark. She kept hearing a small voice telling her to let go. She closed her eyes and exhaled on a sigh. There was no hesitation in her answer when she looked up.

"Yes, I believe that I am."

Benny was gone, but there was a note on the cabinet. Joseph read it and then handed it to Raine.

> I share your grief, but you don't need to share your space, at least not tonight. See you tomorrow. —Benny

Raine laid it on the counter, watching as Joseph began locking up the house.

"You two aren't very close, are you?" she asked.

Joseph paused. "We try." Then before she could get nervous about their being alone, he changed the subject. "You're bound to be exhausted. Why don't you shower and slip into something comfortable. I'm going to clean up, too, then make us something to eat. Okay?"

Grateful beyond words for what he'd just offered, Raine left the room, emerging a short while later in a clean white T-shirt and a pair of shorts. The red Spanish tiles on the entryway floor felt cool on her feet. Her stomach was growling in anticipation as she headed for the kitchen. Halfway there, the delicious aroma of grilling meat wrapped around her senses, hastening her steps until she was almost running.

She entered the kitchen and then stopped short. Joseph was wearing a pair of blue jeans and nothing else. His chest and feet were bare. Drawn to his presence, she moved until she was standing at his side. His hair was still damp from his shower, and when he looked up, Raine saw a single droplet still clinging to the edge of one lash. She reached up and wiped it away before she thought, then stared at it on the tip of her finger, unwilling to test it for flavor in case it was a tear rather than water.

Joseph froze, and in the instant between making a total fool of himself and holding firm, Raine took a hesitant step back.

A little embarrassed, she held up her finger, as if by doing so the slightly damp tip would explain her behavior.

"Water," she said. "I guess you dried in a hurry."

Joseph's eyes were black with emotion, but he didn't move from where he stood.

"I didn't dry at all," he said, leaving her with a

mental image she could easily have done without.

She flushed, but only slightly. After all, they'd shared a lot more than a couple of conversations in their life.

"Something smells good," she said.

Joseph let her change the subject. But just before she'd moved away, he'd seen it in her eyes. She wanted him. Maybe not as much as he wanted her. Maybe not even for the same reasons. But by God, she wanted him.

Joseph tested the steaks and then turned them, watching from the corner of his eye as she began assembling the rest of their meal. The scent of freshly grilled meat drifted up his nose. His belly growled in reply. But there was another hunger within him that far outweighed that of the body.

He was starving for Raine.

It was after midnight when Joseph looked up from the book he'd been reading to realize that Raine was nowhere in sight. The meal that they'd shared had calmed the fever between them. They'd settled into the living room in companionable silence, and the last time he'd looked, she'd been deep in thought, the book in her lap forgotten as she sat staring blindly at a picture on the wall. His one attempt to draw her into conversation had been deftly thwarted and so he'd withdrawn, giving her the space she seemed to need to regroup.

But while he was willing to give her space, he

wasn't sure he trusted her absence. He got up from his chair and headed for the door, instinctively knowing where to look. Just as he'd suspected, she was standing on the edge of the porch, staring toward the rise behind the barns. Even though it was impossible to see it in the dark, they both knew what lay beyond.

"Are you all right?"

Startled, she spun. "You scared me."

His fingers encircled her wrists. Her pulse was rapid and thready.

"Your heart is racing."

She couldn't look away, and in a rare moment of clarity, knew she wouldn't have looked away if she could. Not any more.

"I guess I'm nervous."

His own pulse kicked up a notch. "But not afraid?"

She didn't hesitate. "No. Not afraid."

He moved closer, fingering the feather-soft hair at her neck and then threading his fingers through its length.

Raine put her hands in the middle of his chest, freezing them both at a point of action.

Joseph waited. Would this be the moment she pushed him away?

She centered her hand over his heartbeat. It was a steady, solid beat. She looked up. Just like him. Steady. Solid.

Joseph hesitated, not wanting to put the question into words. But he wasn't the kind of man who let fate call the shots.

"What will it be, Rainbow?"

She kept trying to focus on the question but couldn't get past staring at the shape of his mouth and on a small scar just above his upper lip.

"You already know how I feel," he added. "Nothing has changed. I still want to make love to you."

She closed her eyes and felt his breath upon her face. But he came no closer. She looked up.

"You aren't going to make this easy for me, are you?"

Joseph's fingers slid out of her hair and around her waist.

Before she knew it, she was in his arms.

"That's where you're wrong, Rainbow. This is as easy as it gets."

Her breath escaped on a sigh. "Then make love to me, Joseph. Right now I don't want to feel anything but you."

He swept her off of her feet and into his arms. His skin was warm against her flesh, his arms strong against her back. As he carried her through the house, she locked her hands around his neck and held on. Her pulse was pounding wildly as he laid her in the middle of her bed. He stripped off her clothes and then stood back, staring at her in the dim half-light. At that moment, Raine's body went weak.

He took off his jeans and then he was standing before her. Breath exited her body in a soft grunt. He was so much bigger—in every way—than she remembered. His chest was massive. The corded band of muscles across his belly looked iron-hard. His biceps were much more defined. Her gaze drifted down. He was erect. And proudly so.

Heat burst in the pit of her stomach and spilled downward. So great was her want that her first instinct was to just spread her legs and not delay the inevitable.

But she saw purpose in his movements as he crawled onto the bed, extending his full height beside her. She saw his head dipping downward, felt his mouth centering on her lips, then moments later, heard his deep, gut-wrenching groan as he rolled over and buried his face in the curve of her neck. Once she thought she heard him whisper the word "mine," but she wasn't sure. And after that, couldn't bring herself to care. Facts were facts, and for this night she *was* his. She'd given herself, body and soul, for him to do with as he pleased. She couldn't let herself care, but she could take what he was willing to give.

There was a sense of déjà vu as Joseph moved his hands across the surface of her skin. Although it was a woman he held, rather than the young girl that she'd been, he still knew this shape. The knot on her fourth rib where a baseball had once hit her. The small mole on the lobe of her ear. And he remembered the catch in her breath when his tongue wrapped around the crest of her breast. This wasn't a dream. The urge to sink himself deep into her warmth was overwhelming.

Only after he'd felt her naked body entwined

with his did her realize that he'd waited twelve years for this. But there was a thing that had yet to be said. Protection. He'd left her pregnant once. It wouldn't happen again. He raised himself up on his elbows, fixing his gaze upon her face.

"I will take care of you," he said softly.

Raine knew what he meant, and for a moment, the sadness came back to them both. They'd already made and buried one baby. Making another one wasn't what this night was about. But he needn't have worried. After what she'd been through, babies were a thing of her past.

"I've been told I can no longer have children. But I understand your concern. There are many reasons for still using protection."

*Ah . . . the reasons for bitterness and regrets.*

"I'm sorry, Rainbow," he whispered. "If I could change things for you—"

She put her fingers across his lips. She was tired of talking. Tired of living with emptiness.

"I don't want your pity," she said shortly. "Just make me feel again, Joseph. I need to remember what it feels like to be alive . . . even if it's only for tonight."

The only sign of his emotion was a slight flare of his nostrils. After that, a heavy silence descended between them. They'd made their choices. He was using her to remember. She was using him to forget.

C H A P T E R

12

It should have been easy, this joining of bodies in need of release. For two consenting adults, it shouldn't have mattered that there were no words of love being spoken. Joseph knew all too well how their bodies fit, and despite the years, Raine could still remember the bone-melting sensation of coming apart in his arms. But there was a hesitancy in their kisses, a reluctance to move past foreplay. And it was Joseph who finally reacted.

"Damn you, Raine, I can't do this!"

He tore himself away from her and rolled out of bed.

Raine stared in disbelief, silent for several seconds as her own anger began to surface. Then she tossed her pillow in the floor and crawled out on the other side. With the bed between them, they stood naked and glaring at each other while words of blame hovered close on their lips.

"Say it!" she cried. "Say what you're thinking, damn it!"

He wiped a hand across his face and then turned and stalked to the window.

Again, Raine was left speechless by Joseph's majestic grace. Coming or going, he would be a hard act to follow. And she was more than a little pissed at herself for still harboring an attraction to this man. She was a grown woman with more baggage than most. It should stand to reason that she'd learned her lesson. But from the way she'd willingly let him lead her to bed, it would appear that she had not. She looked around for her things.

"Just give me a minute to get my clothes and I'll be—"

Joseph pivoted. "That's right! Run, damn you. You left me once. Feel free to do it again. Only this time I won't let it hurt."

Raine was shocked into silence by his accusations. It took her several long seconds before she could gather her wits enough to answer, and when she did, it was all she could do not to shout.

"Me? I didn't walk out on you. You're the one who just let me go. I wasn't an adult, Joseph Colorado. I was a girl. My family moved. I moved with them, for God's sake! If you had wanted me to stay with you, you should have asked." When he looked away, she added quietly. "I would have you know."

Suddenly it seemed wrong to be standing naked before this man, even if he wasn't looking. She picked up a blanket and wrapped it around her. When she looked back, he had pulled on his jeans.

"This was wrong from the start," she said. "We just got caught up in the moment. You didn't want to make love to me. You wanted to make love to the girl that I was." She took a deep breath. "She's dead, Joseph. As dead as that baby you buried."

She turned and started out the door. Joseph stopped her with one word.

"Liar."

She spun.

"How dare you accuse me of—"

He said it again.

"Liar."

Fury came swiftly, rattling her senses. "I don't lie," she whispered.

"Why did you come back here if not for this?"

A dark flush spread up her neck and cheeks. "You know why I came. I wanted my baby to be—"

"Our baby."

She glared. "As I was trying to explain, the baby's grave—"

Joseph's chin jutted and there was a look on his face that she knew all too well.

"Our baby," he repeated slowly.

She closed her eyes, trying to calm herself and knowing that if this would ever get said, it would be at his discretion. She met his gaze full force, enunciating each word in quiet anger.

"*Our* baby deserved to be laid to rest on family ground."

"Why now?" he asked. "Why not do this twelve years ago, when it happened?"

She pulled the blanket a little closer around her. It was an unconscious gesture of protection.

"I told you. My life has changed. I will no longer be living in Chicago. If something happened to me, there wouldn't be anyone there to look after the grave."

"Why, Raine? Why leave now at the height of your career? If what you say is true, you were a respected member of the staff."

He took a step forward, frowning when she took a step back.

"I told you," she muttered, unable to look him in the eyes. "I'm going on a trip."

*Liar.* But this time he didn't say the word aloud.

"You didn't just want to bring the baby home. You wanted to watch me suffer."

Even as she was denying his accusations, there was a part of her that knew it was true.

Joseph's eyes narrowed thoughtfully as he stared at the woman across the room.

"But why now, Raine? Why now?"

She turned away and began grabbing for her clothes when suddenly he was beside her. He yanked the shirt out of her hand, then grabbed her by the shoulders and shook her. Not enough to hurt, but enough for her to know that he still cared.

"Why, damn you, why?" he whispered.

The blanket covering her nudity slipped out of her grasp and dropped to the floor between them. Raine gasped, frightened by the look in his eyes. Joseph saw the fear and it made him that much angrier.

"You little fool," he said softly, as his hands moved from her shoulders to her breasts, palming the nipples until they were hard, pouting peaks. "I won't hurt you. I would never want to hurt you."

Raine groaned and leaned into his touch. "You don't understand," she whispered. "You just don't understand."

"Then make me understand . . . help me understand," Joseph said, and kissed her.

Once beside each earlobe.

Once upon each breast.

The heat in her belly was back, only stronger. Her hands slid around his waist as if they had a mind of their own and slipped below the waistband of his jeans, feeling the smooth skin and hard muscle of his backside.

"No," she begged. "*You* have to help *me*. That's why I came."

Now he had a truth. If only he knew what kind of help she needed. So far, all she'd done was talk herself into circles. But that was for later. Now, he was going to make good on his earlier promise.

"I am going to love you," he said softly.

"Then do it. Make love to me."

He lifted her off her feet and lay her back in the bed.

"Don't put words in my mouth, Rainbow. I am going to love you—now, and for as long as you'll let me."

She wrapped her arms around his neck and started to cry.

He traced the curve of her face with the tip of his finger. "No tears allowed, sweetheart. I give joy, not regrets."

He did not lie.

Between the first kiss and the final thrust that triggered her climax, Raine found that joy he'd promised. It was there in the tenderness of his touch, the reverence of his kisses, even the bold sweep of his hands beneath her backside as he plunged himself into her. It came back to her time and again in a mindless sweep as he rocked against the cradle of her hips. And then the climax came, shattering everything that she had been and leaving it to Joseph to pick up what was left.

And he did without hesitation, gathering her into his arms and loving her with touches and words, with soft kisses and shocking promises of other times and places. After twelve years of abstinence from this man, she should have been overwhelmed. But all she kept thinking was that she'd finally come home.

As a child, she'd had to memorize a verse from the Bible that she hadn't understood.

*"Weeping may endure for a night, but joy cometh in the morning."*

She'd wept many tears on far too many nights and up till now, tonight hadn't been any different. Until now she'd convinced herself that she was beaten before she'd started. But that was before coming home to Oracle—and to Joseph.

\* \* \*

Now she lay quietly within the safety of his arms, listening to the even pattern of his breathing and waiting for daylight. The first fingers of gray had just begun to appear on the horizon, ripping back the thick shades of night to let in new light when she rolled over and faced him.

Small shadows lay soft on his cheeks, cast by the thick brush of dark lashes. There was a very tiny flare to each nostril with each intake of breath. Asleep, he looked harmless. Awake, he was imposing. His body was powerful, but it was his gaze that commanded attention. Those dark, all-seeing eyes that burned with equal amounts of passion and anger, but which would soften as quickly with laughter or joy.

She sighed. He hadn't lied. He *had* given her joy. What surprised her more was that the feeling was still with her. Somewhere between last night and now he'd banished her despair. She glanced over his shoulder to the window beyond. The sky was a pale, empty canvas. But the verse that she'd learned as a child kept coming back to her time and again. She closed her eyes and snuggled closer to his chest.

Sometimes joy does come with morning.

Joseph woke up to find himself alone. It took him a moment to remember that he hadn't gone to bed the same way. He rolled out of bed and began scrambling for his clothes. There was a panic within him that wouldn't go away. He kept hearing her vow over and over in his head.

*When this is over, I'm going away.*

"No, Rainbow, no," he muttered, reaching for his boots. "Don't you dare walk out on me now. Not like this."

He bolted out of the bedroom and across the hall. Her bed was made up. He yanked open the closet. Her meager belongings, the clothes that he'd bought her after the fire, were gone. His panic increased. She wouldn't leave like this. Not without saying good-bye.

He ran out on the porch. Her car was still in the yard, but he could see her suitcase on the passenger side of the seat. Pain hit him belly-high and moved upward like the swift slash of a knife. He had to take a deep breath to be able to move. She *was* leaving. In spite of everything they'd said and done last night, she was leaving.

"Where, where, where are you?" he muttered, searching the yard, then the barns. But no Raine. His gaze moved to the rise beyond the corrals and it was then that he knew where she'd gone. To the baby's grave to say good-bye.

Hope left him. It was impossible to interpret that as anything but a final gesture. But he still needed to see her face. He still needed to hear her voice. He had to touch her one more time.

He started running.

Raine sat beside the grave with her legs curled beneath her, feeling the breeze upon her face and the sun upon her back. The creek below was crystal-clear. Earlier, as she'd stood on the banks above, she thought she'd seen one very small fish dart behind a moss-covered rock. She'd smiled and walked back to the tree. Joseph had been right. This was a good place for a little boy to be.

"Your name will go here," she said, pointing to a place just above the raw earth. "Joseph Colorado Beaumont. It's a very big name for a very small boy, but you would have lived up to it, I know."

A grasshopper bounced its way across her vision and she looked down and grinned.

"Something for you to chase, little boy."

And then a shadow passed over the sun and she looked up. Clouds were gathering. It would rain today. But not here. Somewhere up in the mountains, instead.

Even though she knew this weather would stay clear, her good mood was gone. She plucked at a few blades of grass and then glanced at her watch and tossed them aside. It was almost nine. She unfolded her legs, stretching them out before her to work out the kinks. She should probably be going.

No sooner had she thought it than the sun once again shone its face and she lingered. A bird flying overhead suddenly gave a shrill cry. Raine looked up just as it began to dive toward earth. She watched, speechless at the purity of motion and the precision of flight, all the while knowing that if it succeeded in its quest, some small animal must die. Just when the great bird would have crashed into the ground, it pulled up, skimming grass-high along the meadow instead. Moments later, it gave another shrill cry. Raine heard the bird's distress when its prey suddenly went to ground. Only after it went back to the sky did Raine realize that she'd been holding her breath.

At that moment, a simple fact was made suddenly clear. Things live—things die—people included. Raine's shoulders drooped. Subconsciously she'd been blaming Joseph all these years because he hadn't been with her when it happened. Her rational mind knew there wasn't a thing he could have done. It was the irrational part of her that hadn't healed. She'd wasted twelve years on what ifs when she should have been praying for peace of heart.

She looked up at the sky. The bird was already out of sight. She glanced back at the small grave and the wilting flowers she'd left behind last night.

Last night.

It was almost like speaking of another world. Last night Joseph had given her so much more than joy. She looked beyond the mound of fresh dirt to the horizon. Out there were many highways, highways that would take her wherever she needed to go. She leaned back on her hands and closed her eyes, letting the warm sun lick her face, then her neck, spilling its warmth down the front of her blouse, then her lap, to her slim legs stretched out on the ground.

Wherever she needed to go.

And then she heard Joseph calling her name. She sat up with a jerk. Scrambling to her feet, she brushed herself off and then stood in the shade of the tree, watching as he came up the rise. There was an urgency in his steps that she couldn't mistake. Her heart fell. There was only one explanation for his haste. He'd seen her suitcase. He knew she was leaving.

Something tugged at her then. A small voice within her that she couldn't ignore. She thought of the highways beyond the horizon, and the things of this earth she had yet to see. And then she looked back at his face. What if she couldn't find joy out on the highways? What if she searched the world over and there was still no more joy? What if she was making a mistake by leaving? She'd been longing for peace—searching for happiness. Last night Joseph had given her that and so much more.

She leaned against the tree, watching the even swing of his body as he moved up the hill. Guilt hit her. He hadn't seen her yet. The dark expression was still on his face.

That small voice whispered, *What if I don't leave? At least, not today. What if I stay here a while? Not for love, of course, just for joy.* That's what she needed. A little more joy—just enough to get by.

*Go to meet him,* the voice said.

And she took her first step. By the time the sunlight fell strong upon the top of her head, she was already running.

Joseph saw her. First standing in the shade beneath the tree, then now, coming toward him. When she started to run, he opened his arms, catching her as they collided. He laughed, then staggered, shouting out a warning as they fell backward onto the ground. But Raine didn't mind about the ground, or the grass tickling her nose. All she could feel were Joseph's arms around her shoulders, holding her close to him, keeping her safe from harm.

Finally they were back on their feet. Joseph was picking grass from her hair and she was brushing dust from his shirt.

The solemnness of the moment caught her, and she looked up to find his dark gaze fixed upon her face.

"Were you going to say good-bye before you snuck away?" he asked.

She flushed. "I don't sneak," she replied, although she had thought about the simplicity of getting behind the wheel and doing just that.

He shrugged. "I just wondered."

"Would you have cared?" she asked.

He cupped her face with the palms of his hands and then brushed a kiss across the softness of her lips, groaning when she opened them slightly upon his demand. When he could think again, he replied, "What do you think?"

"I think yes."

He almost smiled, then looked away.

*Say it, Raine. Please, for God's sake say the words.*

But she didn't, and there was an uncomfortable silence he didn't know how to break.

Raine fidgeted with the collar of her shirt. As the

old cowboys used to say, she'd made her brag, now it was time to put up or shut up. Joseph bent to brush some grass from the bend of her knee when she laid her hand upon his head.

"Joseph?"

He straightened. *Please, God.* "Yes?"

"About my leaving . . ."

"What about it?"

Suddenly nervous, she looked away. What if he didn't mean it? What if it was just words to say to get a woman in bed? And then she looked in his eyes—those dark ancient eyes—and she knew. Joseph might be a lot of things, but he didn't tell lies.

"I was wondering if you would mind if I stayed on for a bit. Not long, mind you, but just long enough to—"

He put his finger over her mouth and started to grin.

"I was giving you another thirty seconds and then I was going to get down on my knees and beg."

The knot in her belly unwound. She looked over her shoulder to the tree upon the hill, then back at his face.

"I don't think I'm ready to go yet."

He wrapped his arms around her and lifted her off of her feet.

"Far as I'm concerned," he growled. "You can stay forever."

Stuart Rossi had a new lease on life. He'd been in Phoenix a little less than three weeks and he felt bet-

ter than he had in years. Part of it was because he got
more rest here than he did in L.A. Lying flat on his
back on a daily basis in the Phoenix hotel and
breathing the clean, dry Arizona air was like a miracle cure. No L.A. smog to suck into weak lungs, no
late-night hours and heavy foods to tax a waning
heart.

Each day, he sent Edward to a different Realtor,
putting them all to searching for a property on which
he might live. Stuart was ready to move his personal
belongings, all seventeen million dollars' worth, to
this amazing city. His other holdings would be fine.
He could just as easily work from an office in
Phoenix as he could from one in L.A. He had it all
figured out.

Not only was he convinced that if he stayed here
he would be healed from his affliction, but he had
been given a wonderful place in which to wait for it
to happen.

Although he'd called the Colorado residence
twice in the past eleven days, he had yet to speak to
Benny again. But he wasn't bothered. He knew what
to do. Once this house hunting business was over,
he'd send Edward back to Oracle with more money.
There was nothing like the color of green for tilting a
man's morals.

He leaned back in his chaise longue and waved
his glass into the air. Although the pitcher of iced tea
that he wanted was right at his elbow, Edward came
running to do his master's bidding and picked up the
pitcher.

"You're looking fit, sir."

Stuart watched intently as Edward poured. "Damn it, Edward! Don't float my ice."

"Yes, sir, I mean, no, sir, I mean, here, sir," Edward said, and handed Stuart back his glass.

Stuart took a small sip, smiling to himself in satisfaction, then waving Edward away as majestically as he'd been summoned.

"Check my messages," he ordered. "See if any of the Realtors have called. I'm anxious to get out of this hotel and into a place of my own."

"Yes, sir," Edward said.

Once he was alone, Stuart adjusted the flow of oxygen on the tank beside him, then leaned back. Except for the soft hiss of sweet air flowing up his nose and into his lungs, life was just about perfect.


Benny's short romance with being the considerate younger brother was over. It had lasted a little over forty-eight hours. By the time it became obvious that Raine was staying on, he was already pissed. But not at her. Not really. It was just the whole thing in general. He was Joseph's blood kin and he hadn't been welcomed as openly as Raine, who was no kin at all. However, he had to admit that from his big brother's standpoint, she was a whole lot prettier than he was, and probably a great lay.

Most of his current problems stemmed from the fact that on his last trip to Phoenix, he'd made a few bets. Nothing big, just a few dollars here and there on some dogs and some horses. But now he was in the hole to the bookie a little over five thousand dollars. While he knew he could have gotten the money from Joseph, it burned his ass to have to ask. He was a grown man. He shouldn't have to ask for money like a kid going out on a date. In fact, he wasn't going to ask for it. He was just going to take it. He'd scheduled a weekend trip to Las Vegas. He needed some excitement. For Benny, that meant bright lights and easy women.

"I'm going into town," Joseph yelled across the corrals.

Benny waved, then continued to fork fresh hay into each of the stalls inside the barn. He was the picture of industry until Joseph's pickup was out of sight. Then he tossed down his pitchfork and bolted toward the house.

He hit the back porch running and was inside before the sounds had faded. Still congratulating himself for finding the combination to Joseph's safe, he was cornering the doorway from the living room to the hall when he all but ran into Raine head-on.

"Son of a—!" He stopped outright, slightly out of breath from having run all the way to the house and his heart pounding for having been caught. But he wasn't actually caught. It was only his conscience that was dangling in plain sight.

Raine grabbed onto him to steady herself. "Benny! You scared me half to death. I heard you running! Is something wrong? Is someone hurt?"

He was shaking, mostly from the adrenaline rush. It was all he could do to smile, but smile he did. The last thing he needed was for her to tell Joseph he'd been inside the office.

"No, everything's fine," Benny said quickly. "Besides that, you scared me, too. I thought you were with big brother."

She shook her head. "No. He's going one way. I'm going another."

He frowned. "You leaving?"

"Only for the day. I'm going into Tucson to look for a headstone for the baby's grave."

"Oh, yeah," Benny said, and quickly looked away. "Well, I guess I'd better get on back to work," he said.

Raine looked puzzled. "I thought you were just coming inside?"

He grinned and tweaked her nose. "Shoot no, woman. Other than to get myself a clean hanky, I was already on my way out."

He sauntered into his bedroom and as soon as he'd closed the door behind him, rolled his eyes and plopped down on the bed. Clean hanky? Where the hell did that come from?

He sat on the side of the bed, waiting until he heard the sound of her car starting as well. When there was nothing left in the driveway but dust, he headed for Joseph's office.

The room was small. Three of the four walls were floor-to-ceiling bookcases with every kind of reading material imaginable. A painting hung on the blank wall behind Joseph's desk, but he hardly gave it a look. As far as Benny was concerned, one painting of mountains looked pretty much like all of the others he'd ever seen. It was what lay behind the picture that interested him.

He took another quick look outside. Except for the horses, he had the place to himself.

On to the next step.

He swung the picture back on its hinges, revealing a small wall safe. Without wasted motion, he worked the lock, right twenty, left two, right forty-one.

It opened with a distinct click. Benny was smiling as he peered inside.

"Oh man, oh man," he mumbled, then whistled between his teeth as he pulled out several stacks of hundred-dollar bills.

The urge to take all of it was great. He had to remind himself that he wasn't pulling a heist—not really. This was just borrowing a little bit of what was already his. He licked his fingers and began counting, laying money aside until he had the five thousand dollars owed to the bookies. Then he took another thousand for pocket change and shoved the rest back inside the safe.

As far as he knew, there were no large costs coming up and no major outstanding bills coming due. It could be days, even weeks, before Joseph discovered what had happened. And if Benny was lucky in Vegas, Joseph wouldn't find out at all.

Benny's hopes were high as he hid the money in his room and then headed back toward the barn. Maybe this time he'd get lucky at the tables. All he needed was one good night.

## 13

It had been years since Joseph had looked forward to coming home every evening. Now, it was all he could do to get through a day without finding excuses to go back to the house.

Just to see what Raine was doing.

Just to see if she needed any help.

Just to see if she was still there.

It was just after 10:00 A.M. as he stood on the front porch, watching Harlan Winslow pulling out of the driveway with his horse. Dancer was going back to Yuma a better animal than he'd been. The only person who'd needed new instructions on how to take care of Dancer was Harlan's daughter Corkie. There were to be no more indiscriminate treats for the gelding. Just love and attention. Joseph assured the tearful-eyed teenager that it was more than enough.

In a way, Joseph knew he was going to miss the big gelding's begging manner and wily ways. But things were changing in his life. Now that he had someone to come home to, he no longer felt the need to stay with the horses until he was too tired to eat.

Through Raine's eyes, he found pleasure in small things that he'd taken for granted before. Like walking barefoot out on the patio as the sun was beginning to set. The air was beginning to cool, but the stone slabs were still warm from the heat of the sun. And seeing the storm clouds rolling in on the nearby mountains, then watching lightning after dark while lying in each other's arms. Each time they made love it became a new beginning. It was as if the last twelve years had never passed.

But there were times when Raine became quiet— the times when she seemed angry for no reason at all. But never at him. Just with the world. That's when he didn't understand.

Yes, they'd lost their baby. And yes, she'd been told she couldn't have any more. But they had each other. At least they would have if she'd jump off that fence she kept straddling and admit that the love between them was right where they'd left it all those years ago.

But she made no promises, which for Joseph just wasn't enough. He didn't want a part-time woman with a part-time need for love. He wanted it all.


Raine was speeding. She'd spent more time in Tucson than she'd planned and when she'd realized the time, almost panicked. She hadn't thought to leave Joseph a note and he would think she wasn't coming back. By the time she got to the outskirts of the city, she was in a small panic. It wasn't until she passed a gas station that she thought to stop and call.

A few minutes later, she was leaning against the outer wall of a convenience store, listening to the ringing in her ear. She frowned. Why wasn't the answering machine picking up? It took a minute for her to realize that someone had to be using the phone and ignoring the call-waiting signal.

"Darn it," she sputtered, and started to hang up when she heard Joseph's voice on the line.

"Hello? Raine, is that you?"

Sighing with relief, she lifted the receiver back to her ear.

"Yes, it's me. I let time get away from me," she said. "I'm on my way home, but I didn't want you to worry."

Joseph flopped down into the nearest chair, thankful she couldn't see his face or know that he'd just called Evelyn Hart to ask if she'd seen Raine.

"Oh, that's all right. I just walked in the house, myself."

He didn't tell her that he'd been sitting on the front porch for the better part of an hour and staring down the driveway as if wishing her home would magically make her appear.

"Okay, then," she said. "I guess I'll be on my way."

"Where are you?" he asked, and then rolled his eyes. Damn. She'd think he was checking up on her. "Just in case you have car trouble or something, I'd know where to start looking for you."

"I can't see the name of the little store here, but I know I'm on Highway 77 outside of Oro Valley."

He knew right where she was. He closed his eyes, picturing her there.

"I know the place," he said softly. "You should be home in less than an hour."

"Okay," Raine said. "See you soon."

"Raine, wait!"

"What?"

"Drive safely."

"I will. Don't worry."

"Oh, and Rainbow, there's one other thing."

"What?"

"I love you."

She closed her eyes, letting the warmth of the words surround her. Yet as much as she needed to hear that, she couldn't bring herself to say the words back.

"Thank you, Joseph. I haven't heard those words nearly enough in my life."

"I know, but that's because you went too far and almost stayed away too long."

*Oh, Joseph, if you only knew.*

"See you soon," she said quickly, and hung up the phone.

Benny eyed himself carefully in the hotel mirror and then ran the comb through his hair one last time. His smooth brown skin, clean-shaven face, and dark laughing eyes were a perfect foil for the flamboyance of his surroundings. He flipped an imaginary speck from the front of his turquoise blue shirt and took his belt up a notch. His boots were shined. The creases in his jeans were white from having been ironed so many times. He had a pocketful of money and a hard-on that just wouldn't quit. He picked up his Stetson and then looked back in the mirror, setting the black hat at the perfect angle, then giving it a firm tap.

From the sixth floor of the MGM Grand, he could hear the muted roar of the players below. He headed for the elevator with a strut in his walk and a certainty within him that good things were about to happen. He'd show them all. He felt lucky tonight, in more ways than one.

When the elevator stopped and the doors opened for him to get on, the miniskirted girl in the corner was all the proof Benny needed that his instincts were right. Not only was he going to win himself a fortune in Las Vegas, but by God, he was going to get laid.


Joseph was just taking two rib eye steaks off the outdoor grill when Raine drove up into the yard. To say he was relieved was putting it mildly, but he didn't let on. Instead, he waved to her, hoisting the platter into the air in a teasing manner, and then went inside.

Raine grabbed her purse and exited the car, then caught herself running toward the house. She stopped just before she got to the steps, reminding herself that by hurrying she was only wishing her life away.

She made herself slow down.

"Hey, you," she called when she came in the front door.

"In the kitchen," he yelled.

She tossed her purse on the hall table and headed toward the sound of his voice.

"I'm sorry I was—" "You're just in time for—"

They both started and then stopped at the same moment. Joseph grinned.

"Rainbows first."

She smiled. "A rather tardy rainbow begs your forgiveness."

He shook his head. "You don't need my forgiveness, so you'll have to come up with one better than that."

She pointed to the steak. "One of those for me?"

His grin widened. "That's my girl. Always did get straight to the point, didn't you, sweetheart?"

"Let me wash up and I'll help," she said, and found herself giggling as she made a dash for the nearest bathroom. The very idea. Giggling was for very young girls with stars in their eyes, not women pushing thirty.

When she reached for a towel a few minutes later, she caught a glimpse of the woman in the mirror and almost didn't recognize herself.

The towel hung loosely in her hands as she stepped back and stared. *Oh, Raine, what have you done?*

It was obvious. There was a look on her face that hadn't been there since—since she was a girl. And even though she knew that staying here with Joseph had been a mistake, if she had to do it over again, she would still say yes.

She hung up the towel without looking again. It wasn't necessary. She'd already seen more on her face than should have been there. Not only had she seen happiness and peace and even that long-sought-after joy in her eyes, she'd seen love staring back at her.

It wasn't until the nightly news was over and late-night programming had begun that Raine had thought to ask about Benny. He'd made himself conspicuously absent ever since the night they'd buried the baby. She didn't know whether he was doing it out of consideration or if he was angry that she was still here.

Joseph had taken the book she'd been reading out of her hands and pulled her into his lap.

"Where Benny is concerned, no news is good news. Now, come here. You can read that thing tomorrow when I'm out with the horses. Talk to me, sweetheart. Where did you go today? What did you see?"

But now that he'd interrupted her evening, she had other ideas in mind. She turned until she was facing him and began unbuttoning his shirt. He grinned, then stretched his arms across the back of the couch, giving her free rein.

"Why, Rainbow, you just read my mind."

She arched an eyebrow. "I hope not," she muttered as she tried to push a stubborn button through its hole. "I'd guess it was X-rated."

He grabbed the bottom of her shirt and had it over her head before she knew what was happening. She gasped and crossed her arms across her chest as she glanced nervously toward the front door.

"Wait! What if Benny comes in and catches me like this?"

Joseph frowned and then shook his head. "Benny is in Vegas, remember? He won't be home until late Sunday night."

Some of the playfulness had gone out of Joseph's demeanor. "Well, now," she said, a little uncertain as to how to respond.

"Forget about him," Joseph said, sliding his hands behind her back and unfastening her bra.

When she spilled out of the cups and into his hands, he sighed. And when he encircled each nipple with his warm wet tongue and then nipped her, not enough to hurt but more than enough to make her want, she moaned.

"You have on too many clothes," she mumbled, and began pulling his shirt from the waistband of his jeans and then shoving it off of his arms.

"Just hang on to me," Joseph said, and stood up, striding toward the bedrooms with her still in his arms.

*   *   *

There was a pile of clothes in the floor and a tangle of bedclothes falling from the foot of the bed. Silver streaks of illumination from the security light outside broke the darkness inside Joseph's room, marking the consistent rise and fall of their bodies.

He hammered himself against her in gut-wrenching thrusts, too lost in the feeling to slow down, too far in to pull back. Raine took what he gave her and would have taken some more. There was a wildness to their mating that hadn't been there before. It was sex, pure and simple. Man to woman. Punishing each other for the pleasure and still wanting more.

But when their climaxes came within seconds of each other, their need to reach out was instinctive. He had spilled his seed into the woman of his heart.

Raine took it—and him—wrapping her arms around his shoulders and pulling his head down to her breasts while tiny waves of energy ebbed outward from her groin, leaving her spent and weak.

Joseph couldn't focus. The urge to close his eyes was overwhelming, but he kept thinking there was a thing left undone. Just before sleep claimed him, he remembered. He hadn't told her good night.

Hair clung damply to Raine's shoulders and neck, and she was so wired by what had just happened that it was impossible for her to sleep. She kept taking out the memory and reliving it again, from the instant he'd pulled her shirt over her head to the moment his semen spilled down the inside of her leg. She was hot and sticky and it wouldn't have taken much energy to get up and shower. But she wasn't about to move.

She looked down at Joseph. His cheek was pillowed on her breast and his fingers had curled around the narrowest part of her waist. Strands of dark hair were stuck to his forehead and his eyes had already closed. A great surge of love for this man overwhelmed her, bringing quick tears to her eyes. She tightened her hold on him, and right then could not have been persuaded to move if she'd been covered in mud.

*So this is love.*

Tears oozed from beneath her eyelids. She hadn't meant for this to happen.

Friendship, yes.

Companionship, maybe.

Lovers, okay, as long as no one got hurt.

But this wasn't part of the plan. If she gave away this much of herself, in the end it would destroy him.

"God help us both," she whispered, and gave herself up to the night.

*Long tendrils of a brown, snaking vine wound about the metal structure of the old abandoned windmill. It looked as if it had been wrapped in raffia and was awaiting some tawdry decoration to top it off.*

*At the highest point, the fan blades of the windmill were spinning wildly, in spite of the fact that they were not connected to the frame.*

*Joseph was standing beneath the structure, unaware of the danger.*

"Run," Raine screamed, pointing to the fan blades above their heads.

Joseph bolted, heading toward a grove of trees in the distance. When Raine started to follow, she found herself unable to move. She looked down. The vine had wrapped itself around her ankles and as she watched with growing horror, it began winding anew. Up her legs, past her knees, then around her waist.

Struggling frantically to free herself, she started tearing at the vines and screaming out Joseph's name, begging for him to come back. But he'd run too far, too fast, and was already out of hearing.

The vine kept winding, growing tighter with each circle it made until her life began ebbing away. It was around her neck now, wringing the breath from her body like a washerwoman wringing excess water from an old, used up towel. She looked up. The fan blades were upon her.

Raine woke up gasping for breath and choking on screams. She rolled out from under the weight of her covers and staggered to a window, taking long deep draughts of life-giving air.

Joseph was at her side within moments of her exit from bed.

"Raine, honey, what's wrong? Are you sick?"

She thrust shaky hands through her hair, combing it away from her face.

"Bad dream," she muttered, and inhaled again,

taking pleasure in the ability to breathe.

"Wait here," he said. "I'll get you something to drink."

She grabbed him by the arm. "Never mind. I'm going to shower. I'll get it myself."

"You sure you're okay?"

She nodded without looking at him. There was a part of her that was still resentful of the fact that in the dream he'd gone off without her. Left her behind like so much trash. She knew she was being silly. It was only a dream. But as she stepped beneath the shower head and into the spray, she couldn't help wondering how symbolic the dream had been.

She'd been the one to see danger coming. She'd warned him at her own risk and had then been left to fend for herself. That was probably subconscious remnants of her anger at being alone during her pregnancy and then when the baby had died. As for the rest of the dream—the wildly spinning fan blades and the ever-choking vines—she knew all too well what they represented, too. Time was running out and she was choking on her own secrets.

Joseph waited until he heard the water running before he headed for the kitchen. It was just after five. There was no way he'd be able to go back to sleep. Not after that gut-wrenching scream. One minute he'd been lost in a deep, dreamless sleep and then she'd been all but clawing him in an effort to get free.

He measured the coffee and water without thought, but when he slid the pot into place and turned on the switch, light caught and then held on the green crystal in his ring. He paused, staring down at it in quiet contemplation.

It was so much a part of him now that sometimes he forgot it was even there. And then there would be times, like now, when he was forced to remember that he lived his life for others. As much as he loved Raine and as worried as he was about her state of mind, if someone came to be healed right now, they would have to come first.

Raine was a very intelligent woman. If she stayed, would she accept the fact that there was a part of his life he could not share? His mother hadn't. It had driven a wedge between his parents and ended their family before it had barely begun.

Nursing a cup of coffee, he watched the sunrise alone. When morning was patently evident, he tossed out the remnants of his coffee that had gone cold and went back into the house. Just for a moment, he stood in the doorway leading into the kitchen and listened to the quiet.

He didn't want to think about what Benny was doing in Las Vegas. Since Benny hadn't had the guts to face Joseph before he'd left, Joseph had been forced to hear the news from a message on the answering machine.

Somewhere within the confines of his home, Raine was obviously nursing a few secrets of her own. In this house, he lived with one person and slept with another, and at this moment, he had never felt more alone.

Disgusted with himself for giving in to self-pity, he set down his cup and went in search of Raine. Even if she didn't want to talk about what was bothering her, he wanted her to know he still cared.

Raine was sitting in a chair with her head between her knees. Water was dripping from her hair onto the floor as she tried without much success to comb out the tangles from the back of her hair.

"Ouch," she muttered, when her comb hit a snag. To her relief, Joseph appeared, lifting the comb from her hands.

"Hey, sweetheart. Looks like you could do with a little help. Let me, okay?"

She didn't argue. "If I could have seen what I was doing, I would have already cut it out," she muttered.

He grinned. "Boy, I'd hate to think of what your hair would look like if you cut out every tangle you got."

"Most of them aren't this accursed," she said, wincing when his technique hit a snag of its own.

"Sorry," Joseph said, rubbing at the spot where the pull must have been. "I know that hurt."

"No more than what I've been doing to myself," she sputtered.

A few seconds went by and a companionable silence descended. With infinite care, Joseph picked at the knot, easing the tangle looser and looser until one last combing and the knot would be freed.

"Did you know there's an image in this tile that looks like the state of Oklahoma?"

Joseph picked up the hairbrush and pulled it once through her hair, testing for other small knots.

"No, I can't say as I did," he said, smiling with satisfaction as her hair slid through his fingers without hesitation.

Raine thought about what she'd just asked him and then started to grin. Maybe it was from hanging upside down too long, or maybe it was the inaneness of her own remark, but the grin spread to a smile.

"Did you know there's another one with a witch's face?" She pushed at his foot with the toe of her shoe. "Move your foot a little to the left," she urged. "There's something under that one, too."

This time, Joseph took note of her silliness. He took a step backward, holding up his hands to show that he surrendered. At this point, Raine looked up.

"Damn, Rainbow, you'd be a real cheap date. Wouldn't have to spend a penny on you. Just feed you peanut butter and jelly sandwiches and then take you to the bathroom to look at the floor."

She started to laugh. Not small chuckles that beckoned for listeners to join in, but a throw-back-your-head kind of laugh that doesn't care who's listening or if they even agree. She rolled off of the stool on which she was sitting and onto the floor. And every time she thought it was over she would look either at Joseph or at the designs on the floor and erupt into laughter all over again.

Joseph stood with the hairbrush in one hand and

a grin on his face that might never come off. There was a joy in his heart that he couldn't explain. Sharing this moment with Raine was as precious to him as the night they'd buried their child. Different—but every bit as precious.

Joseph tossed aside the hairbrush and hefted her up to her feet. She was still giggling as she combed her fingers through her long, wet hair.

"Ooh, that feels good," she said, rubbing at the spot where the tangle had been. "Thank you so much for your help."

She threw her arms around his neck and planted a very uninhibited kiss on his mouth.

His grabbed her instinctively, returning the affection and adding a couple of bonuses on his own. By the time they were through, both were breathing hard and giving much consideration to crawling back into bed.

But then a horse whinnied loudly from the corral and another answered from a nearby pasture.

"Duty calls," he said with a groan. "The horses are hungry."

"I'm starving, too," Raine said. "How long will it take you to feed and water the stock?"

"About an hour, give or take a few minutes."

She arched an eyebrow. "I haven't used my cooking skills all that much in the past few years, but I think I can manage a pretty decent breakfast in about that time."

Joseph cupped one side of her face with the palm of his hand.

"You don't have to cook for me," he said. "You're not here to be my servant. I want you to be comfortable here, not cleaning and cooking to try and pay for your keep. I already told you that you could stay forever. I don't make idle promises."

*Or threats,* Raine thought, *you just love.* But she didn't say what she was thinking and settled for something safer instead.

"Hey, you told me to make myself at home."

"And I meant it."

"Then I want to make breakfast for my man," she said softly.

Joseph's heart skipped a beat. A funny smile tilted the corner of his mouth as he brushed the surface of her lips with a slow, tender kiss.

"Your man, hunh?"

Raine was struggling with the fact that her toes had just curled inside her socks when she came to enough to nod.

Joseph grinned. "Then have at it, baby. You cook it. I'll eat it."

"Is that a promise?" she teased.

He arched an eyebrow. "Is that a warning?"

She bit the inside of her lip, worrying it a little with the edges of her teeth.

"Well, um . . . maybe not a warning. More like a disclaimer."

She could still hear him laughing as he walked out on the porch.

Stuart Rossi moved into his new home on a Saturday afternoon at ten minutes after three. By four o'clock he was moving among his belongings as if they'd been there all of his life. Besides his favorite things from his L.A. home, he'd had his mother's antiques shipped in from the family estate in Boston and some of the trinkets and treasures he been accumulating during his European travels.

He sat down behind his desk and reached for the phone. The familiar curve of the instrument against his palm did wonders for his attitude. He gazed around the opulent room with quiet satisfaction. The Manet went well on the west wall above his mother's Queen Anne sofa. His collection of jade spanned the north and east walls of the room. The south wall was mostly windows. Stuart liked windows and for the most part, despised artificial light.

He leaned forward slightly, punching in the number he wanted to call. Then he kicked back in his chair, counting the rings and anticipating the voice he would hear. When she answered, he automatically cupped himself. Her husky drawl was the best turn on a lonely man could want.

"Farley Investigations, Georgia speaking."

He gave his testicles a quick massage and then concentrated on his request.

"Hello, Georgia darling. This is Stuart Rossi."

The timbre of the woman's voice rose an octave with her obvious delight.

"Stuart, you sorry ass. Why haven't you called?"

He grinned. "I've been busy moving," he said. "Are you?"

"Am I what . . . moving?" she asked.

"No, are you busy?"

Her anticipation rose, but this time the octave of her voice dropped markedly.

"For you, never. Talk to me, Stuart. What do you need?"

"I want you to find a man for me."

"Why, Stuart, I didn't know you were turned that way."

He laughed aloud. Damn, but this sexy banter did more for him than a pocketful of pills.

"Shut up, Georgia, and listen."

She smiled. "I'm all ears."

Stuart's eyebrows arched as he thought about her hourglass figure and double-E breasts.

"That's a debatable remark, but I'll let it slide for now." Her sexy chuckle silenced as he started to explain. "When you find this man, I need you to make sure that the next time I make him an offer, he won't be able to refuse."

She sighed, pretending to pout. "Basically, what you're saying is you want me to spend all his money, fuck him blind, and leave it hanging."

Stuart laughed again, and then choked. Even as he was working his way through the coughing spell, he knew it was going to be worth it.

Georgia Farley didn't have a heart. At least not the kind that wept for others. But when she heard Stuart choking and coughing and gasping for air, she bit her lip and silently recited as many of the Ten Commandments as she could remember. She was all the way to number eight when Stuart regained control, which for a preacher's daughter wasn't all that much of a feat.

"Sorry," Stuart said quickly. "I, uh, choked on some peanuts."

"Yeah, right. They'll do it every time," Georgia said.

But she knew. Everyone in their circle knew. Stuart Rossi was dying.

"So, what's the lucky man's name and where do I find him?" she asked.

"Benny Colorado. He's in Las Vegas playing the slots. Get out there tonight and give him something else to play with, you hear?"

Georgia grinned. "I hear." Then she added. "Do you have a picture you can fax?"

Stuart frowned. "No. But just look for a smart-ass Indian with a big black hat."

Georgia rolled her eyes. "This is Las Vegas we're talking about. That description could fit a thousand

men on any given day, including some of the enter-
tainers."

Stuart's eyes narrowed thoughtfully. "He's staying at the MGM Grand."

"That's enough to get me started," she said.

"Stay in touch," Stuart said.

"You'll get my bill," Georgia said, then added,
"By the way, where are you? You said you'd moved."

"I'll have my secretary fax you with a new
address. Meanwhile, you can reach me at . . ."

He rattled off his number and heard her discon-
nect. It wasn't until the dial tone began buzzing in his
ear that he remembered he hadn't hung up. He
dropped the receiver back into the cradle and then
smoothed the front of his zipper. There was a time
for everything. He would find himself a woman, and
soon. But right now, he wanted to make sure that
Benny Colorado was deep in his pockets before he
took off his pants.

Benny was riding a high he'd hadn't had since he'd
left L.A. But it wasn't a drug that had sent him flying,
it was the adrenaline rush of being a winner. He'd
gone to the tables with a thousand dollars in his
pocket. Right now he had over fifty thousand in the
house bank and almost that much again in front of
him. His eyes were glittering as he watched the
dealer's hands slipping cards from the shoe.
Although he'd played most of the other tables at one
time or another, blackjack was his game. Right now

his eyes were glittering as he watched the cards being dealt. With little more than a scratch of card to felt, he drew winning hand after winning hand, betting large amounts with wild abandon.

An astrologer might have claimed Benny's planets were all in alignment. A psychic might have attributed his winning to karma. A skeptic might have sneered and added a warning that it certainly wouldn't last. Benny would have thumbed his nose at them all.

At this point, Benny could have had his pick of the unattached women hovering around his chair: stunning, surgically perfect women who had a nose for winners. From where they were standing, Benny more than qualified for their attention. But Benny's interest at the moment did not include any women other than the one dealing the cards. He kept playing and betting and raking it in.

It wasn't until he lost three hands in a row that he looked up from the table. The women were still there, wearing catch-me-and-you-can-fuck-me expressions. Instead of piquing his interest, it turned him off. He tossed in his hand, cashed in his chips, adding those winnings to the others he had amassed, and headed for his room. He'd been at this for more than seven hours straight. He wanted a bath, a change of clothes and a thick, juicy steak—and in that order.

The elevator was full of couples. Half of them were arguing, the other half seemed to be drunk. He got off on the sixth floor, thankful that the bulk of passengers were still going up.

His step was light as he strode down the hall. He kept picturing Joseph's face when he came home with all that money. Then he reminded himself that he would replace what he'd taken before he announced his good luck. Even though he had the money in hand to pay Joseph back, the idea that he'd taken it without anyone's knowledge was beginning to worry him. He was smiling to himself as he shoved the key in the lock and then went inside. Maybe he'd been living with big brother too long. Damned if he wasn't starting to develop a conscience.

The first thing he noticed when he stepped inside the room was that it smelled of roses. But when he didn't see any, he decided he was imagining things.

Shrugging wearily, he tossed his key on a table and sat down on the bed to take off his boots. His belly was grumbling, but he would shower first. By the time he got to the bathroom door, he was completely undressed. His hand was on the doorknob when it dawned on him that the scent of roses was even stronger here. And as he stood, he became aware of a soft, humming sound coming from inside.

Son of a bitch! Someone was in there. And the someone was singing.

He shoved the door inward, ready to do battle, and instead, found himself staring at the woman in his tub. Up to her breasts in bubbles, she had long, curly hair caught high on her head with some sort of a clasp, and her face, completely devoid of makeup, was the most beautiful he'd ever seen. Her features were perfectly proportioned, almost Grecian in style, and the lids of her baby blue eyes were sleep-heavy. She gave his nude form a slow, considering stare, gazing from head to toe and then centering on his middle and the hard, erect member pointing accusingly at her presence.

"Uh . . ."

It was all Benny got said before she stood. Bubbles slid from her hourglass figure and down her double-E breasts. And all the while he was watching them flow, he took note of the fact that she was a natural blonde.

She stepped out of the tub and knelt at his feet. Her lips were wet, her hands slick with the rose-scented soap. Certain that he must be dreaming, Benny grabbed onto the doorframe just in case he was not.

"I'm bought and paid for honey. Enjoy."

She took him into her mouth, and after that, the room took a spin. Benny grinned, then he groaned. Minutes later he was flat on his back in bed. In between the cataclysmic bursts of euphoria that each of his climaxes held, he kept thinking that if this was a dream, he didn't want to wake up.

It wasn't until morning that he thought to ask her name. "Georgia. I'm just a little ol' Georgia peach."

"Well, now," Benny said, thinking he'd become master of this game, as well. "I'm hungry as all get-out. Maybe I'll just have me a little bite of that peach."

Georgia raked her fingernails down his belly and

across his groin, smiling to herself when he sprang erect. There was one thing to say for youth, she thought. They got hot and hard faster than a buck rabbit with a doe in heat.

"I'm hungry, too," she said slowly, leaving him with no qualms as to who was going to consume what first. "And as soon as we've satisfied one hunger, could we work on the other?"

At this point, Benny could have denied her nothing. "Yeah, baby, ooh baby, you know what I like."

"Well, baby, can we?" she asked.

Benny rolled his eyes and then gritted his teeth as her hands worked their magic.

"Can we what?" he groaned.

"Order room service. And after that, let's go downstairs. I'm feeling lucky."

Georgia Farley tossed the key on the bed and blew the empty room a quick kiss. The motel was small and inconspicuous. Added to that, she'd registered under a phony name and she would be impossible to trace. In less than an hour, she would be on her way back to L.A. She'd given Benny Colorado the slip beside the roulette wheel at the Mirage.

"I'll be right back," she had cooed and headed for the ladies' room.

As soon as his back was turned, she'd made for the door. He'd barely nodded. The glitter was long gone from his eyes and there was a small, fixed smile on his face.

She'd wiped him out. Not only had he spent the hundred thousand that he'd won earlier, but maxed out every credit card he owned. If she had stripped naked at his feet and proceeded to screw the next man who came by them, it was doubtful he would have noticed.

An hour passed before it dawned on him that she probably wasn't coming back. After that, he walked out the door, heading back to the MGM Grand to pick up his suitcase. At least he still had a plane ticket home.

He walked in his room, his steps dragging. The message light was flashing on his phone and out of fear, he almost didn't answer. Most of the day was a blank. He couldn't remember who he owed or when he'd promised to pay. He even envisioned Joseph finding out about the money he had taken and telling him not to come home. In spite of all of his guesses, he couldn't have been more wrong.

"This is Benny Colorado in room 628. Do you have messages for me?"

"Only one, sir," the operator said. "Just a moment and I'll connect."

Benny sat down on the side of the bed, staring at a scuffed spot on his boots and trying not to think of how much money he'd had—and how much money he'd lost.

"Colorado, this is Rossi."

If Benny been any closer to the edge of the bed, he would have slid off. The shock of hearing Stuart Rossi's voice was somehow frightening. How had the man found him? Better yet, why here? Why now?

He gripped the phone a little tighter, listening and ultimately understanding who had bought and paid for the Georgia peach.

It was eleven minutes after ten in the morning when Benny's plane landed in Tucson. He walked to the airport parking lot without giving the people he passed, or the condition of the weather, a second glance. A short while later he was on the road to Oracle. Only once did he let himself consider the possibility of turning around and heading west just as hard and as fast as he could go. It would be easy to get lost in L.A. He knew people who would help him. But something had happened to him in the two years he'd been in Arizona. He'd grown accustomed to a clean, decent home and the perks that come from having a good name. He was in hot water right now, but there had to be a way out.

His suitcase was heavy with money. But it wasn't nearly as heavy as his heart. Thanks to Rossi, he could slip Joseph's money back in the safe before he was found out and still have a small fortune left over. And there was the promise of plenty more where that came from. All he had to do was watch and wait. And—when the time was right of course—sell out his brother.

At this point, his mind would blank. He had a way out of one problem, but was shit deep in another. Ever so often he would catch a glimpse of himself in the rearview mirror. But he couldn't meet his own gaze. He kept thinking this was all a bad dream.

Maybe Stuart Rossi would do all of them a favor and die. That would solve everyone's problems, including Rossi's. But that wasn't enough for Benny to count on. Rot had a way of leaving a bad smell behind.

When he turned off the highway and started down the road leading to the Colorado ranch, he wanted to cry. He wasn't a Colorado any longer. He was a Judas. He prayed to God it wouldn't show.

Raine was down at the corrals when Benny parked. He saw her look up and then look away. That suited him fine. He wanted the house to himself. He glanced around the yard. Joseph's truck was nowhere in sight. Even better.

He headed for Joseph's office, trying not to run, but the urgency to hide what he'd done was overwhelming. At least give me back this much, he begged silently.

The trade went smooth. His conscience for six thousand dollars. His soul for the proverbial pound of flesh. Only after he was in his room and the suitcase tucked safely inside his closet, did he start to relax. One hurdle down. Only one more to go. And he couldn't think of it as betrayal, or he would get Joseph's gun and shoot himself where he stood. No, he'd convinced himself that it would be nothing but a phone call. Whatever happened after that was on someone else's head.

When the sound of the engine reached the corrals where Raine was feeding the young colt, she turned, expecting to see Joseph. But it was Benny who got out of the car. She started to wave, but there was something about the way he was staring that made her uncomfortable, so she looked away instead. Afterward, she kept telling herself that she'd been worse than rude. But the damage had been done.

She finished with the colt, giving it a gentle pat on the neck, and then shut the gate behind her as she went to put the bucket in the barn. Even if the task Joseph had given her was a small one, it felt good to be doing something constructive. But that job was over and until he came back from town, she didn't know what to do next.

Her gaze drifted to the rise above the corrals. It was becoming one of her favorite places to be. The creek always ran at a swift, sparkling pace. The shade beneath the big tree was always worth the walk it took to get there. Even the grave itself had taken on an entirely different aspect. It was no longer a reminder of death, but a peaceful place to rest and remember.

Raine gave the house one last glance and then made her decision. The hill it was. Something was going on between Benny and Joseph and she wanted no part of it. She'd stayed in Oracle for one reason, and getting in the middle of a feud wasn't it.

As she'd known, the climb was worth the effort. Last week she'd planted a small rosebush at the foot of the baby's grave and it had taken root as if it had been made for the spot. When she reached the tree, she took down the small plastic bucket that she'd tied to a branch and went to the creek for water. She took off her shoes to wade into the stream, filling the bucket as she walked. A couple of minutes later she was back at the grave and watering the rosebush, then using what was left in the bucket to clean the mud from her feet.

She glanced at her watch. It was almost eleven. Joseph should be coming back any time. She wiggled her toes in the warm, sweet grass. A few more minutes and her feet would be dry enough to put her shoes back on. The sun was hot on her face, and she thought about scooting back into the shade. But there was something patently soothing about sunshine and grass and bare feet. The green hillside beckoned. Her eyes drooped. There would come a time when this would be a memory to cherish. And because she was storing up just such memories for the day when she would leave, she stayed just a little bit longer.

Minutes later, she was asleep.


When Joseph turned down the driveway and saw Benny's car parked in its usual place, his stomach knotted. As he pulled up at the house and parked, he glanced toward the barns. The colt was kicking up it heels in the corral, but Raine was nowhere in sight. For some reason, the thought of Benny and Raine alone in the house made him nervous. The last thing he wanted for her was dissension, and Benny was ripe for it.

"Anybody home?" he called, as he came inside.

Benny walked out of the kitchen with a sandwich in his hand. To Joseph's surprise, Benny was wearing work clothes.

"Long time no see," Benny said.

Joseph nodded. "Good trip?"

*Good? Not unless you like side trips to hell.* "Oh, it had its moments," he said quietly.

Joseph's attention piqued. "Where's Raine?"

Benny shrugged. "She was in the corral with that colt when I drove up."

"You mean she never came to the house?"

"Nope?"

"And you didn't think to go check on her?"

Benny stared at Joseph as if he'd just lost his mind. "Why? Is something wrong with her?"

"Well, no, but she—"

"Hell, brother. Let her be. She's been taking care of herself for a long time without you. I'm guessing she can still handle the job, in spite of the fact that she's here."

Joseph stared. For once, Benny had a good point. A wry grin lifted the corner of his mouth.

"Am I hovering?"

Benny grinned back. "You could say that."

"Do I do that to you, too?" Joseph asked.

Surprised that the conversation had turned personal, it took Benny a moment to answer.

"Well, yes, I suppose that you do," he said. "But don't worry. I hardly every listen to you, anyway."

Joseph stood for just a moment and then he burst into laughter.

"You know, little brother, just when I think you'll never make it, there's a streak of decency in you that keeps floating to the top. It saves you every time."

The grin froze on Benny's face. Decency. He wasn't sure he'd ever know the feeling again. He stuffed the rest of the sandwich into his mouth and then headed for the door.

Benny was halfway out when Joseph yelled.

"Hey, Benny."

Benny stopped and turned. "Yeah?"

"Glad you're back. I hate to admit it, but I think I missed you."

Benny nodded and then jammed his hat a little tighter on his head as he strode off the porch. He kept trying to swallow that last bite of sandwich, but there was a knot in his throat and it couldn't get by. Finally, he spit it out in the bushes and felt like throwing the rest of it up as well. He gritted his teeth and kept on walking.

Joseph headed for his room. Despite what Benny just said, as soon as he changed clothes he was going to check on Raine. It wasn't that she couldn't take care of herself. He just wanted to do it for her.

\* \* \*

She woke with a blinding headache and a fear she couldn't name. Even though she'd been warned it might happen, the sudden onset of the pain was enough to make her panic. She sat up with a jerk, looking around in slow confusion. Grass? She was lying on grass? Where on earth was her bed?

She lay back down with a groan and rolled onto her side, drawing herself up in a ball and holding onto her head to keep from screaming. The longer she lay there, the more frightened she became. The pounding in her head wouldn't stop. What was worse, it was spreading to the rest of her body as well.

It wasn't until Joseph yanked her up from the grass and into his arms that she realized the pounding she'd heard had been the horse he was riding and not her body after all.

"Raine, sweetheart. What the hell are you trying to do, give yourself sunstroke?"

"What?" she mumbled, wishing he wouldn't yell.

"Your head . . . your poor little head. It must be pounding."

She stared. How had he known that? Was it possible to see headaches now? What had happened?

"I don't know what you're talking about," she said.

"You have the makings of a damned good sunburn," Joseph said. "Your face is red and your head is as hot as fire. What were you thinking?"

*Oh, God, just too much sun.*

Slack with relief, she leaned against him, wiping a shaky hand across her face. He was right. As her father used to say, it was hot as a firecracker.

"I didn't mean to fall asleep," she said, pointing to the bucket and the rosebush. "I was watering the rosebush. The next thing I know you're dragging me into the shade and reading me the riot act—which it seems I richly deserve."

Joseph shook his head and then lifted her onto his horse before vaulting into the saddle behind her.

"We'll get you back to the house. You'll want to shower and change and then I suggest some aspirin and about a gallon of iced tea."

Too much sun. She'd gotten too much sun. That meant she would probably blister later on.

Joseph shifted to a more comfortable position, and then glanced down at Raine. She was sitting in his lap with her legs dangling off to one side.

"Are you okay? Are you uncomfortable in any way?"

She sighed and pointed to her nose.

"What do you think?" she said.

He frowned, pretending to study the mess. "Well, on first glance, I'd say medium rare, but I could be wrong."

She laughed. "Just take me home where I can suffer in peace."

He grinned, then jammed his Stetson onto her head.

"This is probably a case of too little, too late, but accept it for what it's worth," he said gently. Then he nudged the horse forward.

Raine sighed with relief at the welcome shade the wide brim afforded her, then leaned back against his arms, relaxing to the horse's smooth, even gait. There was a safety within Joseph's arms that she'd never felt with anyone else. A wave of sadness came and went within her so swiftly, she could almost have imagined it.

Joseph glanced down. There was nothing visible of her face but the edge of her chin. And as he watched, he saw it tremble. A fear came over him then and he tightened his hold. Something was still hurting her. But what?

Was it him? Was it them? Was it the loss of something they couldn't regain? His heart tugged at his conscience. He looked down again, and as he did, saw that the refracted rays of sunlight had caught in his ring.

There was a movement within the crystal that was mesmerizing. A motion of energy and power that made the stone seem alive. He exhaled on a soft sigh as his conscience fell clear. Whatever had happened was over. The past could not be changed. It was the now that mattered, and the future that promised hope. If only Raine would trust him again, he would show her what it meant to be loved. If only—

And then Benny yelled from a nearby corral.

"Is she all right?"

Raine took off her hat and waved it in the air. "You can't call me paleface again."

The vivid hue of sunburn on her skin was impossible to miss. Benny grinned and then waved and pointed.

"Big brother will fix you up. He can heal anything."

Joseph started. In itself, the phrase was innocent. It was true that he often doctored lame horses and cleaned up the remnants of fights Benny used to get into.

He continued to ponder the phrase all the way to the house. He knew Benny was suspicious of the trips he made in the chopper. They'd fought about it more than once. And then he relaxed. There was no way he could know. It was just the coincidence of an innocent remark. Nothing more.

He put it aside as they reached the house.

Raine set Joseph's hat back on his head as he started to help her down. He paused, his hands around her waist, his gaze locked into the clear blue of her eyes.

"Thanks for the lift, cowboy," she said softly.

A wry grin tilted one corner of his mouth.

"My pleasure, little lady. If I can be of any further assistance . . ."

Her feet hit the ground with a soft thud. She straightened her shirt and then smiled as she shaded her eyes to look up at him.

"I've caused enough damage for one day. I think I can take it from here," she said.

"Take a cool shower. There's aloe vera gel underneath the bathroom sink and I recommend a very soft, very large shirt."

She grimaced. "I must look quite a sight."

"You always did look pretty in pink," he drawled, and was rewarded with her quick laugh as she disappeared inside.

# 15

Raine ran her fingers through her hair and wished she'd put it up this morning before she'd left for Phoenix. The trip had taken longer than she'd planned, but at the same time, she was elated by the project.

After more than a month at the ranch, she had gotten antsy about doing nothing but living off of Joseph's hospitality. It had been years since she'd worked as a stringer for a newspaper, but if she could get the story the Tucson editor wanted, he'd told her he would buy it.

All she'd had to do was interview the country music star and two members of his band who'd rescued a woman and two children from a burning car two days earlier. They'd agreed to a backstage interview during a practice session in Phoenix. She'd gotten the story with no problem. Now all she had to do was go home and write it.

She glanced at the clock on the dash. It was a little after three. Barring any problems, she should be back at the ranch around five. After a quick supper, she would work on her notes and then on the story itself tomorrow. It was the first time in weeks that she'd made plans for the future, even if they were no farther away than tomorrow.

But in spite of her optimism, the weight of her hair was still bothering her. Instead of upping the air conditioning, she opted for a natural breeze and rolled down the window. Immediately, her hair began to whip in the wind. For a woman who'd planned to shut down from the world, the simple freedom of windblown hair seemed almost sinful. She leaned forward, cranking up the radio, then accelerating on the gas. When Jackson Browne's golden oldie, "Running on Empty," suddenly blasted at her through the speakers, she laughed.

A while ago, *she* had been running on empty. But no more. Thanks to Joseph, she was full of life and full of joy. She wouldn't let herself remember that she would soon be leaving. Today she was back on track in a way she hadn't been in months. There was a man who loved her who was waiting for her at home, and she had a deadline to meet.

It was just after five when Joseph saw her car coming down the driveway. When he saw the rooster tail of dust she was leaving behind, he started to grin. Success had to be the reason for her haste.

"Hey, Benny. Finish up this last mare for me, will you?"

Benny waved from across the corrals to indicate that he'd heard.

Joseph tied down the horse's reins and gave her a quick, last pat.

"Your supper's on the way, girl. I've got to see *my* girl about a much-needed hug."

The horse whinnied her protest at being tied, but Joseph kept on walking toward the house. He hadn't seen Raine since seven o'clock this morning. He wanted to see that smile in her eyes and hear all about her day.

Raine ran into the house, dumping her briefcase on the bed and the sack of stuff she'd just bought at the pharmacy in Oracle. She kicked off her shoes as she put up the items. Hand lotion and disposable razors. Tampons and shampoo. There was a dull ache at the back of her neck that she attributed to tired muscles and the long drive. But Joseph could fix that. He gave the best backrubs.

Her hair was still sticking to the back of her neck, and as she reached for her hairbrush, she inadvertently knocked the box of tampons onto the floor.

"Shoot," she muttered, and reached down with a grunt, then tossed them into a nearby drawer.

The brush's bristles felt good upon her scalp, and when she twisted her hair off of her neck and fastened it to the top of her head with a clasp, she sighed with relief.

"Hey!" Joseph yelled. "Anybody home?"

She spun, a smile of delight spreading wide across her face, and ran to meet him.

* * *

Benny made it through supper without coming unglued, but the ensuing days and weeks since he'd taken Rossi's money were weighing heavily upon his conscience. Twice in the past week he'd almost confessed the whole thing to Joseph. He'd wanted to. Oh, God, how he'd wanted to. But each time, something kept him silent. Whether it was guilt or just plain fear, Benny's life was still a lie.

He was drinking more and enjoying it less, and it had been more than two weeks since he'd given Shelley Biggers a call. Every time he thought about sex, the image of a soap-covered siren rising out of a tub turned him off. He was sick at heart and too much a coward to confess.

Raine had excused herself right after supper and was hard at work in her room, concentrating on the interview she'd just had. Joseph was in the office working on the books for the ranch. As usual, Benny was the odd man out.

He sat staring at the television with the remote clutched in his hand, searching the airwaves for something to take his mind off the facts. But there was nothing on TV that could make him forget what he'd already done—or what he'd promised to do. Suddenly, he tossed the remote aside and stalked to the door. He grabbed his Stetson and jammed it on his head, then turned and looked around, as if setting the peaceful image of home in his head one more time. Minutes later, he was gone.

Joseph heard the familiar sound of Benny's engine as he started his car. He sighed and then shook his head. Something was bothering Benny, but no matter how hard he'd tried, he hadn't been able to get his brother to open up. Instinctively, his gaze went straight to his father's picture.

"I wish you were here, old man," he said softly. "I need your wisdom and understanding—and most of all, I could use one of your hugs."

The fixed smile on Michael Colorado's face wasn't much help. But Joseph remembered the day that the shot had been taken. He could still hear his father's laughter as the orphan colt had come up behind him and yanked the handkerchief out of his pocket. The colt was registered. Its bloodlines were impeccable and fitting with its long proper name. But from that day on, the colt had answered to the name Sneaky.

Joseph shook his head and then reached for the next bill to record. His dad had died less than six months later and Joseph had sold Sneaky a few months after that to pay for a bunch of Benny's hot checks. He gazed off into space, wondering how two brothers, born of the same parents and with the same blood running in their veins, could be so remarkably different. Then he shook his head and went back to his task.

Raine worked through the night and long into morning, forgoing sleep in Joseph's arms to finish the piece. She fell asleep at the table. She never knew when Joseph came in and carried her to her bed—or when he took off her shoes and covered her up. All she felt was the comfort as she rolled into a ball and fell even deeper asleep.

She didn't know that Joseph brushed a wayward lock of hair from her eyes and then leaned down and kissed the side of her cheek. She didn't hear his soft whisper as he bid her good night.

"Sleep well, sweetheart. You've earned it."

Edward knocked on the library door, waiting nervously for permission to enter. The woman standing a few yards down the hall was making him nervous. If ever he'd seen a man-eater in his life, she was it. Her hips swayed with a constant invitation to sample the wares, and the bodice of her sweater looked as if it might explode. He couldn't remember when he'd seen breasts that size outside of the pages of a men's magazine.

"What is it?" Stuart said.

Edward gave the woman a last glance and then opened the door.

"I thought I told you I wasn't to be disturbed," Stuart said.

Edward gestured toward the hall. "There's a Miss Farley here to see you, sir. I told her you'd left instructions not to be disturbed, but she was rather insistent. Do you want me to—"

"Send her in! Send her in!" Stuart cried, and

thought about removing the oxygen tube from his nose, then thought better of it. Georgia Farley always made his blood pressure rise. He didn't need to be gasping for breath when it happened.

Georgia Farley was waiting just outside the door as Edward stepped into the hall. She gave him a slow wink and then gave his backside a slow squeeze.

"Told you he would want to see me," she whispered, and then winked.

Moments later Edward found himself standing alone in the hall with a very stupid grin on his face and a hard-on any sixteen-year-old boy would have been proud of. He smoothed his hand down the front of his fly and then strutted away.

"Georgia! Darling! You didn't have to come all this way, but I'm very glad you did," Stuart said.

Georgia was adept at hiding her feelings, which in this case proved valuable. To say she was shocked by Stuart's appearance would have been putting it mildly. Although she knew he was still in his forties, he could have easily passed for a man of seventy. His beautiful blonde hair was thin and lifeless. There were dark circles beneath his eyes and wrinkles at the corners of his mouth that hadn't been there six months before. She wanted to throw her arms up in the air and run away screaming. Looking at him like this was too much like facing her own mortality.

Georgia set aside her disgust and slid a pretty pout into place. As long as Stuart Rossi was breathing, he was too rich to ignore and too mean to piss off.

"Stu, baby, it's been too long," she said, and circled the desk before sliding into his lap.

Stuart's eyes widened as her seeking hands quickly found his zipper. Worry tugged at the back of his mind. Would his heart withstand this much excitement? And then her fingers were inside his pants and whatever he'd been worrying about slid to the back of his mind.

"You just let sweet Georgia take care of you," she whispered, and slathered a kiss on his lips before sliding from his lap to kneel before him.

Stuart groaned as his manhood hardened. This is what he'd been needing. A good old-fashioned fuck. And with Georgia, he wouldn't have to exert any effort. Just sit back and enjoy the ride.

She encircled him with her hands, then her lips. He watched until he began to lose control. After that, he just closed his eyes and focused on the moment of climax. It came—and so did he—bucking where he sat and groaning aloud.

Sweet Georgia was as good as her promise. She'd taken care of him all right. He was sated and limp and putty in her hands. She went into an adjoining bathroom to wash up, then came back to relieve her curiosity.

She'd done plenty of jobs for Stuart before, but never anything like she'd done to Benny Colorado. And because the request had been unique, she was curious. What had Colorado done for Stuart to want to ruin him?

"Stuart, baby, can I ask you a question?"

His smile was lazy as he leaned back in the chair, watching as she cleaned him up.

"As if I could deny you," he growled, and threaded his hand through her long, curly hair.

Revolted by his touch, it was all she could do to keep smiling.

"You know that guy you had me total in Vegas?"

Stuart grinned, thinking what an apt description that was. Benny Colorado *had* been totaled—in every way that counted.

"Yes, what about him?"

"Out of curiosity, why? What did he do to you?"

Joseph grinned. "Nothing."

When she saw the evil in his grin, she shuddered. "You broke his spirit for nothing?"

"Not for nothing. For me."

"For you?"

"He's my link to perfect health. He has access to something you wouldn't believe."

"And that would be?"

"A miracle cure. His brother knows a place that can heal me."

"Well, I'll be," she mumbled.

The only good thing about what he'd just said was that she didn't have to hide her shock. Stuart had finally gone around the bend. He was searching for miracles? She arched an eyebrow in disbelief. "Hell, honey, remind me not to ever piss you off. You destroyed a man for an impossible dream."

Stuart grinned. "It isn't an impossibility. You'll

see. They'll all see. Soon I will be one hundred percent cured."

She nodded. "That's just great, Stuie. Meantime, there's a little matter of money still between us."

Stuart swiveled around to his desk, produced a checkbook, and wrote out a check for an exorbitant amount of money. In fact, it was five thousand dollars above the amount they'd agreed upon.

Georgia's eyes widened as she saw the amount. When he handed it over, she gave it a swift kiss before putting it in her purse.

"Thanks, Stuie, baby," she said softly, and gave his lap a final pat.

"No, thank you," he said, coughing slightly as the muscles in his chest began to weaken. As much as he hated to admit it, he'd exerted himself a bit too much.

Disgust for this man hit her square in the face and it was all she could do not to slap him away.

He caught her hand and then lifted it to his lips, licking the center of her palm.

The oxygen tube got tangled on one of her rings and his lips felt as dry as old paper. She bit her lower lip to keep from gagging.

"I've got to be going," she said. "Got a plane to catch, you know."

Stuart turned her loose with great regret. He would have liked a second helping of that generous red mouth.

"I'll let myself out," Georgia said, and then did so with haste.

She was still shuddering. Even after she was in the cab and on her way back to the airport, she couldn't get over what had happened to him. A search for perfect health? Miracle cures? He was crazy. From where she was standing, Stuart Rossi was already dead. He just didn't know it.

Raine woke up with her blouse wadded up beneath her breasts and her jeans twisted around her legs. She rolled over and sat up with a frown, trying to remember why she'd gone to sleep in her clothes. But when she glanced at the table and the typewriter she'd borrowed from Joseph, she remembered.

Her story! Another run-through on editing and she would be through. She couldn't wait to put it on the editor's desk. It was good and she knew it.

She rolled out of bed and headed for the shower, stripping off her clothes as she went. If she hurried, she could have it on his desk before noon today.

Once inside the bathroom, she peeked out the window. Joseph's pickup was nowhere in sight. There was a spark of disappointment as she stepped into the shower. She'd wanted to show him the finished product before she turned it in. But then she shook off the thought. He'd see it soon enough when it came out in print.

She turned on the water and then squeezed a handful of shampoo into her hand before stepping into the spray, scrubbing absently as she mentally reviewed her list of things to do.

A few minutes later she stepped out onto the bath mat and reached for a towel, wrapping one around her head and the other beneath her arms. But as she dragged the towel across her breasts, she winced and then frowned.

That hurt.

She dropped the towel and then stepped before the mirror, giving herself a quick self-examination. No lumps were evident, and yet she'd felt a distinct discomfort. She stared at herself before the mirror, thinking back over the past few weeks and trying to remember if she'd had similar symptoms and ignored them. Nothing came to mind.

She shrugged, then opened the drawer and reached for her brush and got the box of tampons instead.

"Good grief," she muttered, and shoved them aside as she dug deeper toward the back of the drawer to retrieve the big brush.

One stroke, two strokes, the scent of the herbal shampoo drifted around her head, easing the tension in her neck. She kept reminding herself that the past month and a half had been hell. It was no wonder her head was hurting. Surely a person could have a headache without the world's coming to an end.

When the tangles were all gone, she reached for the blow dryer, then turned it on low. And, she reminded herself, headaches were nothing new for her. They came with monthly cramps and—

Suddenly, she froze.

"Oh, God."

The hairbrush fell from her fingers, clattering loudly as it ricocheted from the cabinet onto the floor.

"Oh, God, no," she muttered, staring at her body as the blood drained from her face.

She dropped the towel and raced into the other room, digging through her purse for her checkbook and the calendar that came attached.

She counted once, twice, then three times, and each time she kept coming up with the same forty-six days. Forty-six days since she'd had a monthly period. More than thirty of those days she'd spent in Joseph's bed having unprotected sex because for her, it didn't matter. They'd told her the day the baby was born that she wouldn't get pregnant again. But until she'd come back to Oracle, she'd never tested the theory. What if they'd been wrong?

Dear merciful God, she couldn't be pregnant.

She was going to die.

Joseph put the last clip on the fence post in place and tossed the wire stretchers into the back of his truck.

"Hey, Benny, hand me those pliers, will you? I don't want to leave them lying out here in the field. I'd never find them again."

"Yeah, sure," Benny said, and tossed them over the bed of the truck.

"Thanks," Joseph mumbled, already focusing on what he had left to do today.

He glanced at his watch. It was after two. They hadn't gone home for lunch, but it wasn't the first time they'd stayed out. And Raine was probably still so wrapped up in her story that she never even missed them.

"You got time to help me fix that old wooden gate?" Joseph asked.

Benny paused. Joseph was trying so hard to do everything right.

"Sure," he said. "That's what we're out here for, right?"

Joseph nodded. Benny was changing, and for the most part, for the good.

"I sure appreciate it," Joseph said. "Time was when I'd have to wrestle all of this stuff by myself."

Benny's heart ache grew. He looked at his brother and then looked away. *Say it. Just say it now and it will be all right.*

"Raine was sure excited over her interview, wasn't she?"

Benny nodded as he slid into the truck cab.

Joseph glanced at him and then started the engine. "Do you like her?"

"Who? Raine?"

He nodded.

"Lord, yes, what's not to like? She's pretty. She's sweet, and she puts up with my stuff."

Joseph nodded. "Yeah, that's it, isn't it? She puts up with our stuff."

Benny took off his hat and rolled down the window as they started to move, relishing the blast of air through his sweat-drenched hair.

"You know, if I'm getting in your way, all you

have to do is just say so. I can find myself a place in town, or better yet, I guess I could head on back to L.A."

"No!" Joseph said, and then took a deep breath, trying to calm the spurt of panic that had come with the words. "No way. This is your home as much as it's mine, Benjamin. No matter who comes or goes in our lives, we will always be brothers."

Benny managed a grin and then quickly looked away, unwilling for Joseph to see the tears in his eyes. Brother? He felt more like a traitor.

They didn't speak of Raine again until they were heading for home, and only then after they topped the hill to see that her car was gone.

"Wonder where she's gone?" Benny asked.

"If she finished her story, probably into Tucson to turn it in."

"Oh, yeah," Benny said, and the moment passed.

It wasn't until they walked into the kitchen nearly an hour later and saw her note on the cabinet that Joseph started to worry. The writing was sketchy. Just two words here, three words there, strung together without commas, leaving him to decipher it as best as he could.

*One o'clock*
*Going to*

Here she'd scratched out the next three words, then started over.

*Tucson.*
*Back later*

*Me.*

"Don't you think it's getting kinda late?" Benny asked.

Joseph dropped the note and then walked to the window. Long blue shadows from the trees and shrubs crisscrossed the yard like a geometric design. The sun was hovering just above the horizon, as if waiting for a plug to be pulled. Just as he was turning around, the sudden, shrill peal of the phone made both brothers jump.

"That's probably her now," Joseph said, and grabbed it before it had a second chance to sound off.

"Hello?"

"Joseph, this is Dr. Stanton. Remember me from the hotel fire?"

Joseph's belly knotted. Instinctively, he backed up against the wall, bracing himself.

"Yes, I remember you," Joseph said. And then, before the doctor could answer, he heard the subdued rumble of a woman's voice in the background, and the soft, plaintive wail of a woman in distress. "What happened to Raine?"

The doctor frowned and looked back at the woman on his examining table. Except for the fact that she was pregnant, he'd like to know the answer to that himself.

"She's in my office. It's in what used to be the old Turner grocery store. Do you know where that's located?"

"Yes. What's wrong with her? Was she in an accident?"

"No, no accident," he said thoughtfully. "But I think you'd better come get her. She's in no condition to drive."

Joseph hung up the phone and reached for his hat.

"What's wrong?" Benny asked.

"Something's wrong with Raine," he said. "That was a doctor. He said she was in no condition to drive."

Benny felt in his pocket for his car keys. "I'll take you," he said quickly. "That way you can drive her car home. Save us both a trip later on."

Joseph nodded his thanks, and a short while later, they entered the city limits of Oracle, afraid of what they'd find when they got to the doctor's office. Moments later, Joseph was out of the car before Benny had come to a complete stop.

"Want me to come inside?" Benny asked.

Joseph shook his head. "No need. I'll see you back at the ranch. We'll talk then."

Benny nodded and drove off, but Joseph was already at the door. The clinic was obviously closed for the day, but he could see lights and people inside. He rattled the knob and then lifted his fist, knocking loudly for them to let him in.

Raine hadn't moved or spoken in over an hour. Not since the doctor had given her the news. She sat huddled in a stiff, plastic chair, staring down at her shoes and wondering how she'd gotten that big scratch on the left toe. In the back of her mind, she could hear knocking and shouting outside, but she wouldn't let herself think—wouldn't let herself focus. If she did, she would surely go insane.

"That will probably be Mr. Colorado," the doctor said and then nodded for his nurse to let him in.

Joseph burst inside, his heart in his mouth, expecting to see Raine on a stretcher, or at best, bandaged in some terrible way. But there she sat, alone in that small plastic chair, apparently without a scratch.

"Doctor?"

The doctor shrugged. "She's not ill."

"Then what?" Joseph asked.

Dr. Stanton looked down at Raine. It was her story to tell.

"Other than the fact that she's gotten some unexpected news, I think she's fine."

"What news?" Joseph asked.

"Maybe if you get her home in more comfortable surroundings, she'd feel like talking."

Joseph's heart skipped a beat. Talking? She wasn't talking? He knelt in front of her touched her cheek, then her hair, before taking her hands in his.

"Raine . . . sweetheart, can you tell me what's wrong?"

When she heard his voice, she jerked. Joseph was here? He couldn't be here because he was supposed to be there. She closed her eyes. It was too much to bear.

Joseph was starting to get scared. "Raine, talk to

me, honey. You can tell me anything. I love you, forever and ever, remember?"

She started to cry. That was just it. Forevers meant nothing if they were over tomorrow.

Joseph couldn't stand to see her tears. He reached for her purse.

"Come on, sweetheart. I need your keys. We'll go home where it's safe. Then we'll talk, okay?"

She shook her head, spilling tears from both corners of her eyes.

"Can't run. Can't hide. Still coming." Then she took a shuddering breath and looked up. "Oh, God, Joseph, oh, God."

Her despair was frightening—and it was catching. He was starting to get scared.

"Raine, talk to me, honey. I can't help you if you won't tell me what's wrong."

She blinked so slowly he thought she was falling asleep, but the words that came out of her mouth were like a nightmare. One from which he might never awake.

"Murder."

He inhaled sharply and then glanced up at the doctor.

Stanton shook his head, as if to say he knew nothing about it.

Joseph touched her arm, trying to connect with the woman he loved. "No one was murdered, Rainbow."

"Not yet," she mumbled. "But they will be."

The skin crawled on the back of his neck. "Raine, please, what are you trying to say?"

"The baby's going to die."

He rocked back on his heels in disbelief. "But sweetheart, the baby is already dead. It died twelve years ago, remember?"

"No, not that one," she moaned and grabbed his hand and slammed it on her belly. "This one."

Joseph's eyes widened and his heart began to soar. She'd said it couldn't happen, but as God was his witness, he'd never been so happy about a mistake in his entire life.

"You're going to have a baby?" he asked.

She covered her face with her hands, unable to answer. The doctor stepped in.

"Yes, she's not very far along, but she's definitely pregnant. I'm guessing you're going to be a father about April of next year."

Before Joseph could voice his delight, Raine stood up.

"No one is listening to me," she screamed. "There's not going to be any baby. There can't be. According to five of Chicago's best neurologists, I have less than four months to live. I'm dying, damn it. And oh, God, the baby will die with me."

## 16

It should have been a nightmare. Instead, Joseph drove home with a calm Raine couldn't believe. She kept telling herself that he surely must care, but he was behaving like a man in a trance. *Denial*, she thought. She knew all about denial. But her denial days were long over. Once the shock of her news had worn off, she was about as angry with God as a person could get.

It wasn't fair. Why did some people lead charmed lives while others dodge constant bullets from hell until they breathed their last breaths? She sat on her side of the car, wrapped in fury and unwilling to share anything with Joseph, including her grief. She was shaking so hard it was all she could do to sit straight. But she wasn't willing to suffer in silence any more. God wasn't listening to her prayers, and Joseph was behaving as if he didn't give a damn. But Raine cared. She had something to say, whether anyone chose to listen or not.

"It wasn't enough that he took our first baby." Then she hit her knee with her fist, all but screaming her words at him. "I don't know what game God's playing with me, but I don't care anymore. I'm through trying to outguess him. I'm sick and tired of being slapped down every time I turn a corner. I quit! He can't hurt me anymore, because I don't give a damn!"

Joseph didn't answer. At this point, she wasn't ready to hear what he had to say. He parked the car and then killed the engine.

"We're home, Raine."

"No, you're home," she said sharply. "I'm just passing through."

He grabbed her by the arm. "Stop it! Stop it right now. If your aneurysm is as volatile as the doctors say it is, you're asking for it to blow."

Panic shafted, and then she thought, *Why prolong the misery?* She got out of the car and started waving her arms up at the sky.

"So what?" She kicked at the ground, stirring dirt knee-high on her clothes, then she picked up a rock and threw it upward as hard as she could throw. "What are You waiting for?" she screamed. "What's up? Planning on waiting until the baby starts moving inside me before you pull the plug. If I'm lucky, maybe I'll be conscious long enough to know for sure when it dies."

Joseph groaned. She was out of control. He had to tell her and tell her now. Whether she was ready to hear it or not. He grabbed her by the arm and turned her around to face him.

"Shut up! You're only hurting yourself," he growled.

"You don't—"

"No," he growled. "You don't!"

Raine's fury sputtered. She'd never seen Joseph this angry before, especially with her. But he didn't have a right to be angry. She was the one who was losing everything. But the longer she stood and the longer she stared at him, the more convinced she became that she was wrong. Joseph was losing, too. And what's worse, he was going to be the one left behind.

She took a deep, shuddering breath and stopped. There were tears drying on her face and circles under her eyes. Her clothes were disheveled and her shoes were dusty, but there was a strength on his face that gave her courage.

"Then you tell me," she whispered. "You make me understand. You give me a reason not to hate, because for the life of me, I don't have the strength to do it on my own."

He pulled her into his arms and just held her, rocking her where she stood as if she were a very small child.

"It will be okay," he kept saying. "I can make this all right."

She started to laugh, but the sounds came out broken and turned into more tears.

"It's not okay and you can't make this right. No one can make this right. I have a inoperable time bomb ticking inside my head and a baby growing inside my belly." She shuddered and then pressed her fingers against her lips to keep from moaning aloud.

"My babies," she whispered. "Why do I keep killing my babies?"

Joseph groaned. "No, sweetheart, no. You're not to blame." He hugged her close, smoothing back her flyaway hair and rubbing at the knots of tension he could feel in her shoulders. When she grew very quiet, he leaned closer, whispering softly against her ear.

"How much do you trust me?"

Raine froze. The question didn't fit the scenario. "I'd say with my life, but right now it's not worth all that much."

He leaned back and cupped her face with his hands, unwilling to let her look away.

"If I told you I could save you and the baby, would you come with me? Would you do as I say?"

The expression on her face blanked. And she thought she'd gone over the edge.

"Joseph. You're talking crazy. The aneurysm is inoperable. It's just a matter of time before it—"

"You're not listening to me," he said. "I asked you a question. If I told you I could save you and the baby, would you come with me? Would you do as I say?"

She frowned. There was a calmness within him that made no sense. But he'd asked her a question she could answer. In a way, it was easy because she had nothing to lose.

"I will go where you take me. I will do as you say."

A muscle was working in his throat as he closed his eyes and pulled her close.

"We leave in the morning before dawn."

"Where are we going?" she asked.

"To the mountain that embraces the sun."

Benny knew something was wrong. He'd heard them fighting out in the driveway. Later, after they'd come inside, he could still hear an occasional sob coming from her room.

Joseph had come out long enough to ask Benny to take care of the ranch. Benny quickly agreed, but his heart skipped a beat.

"Is it Raine . . . is she sick?" he asked.

At first Joseph didn't answer. Benny watched the expressions changing on his brother's face.

*Say it, Joseph. Spit it out. Dear God, can't you just once tell me the truth?*

Then Joseph sighed and looked away.

"She's pregnant," he said quietly. "The news unsettled her, that's all."

Benny frowned. *You lie.* "Are you going to marry her?"

"If she'll have me."

*Then she has nothing to cry about.* But all he did was nod.

No woman screamed at the top of her lungs and threw rocks at God because she was pregnant.

"Is that where you're going tomorrow . . . to get married, I mean?"

Joseph shook his head. "No. We're not getting married tomorrow."

Benny managed a smile. "Good. I may not be the best man for the job, but I would like to be your best man."

Joseph smiled and at that moment, the bond they'd been born with seemed real.

"It's a deal," Joseph said. "Talk to you when we get back."

"You can take my car if you'd rather drive it than your truck."

Unaware that he was being set up, Joseph answered truthfully.

"No need. We're only going as far as Tucson. After that, we'll take the chopper."

Benny's eyes narrowed. *I knew it.* "Safe trip, then," he said shortly.

"I'd better get back to Raine," Joseph said.

Benny nodded. "Good night."

"Yeah, little brother, it is a good night," Joseph said, and then he was gone.

Benny went back in his own room, his mind spinning with questions. Joseph was leaving again, and in the chopper. It had something to do with Raine's pregnancy, all right, but there was something else involved, he just knew it. Why else would she have gone to the doctor and then become too distraught to drive?

He thought of the wounds on Joseph's leg that had miraculously healed overnight, and of the strangers who'd knocked on their door and then never came back. Instinct warned him that this was what Stuart Rossi had been waiting for. This was his chance to get out from under the debt. All he had to do was make one quick phone call. It wasn't as if he was putting anyone at risk. He just wanted Rossi off of his back.

But what about Raine? She was a great girl and had been through a lot. What if his phone call put her in jeopardy? He sat on the edge of the bed, wrestling with his devil until long after midnight. In the end, Benny's fears outweighed his conscience. He picked up the phone and made the call.


Stuart was flat on his back and sound asleep in his bed. The remote control was beside his pillow, although there was nothing left on the screen but what Edward called ant races. The snowy pattern fizzed and buzzed in a steady monotone—a perfect accompaniment to Stuart's occasional snore. Somewhere in another part of the house, a phone began to ring, but Stuart didn't hear. He was dreaming about women with hourglass figures and double-E breasts.

It wasn't until Edward came racing down the hall with a portable in his hand that he began to rouse. When Edward burst into his room without knocking, Stuart started to curse.

"What the hell do you think you're—"

"It's Mr. Colorado, sir. He says it's urgent."

He grabbed the phone out of Edward's hand.

"This better be good," he growled.

"He's taking the chopper up tomorrow—early. Other than that, I have no new information."

Stuart frowned. "Maybe he's just going for a joyride, you fool. Didn't you ask him?"

"No one was laughing," Benny said. "Something is wrong, but they won't tell me what. Now you wanted to know when he left in it again, and damn it, I'm telling you. I've betrayed his trust. After this, we're even, do you hear me?"

Stuart's eyes narrowed angrily. "You aren't calling the shots, boy, I am. And I'm telling you to be ready in the morning."

Benny frowned. "Ready for what?"

"A ride. Wherever Joseph goes, I go, and until I get what I paid for, you're going along, too."

Benny groaned. "That wasn't part of the deal. What if Joseph sees me?"

"So I'm changing the deal," Stuart said. "And if you're lying to me, it won't matter whether or not your big brother sees you, because I'll tell him anyway. Do we understand each other?"

Benny closed his eyes and bowed his head. "Yes."

"Good," Stuart said. "You'll be picked up no later than eight A.M."

"How will we know where he goes?" Benny asked.

Stuart smiled. He'd already thought of that. "His chopper is bugged."

Gorge rose in the back of Benny's throat. Dear God, what had he done?

"What if he doesn't leave on time?" Benny asked.

"I'm not a patient man, Colorado. You'd better pray that he does."

When the line went dead in Benny's ear, he wanted to cry. He kept telling himself to get up now. All he had to do was walk across the hall and confess.

And then lose everything he'd come to cherish.

He dropped the phone back on the cradle, then curled up in a ball on the bed. He closed his eyes and began to shake, but sleep wouldn't come. Instead, he lay facing the window, staring into the darkness until his eyes began to burn and his head was one big ache.

Just after daybreak he heard footsteps outside his door and rolled out of bed. This was it! This was his chance! Tell him now before it was too late!

He dashed across the floor. By the time he opened the door there was no one there. He stepped out in the hall, calling Joseph's name just as a lock clicked in the front part of the house.

*Oh no. They're already outside.*

He grabbed his jeans, running as he put them on.

An engine started.

*Wait, Joseph, wait!* While his mind was screaming, he was dodging tables and chairs, trying to get to the front door. Less than ten feet from his objective, he tripped, falling into an ungainly sprawl on the living room floor.

Someone had just shifted gears.

"Joseph! Wait!" he yelled, scrambling to his feet and yanking open the door.

He saw them then, halfway down the driveway

and disappearing in a cloud of dust. His shoulders slumped. All his good intentions were wasted. He'd left it too long.

He watched until there was nothing left to mark their passing but the faint odor of dust. Then he went back in the house and shut the door. He would have to hurry now. If Rossi made good on his promise, he would be here within the hour. Benny didn't know where, and he didn't know how, but now it was up to him to protect whatever it was that his brother held dear.

Raine stood beside Joseph's truck, watching as he went through a preflight check of the waiting aircraft. She kept trying to picture herself inside that thing with Joseph at the controls, then flying too far away to be found.

It would be her salvation, because she was convinced that Joseph had lost touch with reality. Every time she'd pushed him for answers, his only response was a question.

Did she trust him?

Yes.

Then she had a silent question of her own.

Did she trust herself?

No.

A slash of midmorning sun cut through the hangar window and into her eyes. She winced and turned away, and when she did, felt the ground tilt at her feet.

She shaded her eyes and looked away. A low throbbing was beginning right behind her eyes, pushing and pushing, spreading like spilled water across a kitchen floor.

Headache? Dizzy?

They were the beginning of a series of symptoms the doctor had warned her might come. Oh, there were others. Her favorite had been the last doctor's warning—more of a promise, actually—that she wouldn't feel a thing. It would be a "here one second, gone the next" type of death. If she believed in God, a nonstop ticket to infinity.

And then she made herself calm. What if she was just borrowing trouble? She'd had the occasional headache all her life, and slight aches and pains, and head rushes of all kinds. They hadn't killed her then; what made her think that today was the day? Besides, she reminded herself, they'd promised her four more months.

At this point, her pulse skipped a beat. But, she reminded herself, she hadn't been pregnant when the promise had been made. She knew what drastic changes a woman's body would make during pregnancy, not the least of which was a change in blood pressure.

She glanced back toward the chopper. Her headache was getting worse by the moment, and Joseph was nowhere in sight. Panic seized her. She didn't want to die alone out on an airport runway. She took a step forward and it felt as if the world turned half a notch off center.

"No," she muttered, and grabbed hold of his truck and held on.

"Joseph!"

She waited for him to appear. Now beads of sweat were beginning to run down her forehead and down the middle of her back. Fear had hold of her legs and wouldn't let her go.

She glanced back at the hangar and frowned. It was getting dark. Must be a storm. That meant they wouldn't be flying. She looked up at the sky, expecting to see a mass of great thunderheads gathering overhead. But it was clear, as far as she could see.

Her pulse began to hammer. Oh, God, it wasn't the day that was growing dim, it was her vision.

"Jooossseepphh!"

The scream that came out of her brought everyone running. She saw Joseph emerging from inside the hangar and knew a swift sense of peace. She reached for him.

Moments later, he caught her, then lifted her up. Frozen with fear, he kept calling her name, but she was too far away to answer.

Joseph had never been afraid before. Not like this. Oh, there had been times when he'd worried that the families who'd asked for his help had waited too long to bring a loved one to him, but he'd never flown with the fear that was inside him now. Raine was his woman, his life. She was carrying his child, and she was dying.

He glanced at her face.

She was too pale. Too quiet.

"Raine!"

She didn't answer.

"Raine, can you hear me?"

She didn't move.

He looked up at the sky and the sun moving toward its daily zenith, then back at the horizon, frantically searching for the landmarks that would tell him he was almost there. His heart was heavy, his mind shot with a panic he couldn't name. A single phrase kept running over and over through his mind.

*Don't let her die. Don't let her die.*

But he didn't know who he was praying to—the ancients who'd come out of the sky, or God who'd created them all. The healing place was mixed up in his mind with God's benevolence and all-healing powers. The legend claimed another race of people had come to the mountains that embraced the sun, but could it have been angels instead?

Something brushed past his cheek and he turned, his eyes wide with panic.

"Raine! Can you hear me?"

She didn't move. Didn't speak. Had that been her spirit? Was she already dead?

Before he had answers, his destination suddenly loomed to the west.

"Thank God," he whispered.

Like an eagle diving for prey, Joseph Colorado took the chopper in through the arms of the mountain, landing at the base of its breast.

Within seconds of setting down, he was out and reaching for Raine. Thrusting his fingers against the base of her throat, he prayed for a pulse and got it. He looked up. The sun was almost directly overhead. There wasn't much time.

"Raine, I know you can hear me," he said, as he carried her to the base of the wall. "Don't leave me, sweetheart. You promised to trust me, remember?"

He laid her on the ground and began tearing off her clothes, scattering them like a madman. Only after she was as naked as the day she'd been born did he stand. Thrusting the ring into the lock, he counted the seconds as a portion of the rock slid away. Then he spun and scooped her up in his arms and disappeared into the belly of the mountain.

"There, damn it! He went there!" Stuart raged, and pointed toward the valley between two upcoming mountain peaks.

Gunnar Jax, the mercenary Stuart had hired to pilot his chopper, was already responding to the blip on radar, but Stuart was too crazed to notice.

Benny sat hunched in his seat, airsick and heartsick. Stuart had been as good as his word. It was eight minutes after eight when the helicopter had landed in an open area beyond the barns to get him.

Benny had been waiting, and the first words out of his mouth had been a plea that had quickly turned into an argument. Stuart had hit Benny then, first a slap in the face, then in the head with his cane. At

Stuart's instructions, Gunnar had dragged Benny into the chopper and tied him into his seat, then taken off toward Tucson.

They'd been several thousand feet north of the airport and circling when the blip suddenly showed on the screen. Joseph was in the air. After that, they'd been with him all the way.

"He's down," Gunnar shouted.

Stuart cursed. "Hurry, you fool!"

Benny groaned. Just when he thought it couldn't get worse, it was happening.

"Please, Rossi, you have no need to make threats. If there's anything there that can heal, I know my brother. He won't deny you."

"He already has," Stuart snapped. "But he won't this time. I have something he wants. We're going to make a trade."

Benny's heart stopped. Now it made sense. This was why Rossi had insisted he come along. He was planning to use Benny for bait.

"There's the chopper," Gunnar said as he circled over the area. "But I don't see live bodies anywhere."

Benny shuddered. Live bodies. Oh, God. Oh, God.

Stuart started cursing and then coughing. His face was a pale, ashy gray as he leaned back in the seat, forcing himself to stay calm. A few seconds later his skin took on a pinkish hue and he began to relax.

"Set it down there," Stuart said, pointing to a small arroyo a couple of hundred yards from the black Ranger.

Moments later, they were down. At Stuart's command, Gunnar yanked Benny out of the seat and began dragging him toward the other aircraft. From the angle in which they were moving, there was nothing visible but the flat, imposing face of a mountain.

"They're not here," Benny said, unable to hide his relief when the aircraft came up empty.

Stuart spun and hit him across the other cheek with the head of his cane.

"Shut up!" he hissed. "They're here! They have to be here!"

But Benny wouldn't be hushed. Rebellion felt good. He wished he'd tried it weeks ago.

"Yeah, and they're probably skinny-dipping or something. You're gonna look as crazy as you really are when you start talking about miracles."

Gunnar pulled a pistol and jammed it against Benny's cheek. He broke out in a cold sweat. This kept getting worse.

Then Gunnar pushed Benny forward.

"Move," Stuart growled.

He started walking, all too aware of the round, black barrel pointing at the middle of his back.

The air inside the mountain felt colder than Joseph could ever remember, and he wondered if Raine felt the chill. He ran without stopping to check on her condition. At this point, there was nothing he could do to save her except get into the chamber on time.

Last night she had been standing in the middle of his yard and throwing rocks at God for what she viewed as betrayal. Now he knew what had driven her to that end. If he lost her and this baby, he would go mad.

He kept picturing an explosion inside her brain, then every beat of her heart becoming slower than the last. He kept seeing a new life, hardly more than a thought, motionless inside her belly. And he saw himself, with the years stretching out before him, trying to come to terms with their fate.

"No," he gasped. "You can't have her. She's mine."

With what amounted to a last bit of superhuman strength, he threw her over his shoulder in a fireman's carry and began to run.

When he finally burst into the chamber, he laid her in the middle of the floor and then folded her arms across her chest. Once again, he felt for a pulse. It was there, but fainter. He got down on all fours and leaned close to her ear. He didn't know if she could hear him, but if there was a conscious part of her still living, it had to be said.

"Rainbow, I know you can hear me. Now you've got to listen. In a few moments, your healing is going to begin." He cupped her cheeks, speaking directly at her as if she was looking him straight in the face. "If you love me . . . if you ever want to hold this baby you're carrying in your arms, then whatever you do . . . don't open your eyes and don't move. You'll know when it's over. Follow the green lights back to me."

She took a deep breath, and then gave a great sigh.

Joseph stared, waiting for another to follow. It didn't come.

"No!" he groaned, and grabbed her neck with his fingers, frantically searching for a pulse. There was none there. "No, damn it, no!" he screamed, and bolted to his feet.

Seconds later, he thrust the ring into the niche, waiting only long enough to see the first ray of sunlight piercing the stone at her head.

Then he ran.


"Where the hell could they—"

"There!" Gunnar shouted, pointing as Joseph suddenly appeared out of nowhere.

For a moment, the trio stared in shock, unable to believe what they'd seen. One minute they'd been staring at what appeared to be solid rock and then Joseph was on his knees in the dirt.

They watched as he scooped up a handful of earth and then stood. When he lifted his arm to the east and began to chant, Stuart's eyes narrowed.

"By God, I was right! He's performing some ritual. And where's the woman? You said he took a woman with him?"

"I don't know," Benny said. "She was with him when they left the ranch."

Benny glanced at Rossi. Rossi was so taken with what Joseph was doing, this might be his chance.

Whatever happened, Benny had already decided he wasn't going to be the pawn.

Joseph saw them as the last of the earth ran from his fingers. And when he saw Benny, the look on his face said it all.

*This is it,* Benny thought, and hit the pilot in the back of the neck with both fists.

"Run, Joseph, run!" he screamed, waving his arms at his brother as he ran, in a last-ditch effort to stop what was already coming undone.

Joseph hesitated briefly, then took a dive toward the skids of his helicopter, flattening against an unexpected onslaught of gunfire.

But there was only one short burst, and it was Benny who went down.

"No, dear God, no," Joseph groaned, and was on his knees and crawling toward Benny before his brother stopped falling.

When Stuart saw Joseph Colorado crawling into the line of fire, he panicked. If they were dead, who would show him how to be healed?

"Stop! Stop! For God's sake, don't shoot," he cried, and hit Gunnar Jax across both arms with the head of his cane.

The gun fell to the ground with a thump. Cursing with pain, Gunnar swung at Stuart with a double-edged knife.

"Rossi, you crazy son of a bitch! No one hits me and gets away with it."

Stuart fell back against the chopper, then down on the skids. The oxygen tube had fallen out of his nose. His skin was losing color and he was gasping for air.

"I didn't give the order to shoot!" Stuart hissed, then grabbed the gun from the ground and shot the man where he stood.

He didn't think about who would pilot the chopper or how he'd get home. Nothing mattered except
ridding himself of his afflictions. Something warm ran
down his arm and onto the back of his hand. He
looked down, puzzled by the unfamiliar sensation.

Oh, damn. Gunnar Jax's knife.

Blood was dripping from the ends of his fingers
and onto the ground.

Steady. Flowing. Red.

Red like Georgia Farley's lips.

It kept dripping and dripping and dripping. His
treatments. He'd been letting them slide. Treatment. It
was a stupid thing to call it. Bloodsucker would be
more apt. Stuart might have been a blue blood when
he was born, but he'd had so many treatments of
plasma that he was now a conglomerate. A real mutt
in the truest sense of the word.

He looked back at the blood, then at the oxygen
tank on the ground and started to laugh. It didn't
matter now. He was safe. He couldn't choke on his
own spit. He wouldn't bleed out on the floor of this
Arizona mountain. All he had to do was get inside the
cave and he would be cured.

He started to run, his heart hammering irregu-
larly, his breath coming in fits and jerks. But no matter
how he tried to pace himself, the oxygen tank he was
dragging kept hindering his steps. In a fit of anger, he
ripped the tube from his nose, tossed it aside with the
discarded tank, and headed toward the mountain with
blind intent. His focus was starting to cloud as he
stumbled toward the place where Joseph had emerged.

Ten steps. Nine steps. Eight, then seven, and suddenly it was there! He could see it now! The dark slit in the wall that looked to be more shadow than truth. Salvation was in there. He knew it.

He didn't hear Joseph shouting. He didn't hear the strange roar that kept gathering energy. He was too busy following Wynema Littlefish's image. It kept dancing before him, beckoning him onward, showing him the way.


Benny groaned and then coughed. A thin stream of pure red suddenly emerged at both sides of his mouth, and when he tried to speak, he choked on his own blood instead.

Joseph looked toward the opening, but the air was already shifting, stirring, thickening. A high-pitched hum had begun to pour from the mountain. Raine was not breathing when he left her. He knew the chamber healed, but would it bring someone back from the dead?

He leaned over his brother's body, sheltering him in the only way he knew how, but Benny's eyes were glazing. Fear engulfed him, leaving a cold, bitter taste in his mouth. After all of these centuries, after all of the care to protect the great gift the People had been given, it had come to this.

Benny moaned, and Joseph cradled him as he would have a child.

"Cold," Benny whispered.

Joseph pulled him into his lap. His voice was

shaking, his eyes blurred with tears.

"Here you go, buddy. Stay close to me. I'll keep you warm."

Benny exhaled slowly, and it sounded to Joseph as if all the life in his body went out in the sigh.

"Joseph . . . sorry. So sorry."

Joseph shook his head and laid his face against the back of his brother's head.

"I know you are, Benny. It's okay. It's okay."

Benny's eyes closed. Slowly. Peacefully. It was finally okay.

Joseph felt his brother go limp. Even then, he couldn't bring himself to look. Instead, he threw his head back and let out a great cry of despair. It was too late. It was all too late.


*Raine, I know you can hear me.*

Bathed in the bright white of peace, Raine paused and then turned. Behind her she could hear Joseph saying her name.

*Yes, I can hear you,* she thought. But she didn't call out to him. The urge to keep moving was strong . . . so strong.

*Don't leave me. Don't leave me.*

Again, Raine turned, this time frowning. What was wrong with him? Didn't he understand? She had to go. She was on the way home.

She looked toward the light. It was brighter now, more focused. It took her a moment to realize that she was moving away, not toward it.

No. No. Don't send me back.

And then a knowing came upon her. She heard a voice, and knew love, and felt peace.

*"It isn't your time."*

It was then she let go, turning back to the sound of Joseph's voice. She could still hear him in the distance, begging her to trust him, telling her it would be all right.

She started to move. He needed to know what was happening to her. He needed to know he'd been right.

Stuart could see it ahead of him—a massive green light, pulsating, spinning, a mythological siren singing a song of destruction. Blood was coming out his nose now, and from his ears, and around his teeth. His bones were shattering as he dragged himself along, inch by painful inch. The skin on his arms was blistering and bursting and blistering again. But he didn't know, didn't care. The glow from the cavern had become his Holy Grail.

And then he was there, standing in the doorway to what he believed to be heaven. The woman was flat on her back. Suspended between the floor and the ceiling with nothing in between and pierced through and through with thousands of thin verdant spears; tiny laserlike wands of bright light.

Stuart trembled with awe. Wynema. This is what cured her. This is what took her afflictions away. He reached into the chamber, shaking with joy as the first of the translucent green rays pierced his hand.

Healed. He was going to be healed. He walked the rest of the way in, holding out his arms and tilting his head back so that every part of his body would be swept clean of the infectious debris.

He saw them coming; cleansing—sweeping— green slashes of power. He was still smiling when they burned out his eyes. And when he started to scream, his tongue turned to ashes. Then his heart, then his lungs, then all that he was turned to dust.

He had been, but he was no more. In the space of a heartbeat, Stuart Rossi had ceased to exist.

The sun had moved from its zenith and was angling westward. Joseph had been at the entrance to the tunnel for over an hour. He hadn't moved and he couldn't have spoken to save his soul. He'd cried for his brother. But he wouldn't let go of Raine. He wouldn't let himself believe that she was dead now. He couldn't face the world without her in his arms.

Her clothes were dangling from his hands; colored swatches of fabric that he'd torn off of her in distress, and that he was now waiting for her to come claim. His brother's blood had dried on his arms and on his chest and there was a finger-wide streak on his forehead above his nose.

There was a dark, savage look to his appearance that colored the truth. He was no savage. Never had a man shown more compassion than Joseph had on this day, and yet he stood alone, waiting for his miracle. Here in the sacred place of the People and encircled by the spirits of those who'd gone before him, he was Apache—guardian of the healing place—keeper of the secret of the mountains that embrace the sun. And a man without his mate.

*For her. I'm waiting for her.*

Her cheeks were wet. She reached up and touched them then, brushing her fingers across her lips as her brows arched in surprise.

Tears? It didn't make sense. She didn't feel like crying. In fact, she felt like singing.

She sat up and then frowned.

*I'm not wearing clothes. Why am I not wearing clothes?*

She stood, looking at her surroundings with renewed curiosity.

She was inside a cave that branched off to a tunnel. And as she stood staring around in confusion and waiting for Joseph to appear, she had a vague recollection of hearing his voice, of him begging her to come back. She wrapped her arms around herself and shuddered.

*Come back? Where did I go?*

She took a step forward, only then realizing that the floor on which she was standing felt strange. Nothing was sharp, but it was very irregular, like a cobblestone path made of glass.

*When it's over, follow the green lights to me.*

She spun, expecting to see Joseph. It was his

voice. But he was nowhere in sight. The urge to find him was strong and she moved toward the opening, feeling, as much as seeing, her way through the faint, glowing light.

*Do you trust me?*

"Yes, I trust you," she whispered, and then jumped when she heard her own voice. It echoed strangely, as if she was hearing herself speaking from a long distance off.

She reached out, tracing the shape of the green crystal embedded in the wall, then fixing her sight on the next one a short distance ahead.

"Okay, I'm following the lights. But where are you, Joseph, where are you?"

Even before he saw her, he heard her calling his name.

"Here!" he shouted, and moved closer to the entrance. "I'm here!"

Moments later she burst into the sunlight and leaped into his arms, smiling and crying and clinging to him as if he might disappear.

"I couldn't find you," she kept saying. "I called and I called."

Her body was cool and her spirit was strong. He kept running his hands up and down her arms and then tangling them in her hair.

"I'm sorry, Rainbow, I'm sorry. I could take you in, but you had to be the one to come out. Here, let's get you dressed, okay? We can talk on the way back."

He handed her the clothes, one item at a time. It

wasn't until she sat down to put on her shoes that she saw the tarp-covered body on the other side of the chopper. Her smile stilled and she pointed.

"Joseph?"

He didn't have to look to know what she was asking. Even after living with the knowledge for two hours now, his voice still shook from the pain.

"It's Benny."

Shocked, she got to her feet, barely able to ask. "Benny? How did he get here? What happened?"

"What do you remember?"

"Practically nothing. The airport. I had a headache. I remember calling your name, then—"

She froze, her eyes widening in disbelief.

"Oh." She touched her eyes, then her head, then ran her hands across the flat of her belly. The last thing she remembered was knowing she was going to die.

"Dear God, how did—"

"Don't ask me."

She bit her lip. It hadn't been a request, it had been an order. She remembered his promise. Trust me and I will heal you and your child. Even though she had yet to have a doctor's diagnosis, in her heart she knew it had been done.

"What are we going to do?"

"Hide my brother's body."

The question was on her lips, but she waited.

"There were others here, as well." He pointed to the other chopper, then his voice broke. "He died trying to save me."

"Tell me what you need and I'll do it," Raine said.

Joseph took her in his arms. "I already have what I need. I have you."

But later, she turned away as Joseph lifted Benny's body into his arms. When she looked back, Joseph was walking toward her. His arms were empty, and the opening to the tunnel was gone.

"You better get in now," he said, helping her into the chopper and then buckling her in place. "Wait for me. I'll be right back."

Wait for him? That was a joke. She'd been waiting for him all of her life. She wasn't about to walk out on him now. And then she looked around at the desolation of the place. Where on earth could she possibly go?

A short while later they were airborne and circling high above the other chopper. Joseph kept glancing at his watch. A few moments later, a large ball of orange flame suddenly erupted from the site, sending burning debris in all directions.

"Oh no!" Raine cried. "That helicopter just blew up!"

"Yeah, it did."

She stared at Joseph and suddenly understood.

"It looks like it crashed, doesn't it?" she said.

"That's what they'll think for a while. By the time the FAA figures it out, it won't matter."

"They're all dead, aren't they?" she asked.

He looked back toward the horizon without comment.

Anxious to change the subject, she glanced down at the place they'd just been, looking past the column of black smoke and the burning aircraft.

"Look," she said, pointing below. "That mountain has arms.

There was a terrible sadness within him. He didn't have to look to know what she meant.

"Yes, I've heard them called that before.

She was quiet for a moment, and then she sighed.

"Bad things happened there today."

He nodded again.

"Because of me?"

He reached for her hand. "No, baby. Because of greed."

"Joseph?"

"What?"

"I'm cured, aren't I? I'm not going to die."

Joseph looked at her. There was such hope on her face—such expectation. At least one good thing had come from this day of horrors.

"No, you're not going to die, and yes, you're cured."

Shuddering with an exultation she couldn't quite believe, she had to ask.

"And the baby?"

His voice softened. "The baby will be fine, too."

Tears shimmered across her vision as she shook her head in disbelief.

"I don't understand—but I really don't care. What matters is that it happened." Then she gripped his hand, pulling his attention from the controls to her. "Thank you, my love, more than you will ever know. You did the impossible."

He shook his head. "I did nothing."

Then he slid his sunglasses into place and aimed the black Ranger south.


For three days and nights Joseph wrestled with dreams. Dark dreams in which the spirits of his ancestors hovered over his bed, speaking to him in a tongue he could not understand. Each morning upon awakening, he was left with a feeling of a thing left undone.

Raine knew he was troubled and saddened by the loss of his brother. Yesterday she'd stood beside him at the feed store and listened while he mentioned, as if quite by chance, that he would be missing his brother's presence at the ranch.

The clerk shoved the ticket across the counter for Joseph to sign and shook his head with regret.

"So, he finally made good on his promise to go back to L.A., hunh?"

"L.A.'s sure not my kind of town," Joseph said. "But Benny liked the nightlife."

Raine wouldn't look at his face. She couldn't. The loss was too fresh between them. And so she busied herself by examining her list, thinking to herself that Joseph hadn't really lied. He'd simply stated two facts. He would miss his brother—and he would never live in L.A. More importantly, he'd given the townspeople a reason not to question Benny's absence.

Later that same night Raine turned on the TV and found herself staring at a closeup of a burned-out helicopter. A few moments later, the camera pulled back and then swept the surrounding area, giving the viewers a picture-book look at the mountain that embraces the sun.

"Joseph!" she shouted. "Come quick!"

He came running out of the bathroom, dripping water and wrapping a towel around his waist. Only after he saw that Raine was fine and that her excitement was a result of something on TV, did he relax.

"Damn, Rainbow, you scared me half to death," he muttered, and then flipped water at her nose to make his point.

Ducking the water, she grabbed his hand and pulled him closer to the screen.

"They found it!" she said. "Listen."

Joseph's gaze flew toward the TV. When he saw the skeletal remains of the burned chopper, his belly rolled.

"Although Bel Air billionaire Stuart Damon Rossi's body has yet to be located, the burned-out wreckage of his chartered aircraft was found only hours ago, as was the body of the pilot. Little hope has been given for Rossi's safe return, since the billionaire has been suffering from congestive heart failure for some years now and was dependent on a personal oxygen tank for sustenance.

"Rossi had no heirs, and according to the terms of his will, except for ten thousand dollars to an Edward Belkin, who was his chauffeur, and an original Manet to a woman named Georgia Farley, the bulk of his estate will go to various charities scattered throughout the state of California.

"Stay tuned for . . ."

Joseph turned away. Their search would be hopeless. Even if they knew where to look, they wouldn't find him, because there wasn't enough left of Stuart Rossi to sweep up.

He hit the mute button on the television and then looked at Raine. He didn't know what he expected, but it wasn't the sweet smile on her face. When she held out her hand, he took it instinctively.

"I'm not hungry anymore," she said softly.

"If you don't want to eat, then what do you want to do?" he asked.

"I want you to take me to bed."

Ah, God. How can something so simple make everything all right? He threaded his fingers through hers and then dropped his towel where he stood.

"I don't think I can do that," he said softly, and pulled her into his embrace.

He smelled of lemon soap and her herbal shampoo. She wrapped her arms around his waist and leaned into his bare brown body, all too aware of his growing desire.

"And I'd like to know why not?"

"I think it's too far away."


It was what some people called "the witching hour," the halfway mark between night and day. Raine had rolled toward the edge of the bed. Secure in the knowledge that she was loved and in love, she slept soundly, wrapped up in the sheet and the warmth of her dreams.

Joseph lay flat on his back. One arm was up over his head, the other outstretched toward Raine. Even though he slept without nightclothes or covers, the burden of his duties kept weighing him down.

They surrounded him. They moved through him. Whispering, always whispering. Things he must do. Things not to say.

The muscles in his legs began to twitch, as if his body was trying to follow his mind as it raced with the past.

They were chanting—wailing the same phrase over and over. He began to run, desperate to get close enough to decipher the words, but he couldn't catch up.

The sky began to darken and the wind began to blow. He found himself standing on a precipice and staring down into a valley. They were all around him now, their voices moving in unison, flowing through his mind like fire across a prairie. Louder and louder they cried, shouting the same words over and over, wailing in sorrow at the wrong that had been done.

Joseph answered their cry.

*I did as you asked.*

But they hadn't seemed to hear. Their ancient faces were etched with sorrow. Their mouths wide in mute despair.

*What? Tell me what I need to know.*

Closer and closer they came. He turned now. His back was to the great void beyond the precipice, his attention completely focused on fulfilling his obligations.

From the chaos of voices, one suddenly stood out and he could almost hear what they said.

*Dad? Dad? Is that you?*

As he watched, his father emerged from the swirl of dust and feathers to stand before him. He was there—and yet he was not.

Joseph wanted to hold him, and to be held within the strength of Michael Colorado's embrace. Instead he stood motionless, mute beneath the power of their countenance. Their voices rose in unison.

*The circle is broken.*

Joseph groaned beneath his breath and threw his arm across his eyes.

They inhaled as one and exhaled on a cry.

*The circle is broken.*

Then they moved toward him as one. He felt their tears. He heard their cries. There was a sudden and terrible pain within his body, and then they were gone.

Joseph sat straight up in bed, heart pounding and drenched in sweat.

*What was that? What the hell just happened to me?*

Raine was still beside him, sleeping like an innocent. He groaned silently and started to wipe his face when he realized he was holding something in his hand. Careful not to wake her, he slipped into the bathroom and turned on the light.

The ring! He was holding the ring!

He broke out in a cold sweat, unable to believe his own eyes. This was no accident. That ring wouldn't have come off if he had tried to force it. He closed his fist around it, feeling the shape of it next to his skin and remembering the voices.

*The circle is broken.*

There had been pain when he took it unto him. He inhaled harshly, staring in disbelief. And there had been pain just now when they tore it from his hand. Finally he understood.

The circle was broken.

The healing place was for the living. It was a place for renewed hope and new beginnings, not for lies and deceit.

The circle was broken.

He looked at the ring again.

"Yes," he said softly. "Yes, I understand."

There could be no healing where death had occurred.

He bowed his head. The guardians had spoken.


"I'm afraid for you," Raine said, standing by the truck as Joseph tossed his bag inside the cab. "They're still searching for Rossi. What if someone sees you there?"

But Joseph wouldn't budge from his decision to go into the Superstitions alone. He had no answers

for her questions, but he knew in a way he couldn't
explain that he would be protected. So he told her the
same thing he'd been telling her since his decision had
been made.

"They will not see me."

She threw her arms around his waist, molding
herself to his body.

He tilted her chin, angling it upward until her
mouth was at the perfect angle to kiss. So he did.

"I'll be back."

She leaned against his arms, searching his face for
a reason to panic. His gaze was steady.

"I'll be waiting," she said.

Within minutes he was gone. Raine watched the
road until there was nothing to see and then started
walking toward the rise beyond the barns.

The sun was out. The day was clear. It was a good
day to wade in the water and lie in the shade of big
trees.


The trip was surreal. Every landmark that he flew
over took on new significance. The cluster of red
barns that marked the boundary of Robert Horse's
place. The small grouping of buildings that he knew
to be Oracle. One mountain range after the other he
flew—through narrow passes dark with green, above
low hanging clouds on top of a peak.

He would never come this way again. And even
though he knew he was right in what he was doing,
there was a sadness within him he couldn't express.

Tears wouldn't heal it. Anger wouldn't change it.

A centuries-old legend was about to end.

Joseph felt like a dinosaur who'd outlived his time. He would have to find new direction for his life.

Then he smiled. Not much, just enough to remind himself that his direction had already been set by a long-legged woman who lit up his dark.

Lost in thought and flying by instinct alone, he was startled a while later to see his destination dead ahead.

The green peaks beckoned, as if to say come here . . . stop here . . . this is a good place to rest. And as he had so very many times before, he shoved the control stick forward and sent the black Ranger hurtling toward the face of the mountain that embraces the sun.

Although it was midafternoon, the day was cool. He could see it had rained, but the scent of burned metal and fuel still hung in the air. Joseph chose not to look toward the site. He'd seen it once. There was little to be gained from remembering.

A bird cried from a nearby tree and another answered in the distance. Joseph stopped, then turned, surveying all before him with a careful eye. A strip of yellow crime scene tape had caught in the low branches of a bush and it fluttered in the breeze; a bit of modern civilization that had no business in this place.

His eyes narrowed. His jaw clenched.

*The circle is broken.*

The guardians had been right. The circle of life was broken in this place. Man had come into Eden and tried to change all the rules—again.

Then he frowned. Will we never learn?

The face of the mountain loomed before him. It stood perpendicular to the ground with hardly a slope. Joseph stopped before it, needing to pay homage one last time.

He knelt and took a handful of earth, then stood proudly. Lifting his arm to the sky, he let the Arizona dust flow free.

To the north.

To the east.

To the south.

To the west.

Speaking in the tongue of the People, he made one last prayer. Only this time, it was the mountain in need of repair.

Then, without further delay, he took the ring from his pocket and thrust the green crystal into the lock.

Nothing happened.

The hair rose on the back of his neck. Was it already too late? Then he heard a sound, like the deep groan of something in pain, and the rock slid back, revealing the inside of the mountain's belly.

The tunnel was there, marked by the trail of green light. But there was a new darkness within that had nothing to do with the absence of light. Joseph stood in the opening as it passed around him and knew it for what it was.

Decay. There was a scent of decay.

He looked down at the ring, staring at the clear green crystal, remembering the hands who had worn it and the burden of their commitments, staring until it and the ground below blurred before his eyes.

He lifted his head. Tears ran freely down his cheeks.

"Let it be over."

Once more, he shoved the ring in the lock, and just before the rock slid shut, fed the circle of silver back to the mountain from whence it had come.


She'd been watching for hours. And when she finally heard the sound of his truck, the knot in her stomach relaxed.

He was back.

She gave the small grave and the new rosebush one last glance and then started for home. As she reached the crest, she saw him look her way. She stopped and waved, and then began walking again, only this time faster. By the time she got to the bottom of the hill she was running.

He caught her on the run, lifting her off of her feet and into his arms; laughing and kissing and making promises she didn't have to hear. She knew her man.

He was as good as his word.

# EPILOGUE

"**D**addy, Daddy, Daddy, tells me a story."

Raine smiled up at the man who had just appeared in the bathroom doorway.

"We're taking an early bath," she explained.

Joseph grinned at the little brown-eyed imp smiling up at him from the middle of a tub full of bubbles.

"Dare I ask why?"

Raine shook her head. "Not if you want to keep that smile on your face."

He arched a brow. "Was it anything of mine?"

She rocked back on her heels and laughed. "Does it make a difference?"

"It might," he said.

But when the little imp made a very sad face, he made a face back and added a loud pretend growl for good measure.

Belinda Colorado squealed, partly with relief that her daddy wasn't too mad, and partly with delight that he would play. Besides, he would be very happy when he saw how pretty she'd made his good boots.

Magic markers were her favorite toy of the moment. Today she'd used all the red.

"Have mercy," Raine yelled, as the soap bubbles flew and the imp disappeared out of sight.

But before mother or daughter could panic, Joseph had Belinda up in his arms, sputtering over the fact that she'd gotten bubbles all over his shirt. Whatever fear the child might have felt when going under had disappeared like the bubbles that kept popping around her.

"Will you, Daddy? Tells me a story, please."

He winked at Raine as she handed him a towel.

"She's all yours," Raine said, and started out of the door.

"Hey!" Joseph yelled. "Where are you going?"

"To finish my column for the Tucson paper and then, I think, take a bath of my own."

He winked at Raine and blew her a kiss as their daughter wiggled to be put down. He was still chuckling to himself later as he pulled her nightgown over her head.

"There now, baby girl, I'll bet that feels better."

"Daddy! I'm not baby girl. I'm Belinda."

"Well, excuse me," Joseph said, as he tossed the wet towel on the bathroom floor.

He'd clean it up later. He'd made a promise to a three-year-old that he needed to keep.

He started to sit down in the rocker with her in his lap when she squealed and pointed toward her bed.

"My blankie. My blankie. I needs to have my blankie."

"I knew that," he muttered, more to himself than to her, and scooped it from the pillow before returning to his seat.

Almost instantly, Belinda leaned against his chest, her blankie tucked beneath her chin and her thumb poked in her mouth.

"Story," she mumbled around her thumb.

"Right. Now let's see . . ."

She yanked out her thumb long enough to make one more demand.

"Tells me, Daddy . . . tells me about the mens who comed out of the sky."

Joseph's smile softened while his mind slid back to the past. "Are you sure?"

She settled back down against his chest. "I's sure."

He started to rock.

"Many, many lifetimes . . . before the men in metal clothing . . ."

He felt her sigh and he softened his voice. ". . . came riding into the land of the People . . ."

"That's us, wight, Daddy?"

"Yes, baby, that's us."

She nodded, satisfied with her place in the world.

". . . on the four-legged beasts, other men came out of the sky and stayed among the People."

He was rocking now, although she'd already fallen asleep to the soothing cadence of his voice. But there was a peace inside him that came just of the telling, and so he continued to tell it—not for her, but for himself.

"We could not hear their words, but we knew

their thoughts. They dug deep into our land, taking the heart out of the mountain that embraces the setting sun."

He continued to talk, his voice falling lower and lower until it was all but a whisper. Then he looked down into his sleeping daughter's face and knew that her life had been the renewal of his faith.

On the downswing, he got up from the rocker without missing a beat and laid Belinda in her bed. Her blankie was still clutched tight beneath her chin. Her thumb was still soaking in her mouth. He pressed a soft kiss against the black, silky hair and then whispered very close to her ear.

"So it is said. So I believe."